—— THE ——
MAGDALENE COMPLEX

— THE —
MAGDALENE COMPLEX

REVELATION FROM THE SILENT APOSTLE SERIES

ANDREW DAVID DOYLE

iUniverse, Inc.
Bloomington

The Magdalene Complex
Revelation from The Silent Apostle Series

iUniverse books may be ordered through booksellers or by contacting:

iUniverse
1663 Liberty Drive
Bloomington, IN 47403
www.iuniverse.com
1-800-Authors (1-800-288-4677)

ISBN: 978-1-4759-8127-8 (sc)
ISBN: 978-1-4759-8129-2 (hc)
ISBN: 978-1-4759-8128-5 (ebk)

Library of Congress Control Number: 2013904799

Printed in the United States of America

iUniverse rev. date: 03/13/2013

CONTENTS

ACKNOWLEDGEMENTS

It is with great joy that I extend my thanks to those people of whom have made this project a certain reality that I thank the most, and who collectively contributed to my work by way of their anecdotes and fascinating stories that have triggered a certain 'spark' in my fact finding and many literature reviews whilst compiling this work.

As with both previous published novels that make up the primary backbone and structure of 'The Magdalene Complex' I feel that further thanks should be extended to Robin Linn for her analytical eye and recommendations that have been incorporated into the work, and to 'Crystal Clear' publishing who provided oversight of the final edit prior to submission for publication, and respectfully to iuniverse who have paved the way for many of my supporting projects

Andrew.

Author's Preface

Andrew David Doyle

This particular edition has previously been exposed to the pending audience in the form of two novels: The Silent Apostle & The Silent Apostle II 'Assignation' of which will undoubtedly become objects of desire for any serious fantasy/biblical fiction reader.

Therefore, any misunderstanding or misinterpretation are purely intentional and a luxury that is afforded to the fantasy fiction writer.

I have, in certain accounts from the varying sources, condensed such detail and information so as not to cloud the work by overwhelming, analytical detail that often lurks behind simplicity and study—especially in such subjects as 'mythology' 'folklore' and subject matter relating to the church in general, and of which are complicated subject matter in their own rights.

The lapse of nearly a quarter century since writing the original scripts for this edition has called for many alterations to the accounts of the later condition of information availability. therefore, I have not departed from the original and intended scope of the work.

Andrew David Doyle

The list of hidden contributors from web searches and other resources consulted coupled with personal visits to locations of interest have made this labour of love a reality whilst brining 'The Magdalene Complex' into the public domain.

ABOUT THE AUTHOR

Andrew David Doyle was educated in Dundee, Scotland, prior to joining the ranks of the British Armed Forces (Royal Artillery), with a successful career that stemmed almost fifteen years, after which Andrew had embarked into the commercial world of hydrocarbon exploitation and currently works for a major operator on global deployment.

Andrew enjoys his 'hobby' as an author and is a member of the Society of Authors.

Other works written and published by this prolific Scottish author are:

- *Agnus Dei—Templar Knots +Krosses*
- *The Circle of Swords*
- *The Lost Monks of Avalon 'The Avalonian Traveler's Guide*
- *The Magdalene Complex*
- *The Silent Apostle*
- *The Silent Apostle II 'Assignation'*
- *The Whispering Swordsman*

Chevalier Andrew David Doyle, OSMTH, KT, Scotland

CHAPTER ONE

THE HOST

'Mathew, Mark, Luke and John,' cried Doctor Darlene Gammay with succinct authority, as the tutor was laying down the proverbial foundations and setting the exacting tone of her special presentation about the life of the Apostles to a group of biblical scholars from the University of somewhere or other, who looked back at her politely, each attendee anticipating to hear a revelation from the ancient world of holy wisdom.

'These are the names of four of our most famous biblical characters, or Apostles, of the Bible. They are all well documented as being the followers of Christ, and may have interfaced with him or many of the other historical figures in biblical times.

Although we are generally told that there were twelve Apostles in total, we can deduce from various writings that they all appeared at different times throughout 'Jesus' life, and appeared to have had an equal standing in their own special hierarchy of biblical writing. But in fact, as we work through this lesson, we will find that the Apostles did in fact all fall into a specific ranking structure and may have varied in their numbers at specific gatherings or meetings.

Therefore, it is widely accepted that the Apostles as we know them were not all scholars, but in fact were key figures in their particular societies. Perhaps they were the ones who could read and write and therefore, they chose to write about the many exploits of this one man, eventually sending many stories throughout the Holy Land of some rather remarkable goings on, and thus, documented most of what we know about the life of the man Jesus from Nazareth. And indeed over time these writings do not let us forget his existence, nor his death; these writings by the Apostles collectively ensure an archive of amazing detail. The many writings and texts are delivered with such a passion that we simply cannot dismiss or ignore, especially today as it is corroborated in so many academic ways.'

A single hand went up in the audience and the tutor acknowledged: 'Yes, you, the lady in the middle, with the shawl.' A clear decisive pointing of her pointy finger spotlighted the mantle-clad maiden. It was one of those exaggerated movements of the finger that university tutors learn as a mandatory requirement for responding to being asked questions out of turn: the distinctive body language frozen in the given direction, which must have been taught on the curriculum for tutorials as part of the secret school of arrogance and ignorance.

The middle aged woman stood up and asked a question about Saint Matthew. 'Doctor Gammay, how do you interpret how Matthew actually knew about the existence of the three wise men and how would he know that they were en route to Bethlehem from the East, do you suppose that he may have received written word in advance from other prophets or was he informed by a dedicated messenger?' The Doctor stood for a few seconds and pondered the question. 'Good question,' she said.

'It is easy to say that in this case, John the Baptist was preaching in the wilderness well in advance of these events, and any follower could have made their way across the desert and met with

Matthew, or may have passed messages along the many carnival or camel routes along the winding roads to Damascus and indeed, Bethlehem. I would say however, that we should aim this question at John, as he was perhaps more likely to be more informed than Matthew, although they may have been very close to one another in the first place.

And then again, if we take the Bible in full context, we would discover that there are other prophets networking with one another and laying the many seeds of history. In order to answer your question we can turn to yet another documented prophet mentioned in the Bible, one named Esais, who is clearly documented in the holy gospels written by Matthew as discussing repentance in one of his many sermons.

He would have perhaps been an implantation within the crowd to support any message being delivered, a person who would travel ahead to the next place of preaching and start to "gee" the crowds with idle gossip, but we should always err on the safe side in academia and work to the facts.

I must say it would be difficult to clearly define if these words were spoken or written in advance or after many events, and therefore, from a scholarly standpoint, we must assume that all events are recorded thereafter. But I do take your point as to the origins of such information, we must work to the ethos that archival evidence will never ever be fully corroborated or brought to modern day thinking as decisive, or will ever be declared the ultimate overarching body of evidence to substantiate such a claim.

I mean, could you imagine resurrecting any of the Apostles today, and asking them what they thought of today's real world, asking them for their opinions as they view modern society through the eyes of a layman? Ask yourself this: what would they really see? Global war, famine, floods, corruption, genocide, racial abuse, hatred . . . All the 21st century favourites, and we haven't even touched on WMDs—Weapons of Mass Destruction—yet, our pending Nemesis, our demise, and most definitely our Armageddon. I am sure they would record our current status of the world as a 'literal living hell.'

A hell with so much uncertainty going on that we do not know where we will be in five or ten years' time. As an example, imagine if you will the following circumstances: let us say that during an archaeological dig in the distant future, the 29th century for example, a researcher discovers a single book that was completely unknown to the finder. This book was hidden away from prying eyes for whatever reason, the subject matter was the demise of the earth, and the work was preserved in a bone-encased casket with a few modern day items such as an empty bottle of Coke and a packet of cheese and onion crisps.

Now how would the archaeologists research its contents, how could the team research the author or even the author's origins, how could you establish any credible evidence to say that this person did in fact write this work? How would you decipher the language if it was written in a foreign language, how would you test the inks or bloods for authenticity or age? These are just some of the questions we must ask before we commit ourselves to ascertaining the authenticity of documents or indeed any artefacts.

To add a little bit of even more complexity regarding our mystery, let's say this parchment was written in the calligraphy of the 3rd century Aramaic language. But do we know that cheese and onion crisps were on the market then? How would the scholars interpret what conditions of the times were actually like, six or seven hundred years ago, what was society suffering as this book was being hidden in an attempt to tell the world of the future what was really afoot?

We can look at the internet or review newspapers today to see what is happening globally, but back in the days of Christ it would be very difficult to decipher fact from fiction or find the resources to corroborate your findings, a real dilemma we face today. We have military records, we even have Templar records and at a push we could ask the Vatican to release some documents, but how would you get to the nitty-gritty detail?

This is why the work of the Apostles is so important; it's not just the life of Jesus that is documented but a whole way of existence and belief, which was captured by so many. So, yes, an excellent question to ask, thank you, my apologies for drifting away from the main question, still, all this is relevant to our session.' Doctor Gammay stopped for a few seconds and stared out the window, her mind momentarily wandering.

She collected herself, and began again. 'We must bear in mind that not all the Apostles were men of education either. It is imperative that we remember that fifty percent of the Apostles were, in fact, normal, everyday fishermen who worked to support their families day in and day out. And we may even have an element of artistic licence creeping in from certain angles, where, maybe not all the true facts have been recorded.

Who is to say that John may have disliked Mary Magdalene and discredited her at every opportunity? Let's face it, women were not treated or viewed as equals in those earlier times. Perhaps Mary was starting the suffragette movement well in advance of Emily Pankhurst, very hard to pinpoint, I don't really know.' There was a slight shift of atmosphere at these impromptu humorous comments, and soon a few chuckles emanated from within the group.

'The finer, more sensitive and succinct detail we would wish for as academics is never readily available, and that's what makes Bible Studies interesting. Of course, we must remain sceptical, as the works and their origins are often shrouded in mystery, and may not even have been written by the assumed authors in the first place.

In essence, these authors may have just been simple fishermen who worked on the river Jordan or advanced further afield, to the Black Sea, the Sea of Galilee, perhaps even to the Dead Sea. A sea where the phenomenon of super salinity is an amazing geological anomaly, one that could certainly provide enough salt for all our fish and chips for many years to come.'

Darlene watched the faces of the assembled group; they were hanging on her every word, but failed to see the humour in the Dead Sea angle. She would either have to change her audience or change her subject matter. The latter was not going to happen; she had a passion for this line of study, it was her bread and butter, and any move away from the subject would be intellectual suicide for her. Darlene was not by any account a religious fanatic, nor did she attend Church four times a month. Sunday for her was usually a recovery period after a healthy night out on the tiles. The university campus life provided her with all the excitement and solace that she required.

The discussion in the room continued as the tutor presented her lesson to a mixed jury of religious enthusiasts. Kemp Hastings sat quietly at the back of the classroom with his little red notebook neatly spread across one of his knees. He was absorbing the lecture that Doctor Darlene Gammay was presenting to the assembled crowd of just eleven people, her first public session since walking out of the university just over two weeks ago in a cloud of mystery.

One seat in the room remained empty, a large name tag lying on its flat surface. The tag read: 'St Andrew', printed in bold black lettering. 'How ironic,' thought Hastings, and watched the tutor as she traversed amongst the group providing each individual with a quick overview as to what each Apostle had brought into the storyline of the 'good book'.

Hastings watched and listened as she sold her ancient world of biblical life to the modern day media presenters. The group were actually a cross section of reporters and bible thumpers; it was a joint effort in selling the good Lord to the next generation. The assembly ranged in age from eighteen to twenty four with the addition of two teachers, both slightly older, who had changed careers from social work to God's work. He smiled inwardly as he watched the students sitting on the seats in front of him, each of whom was holding a name plate with the designated Apostle's name written upon it. He could feel the obedient and very much captured audience waiting to be informed about the exploits of these ancient ecclesiastical storytellers and their exposure to the world's most famous man apart from Elvis.

The lesson ran over the scheduled time by thirteen minutes, mainly due to an open question forum that the Doctor appeared to be quite uncomfortable with, although it was not surprising that newcomers to the world of the Apostles had a million questions that required attention. Eventually the questions ended and the assembled group of pseudo-Apostles dispersed in a hail of texting and key rattling.

Kemp waited patiently at the back of the room until it had emptied, a single earpiece feeding him the music of Puccini's 'Humming Chorus', a soft encore taken from the Madame Butterfly opera. He kept the volume at just the right level, drowning out the drone of the room as the students escaped into the large hallway, then picked his moment to grab the Doctor's attention.

'Doctor Gammay, great session, although I think some of the younger generation may need a lesson on how to dress, I mean look at that dress sense,' he said, pointing to one of the students. 'Or at least get themselves a clothing reality check, what do you think?' he said, pointing again to the 21st century example of student attire. It was truly a sight that needed a little more than just a quick haircut to fix, especially with the fashion police of modern society on the loose: they would have had a field day with some of the anti-societal student freaks, with their bleached jeans and torn t-shirts depicting the logo 'FCUK de Pope'.

'Oh, most definitely,' she replied without looking up. 'Did you enjoy the session, mister . . . ?' There was an awkward moment of silence, as he fumbled with his notebook. 'Hastings,' he barked. 'Kemp Hastings. Not really my cup of tea I am afraid, if I was to be brutally honest, but it explained a few things that I was certainly vague about, especially Andrew.'

He offered his help, and then assisted the lecturer in gathering her bits and bobs together. 'It's a pity St Andrew wasn't playing today, it would have been great to hear his side of the biblical story.'

Doctor Gammay smiled at Kemp. 'Maybe he was in attendance. History tells us that probably no one was listening to him anyway.' Kemp smirked a boyish kind of grin.

'Fact is stranger than fiction, they say,' he riposted, passing her the bundle of name tags. 'Copious amounts of evidence point to the fact that the Apostle St Andrew remained on the periphery of the central group, and would often not sit amongst the three top seats as it were, but often found himself in the middle ground between conclave and the masses.

Most of which was corroborated and recorded in the good book by some of the other Apostles in their many interpretations,' Gammay replied. Kemp changed the line of questioning to ease the tension in the air.

'Is this your new full time occupation then, running from academy to academy, teaching the "good book"?' he said, then smiled. The Doctor stopped and stared directly at him. 'Mr Hastings I do not teach the "good book",' she intimated the commas with inverted fingers held high. 'I merely relay what has already been written by the learned scholars of the ancient world, we just put it into a more comprehensible context for the students to understand.'

Kemp almost stood to attention as the lecturer grabbed her bag and stood directly in front of him. 'This lesson was geared towards identifying some of the Apostles who left their mark within the Bible literature and not some haphazard attempt at correcting history.' If Kemp was honest with himself he found the lesson was quite an interesting subject nevertheless.

Doctor Gammay continued. 'It is difficult enough getting translators to get the translation right in the first place, there is so much inconsistency within presented work. It is a very complex procedure to pin point the exact meaning of the language, let alone educate the misguided academic world in their entirety. Who, incidentally, think they know it all about the lives of perhaps the most famous group of people apart from The Beatles Mr Hastings.' She cut off and momentarily stepped off her pedestal, realising she was having a moan about her recent departure from the academic world to a complete stranger.

'Well actually Doctor, it's Kemp, and I think you are doing a great job, people need educating. I can see the trials and tribulations of university campus life have left their indelible and insidious marks on your psyche, not easy to walk away from five years in residence, trust me, I know. But look at the upshot, you have escaped into the big wide world, good on you, fancy a cup of tea or coffee?' he said in a rush, clasping his hands in prayer.

Darlene Gammay took a deep breath and a few seconds gazing over Kemp Hastings and his ego. 'Are you trying to chat me up Mr Hastings?' Kemp smiled one of his broad smiles.

'But of course I am! But I want your brain, well, not your physical brain, I want access to the deep secret vaults within it, and of course to your scholastic knowledge of Medieval folklore and the biblical library.

Most importantly, your knowledge in and around the work of the gospels, and the Apostles who wrote them. That's basically why I am here. Dare I say, I wish to hear more of your Matt, Markus, Lukey and Johann. They are of great interest to me,' he said, rubbing his chin. 'What about it then?' he posed the question knowing full well that Dr Gammay was not going to give up the opportunity to conduct a few further lessons or, indeed, miss out on any potential income.

The Doctor tilted her head and smirked. 'Mathew, Mark, Luke and John, the typical four that everyone seems to remember. But, Mr Hastings, can you remember and name the other eight? I don't know why people remember this group, I mean they are not even in alphabetical order for goodness sake. You can pay for the coffee as well Mr Hastings, I am still waiting on the bloody University paying my final salary.' Kemp smiled again. 'But of course dear lady, after you,' he said motioning the Doctor to pass by with a pretentious cavalier bow, and a sweep of his imaginary peacock-feathered hat.

The usual students' corner café was closed. Kemp spied the local bar adjacent, noticing as he did so that its name was 'Deacon Brodie's', then he gave out an inexplicably loud laugh and made a quick apology. 'Sorry about that, something I read recently about the infamous Deacon Brodie, you must excuse me.' He opened the car door for his new-found friend. 'After you.'

Darlene was about to step into the car when he offered his limited response to her question. 'So, here goes, this is how I remember the Apostles in their entirety, each capital letter indicates an Apostle's first name: "The Scriptures Tell Lies about Mary Magdalene's Apocrypha Because Justice Misled Jesus and Judas". So, therefore, Thomas the Tank Engine and Simon the snorkel were called to a-'

Darlene suddenly stuck both her hands straight up in the air in protest. 'Stop! Stop! Stop! No way are you going to recite the names of all twelve Apostles using everything from the Simpsons to the Muppet show mister Hastings, no way José, it's not quite PC now is it? I believe you mentioned coffee.'

Kemp huffed. 'Okay dokey then, what about Thomas, Simon, Thaddeus. Luke, Andrew, Acts, Mark, Mathew, Bartholomew, James, John and Mathias and on a second visit you could add Magdalene or even Judas.'

Darlene smiled. 'If you had said Phillip instead of Mark then I would have let you off with ninety nine per cent.' Kemp tilted his head in thanks. 'Of course Jesus himself would also have been recognised in the modern day as an Apostle, yes or no?' She smiled but did not answer and simply evaded his question completely.

'Nice car, I do like Jaguars. It's the older styles that keep their looks, don't you think?' Kemp was touched, he had discovered a female of the species who saw the car as an example of fine engineering and not the male appendage extension as popular myth would usually have it.

'After you,' he said again. The doctor stopped and pointed across the road.

'Ah look, Deacon Brodie's is still open,' she said, pointing to the illuminated door sign, then stepped away from the car heading towards the café. Kemp closed the door of the jaguar very gingerly behind her.

'As if Deacon Brodie hasn't tortured me enough,' he said quietly, walking behind the Doctor taking in her slender round shaped bottom slinking away under her black skirt. Deacon Brodie's was very quiet, just enough people inside the café bar to guarantee a relatively quick service. The couple sat down and draped their

11

jackets over the same chair. 'So, Mr Hastings, what is it that I can do for you exactly?' Kemp placed a photocopy of an illuminated manuscript on the table.

'Take a look at this and tell me what you think.' Darlene Gammay leaned forward and spent a few seconds tracing the text on the page with her index finger. Then the waitress interrupted. 'What can I get you?' she asked in a half almost very dis-interested way, whilst still chewing her piece of bubble gum and was poised with pencil and paper at the ready.

'Café latte for me please.' Requested Darlene.

'I will have a mug of hot chocolate. And can you also bring a small glass of brandy please?' The waitress smiled and walked away. Darlene waited a few seconds then offered a response.

'Where in hell's half acre did you get this from?' she asked, and alerting Kemp to the potential reality that this parchment could be genuine, and from his investigative background experience he would be safe to assume that this was normally the first question asked when someone is genuinely interested in something. He leaned back in the wooden chair.

'It was found in a grave, not too far from here actually.' He said no more. The Doctor began to mumble a few words, then stopped and stared at Hastings. She pulled out a pair of modern gold-rimmed reading glasses and read again.

'My Aramaic and Latin are a bit rusty, it will take me a few minutes to get my head around some of this older Aramaic stuff. It's difficult when it's a photocopy full of splatter; one loses so much fine detail in copies. I would have to see the real thing of course. I mean what I am observing here is probably a copy of a fake anyway, but get the little buggers under an electronic microscope and there is no hiding from science.'

Kemp slid a beige A4 folder in front of her. 'Try this then.' The Doctor shook her head and flicked the cover page very nonchalantly, exposing the next page down, then momentarily froze whilst taking a very deep breath. She was obviously overwhelmed by what was staring back at her from the colourful page.

'This cannot be what I think it is?' Kemp pursed his lips.

'It all depends on what you think it is,' he answered. 'We think St Thomas of Aquinas, one of your so called Apostles, was the custodian of this little chap for quite some time. He was keeping it hidden from prying eyes, pretty well secreted in his own tomb in India along with some rather interesting Knights Templar artefacts.

A second parchment was also apparently found not too long after the Nag Hammadi was discovered, and was presented to the academic world with the cautious statement that it might be the original. This other document was a sort of map, not quite sure how exact it was, but it certainly brought this little gem to light.

This new revelation started a series of events and investigations that led to this particular manuscript being discovered. It's not a coincidence that it was deliberately secreted in this specific grave, it's there for a very good reason, placed there to ensure its ultimate safety. It was discovered in the tomb of a Cistercian monk only known as 'Wishart', and we think it was hidden there for about 500 years.'

Darlene was clearly excited, almost jubilant, as she cast her eyes around the room. She reverently touched a corner of the parchment.

Normally she would have donned white latex gloves and placed the work under controlled lighting in the secured laboratory, a precaution to reduce any chance of distraction or indeed theft, but the excitement of the moment had definitely got the better of her.

The page was immaculate, each symbol was clearer than clear, the colour was free from imperfections, the text was perfect. In her meagre opinion, having only spent five years at Nottingham University completing her PhD in Theology and Religious studies, not to mention a further couple of years in London covering Biblical interpretation theory, she felt confident enough to say that this was a genuine and pristine example of an original illuminated manuscript. 'This vellum feels as if it is sweating, you know, like, still breathing, not dry and brittle like most samples of this age are, but alive.' Hastings nodded his head.

'Yep, an Incorruptible Epistula or IE for the studious types, I haven't touched it myself. I keep thinking that dead skin contains little virus things that make you sick.' Darlene really smiled for the first time, and Kemp stared at her longer than he should have. 'Miss Gammay there's something else you should know about this manuscript which is very interesting.

This document was once contained in a wooden box held in the vault of the London Bond building waiting to be exported to Italy. It was there in 1666 which, I am sure you are aware, was the year that the Great fire of London occurred. Well, this little artefact actually survived an intensity of heat that incinerated everything else in the casket and of course the casket itself, along with half of London's inner city. It appears that this vellum is quite impervious to heat or direct flame.'

She stopped reading the page and raised her head. '"Incorruptible Letters" Mr Hastings? Are you 'shittin' me. Now let's be serious here, all animal flesh eventually dies, tissue does not live for more than a few hours after death, it decays and dies. I suppose you could argue that during putrefaction one could add anoil or something into the stripping mix to preserve the parchment, but to make it flame proof?

I would certainly have my reservations. But this parchment, by my reckoning, is easily 2nd or 3rd century, and is of a greater quality than most I have seen. In fact, if I did not know any better, I would say this was written as recently as yesterday given the quality of the colours.

Kemp found himself staring again. 'Actually Miss Gammay it is indeed second century or even first, we think it was scribed about the same time as the Apostle John's other work, just after the crucifixion, if you go for that sort of thing.'

Darlene leaned forward and tutted. 'Mr Hastings I teach biblical studies, I do go for that kind of thing, but this is not the work of the Apostle John. This author is left handed, and more adept in this type of subtle script, look at the flow of the handwriting: it is not heavy but light and matter of fact. I almost get the inclination to go as far as to say that this was written by a woman.'

Hastings was trapped. The quick-witted Doctor had captured his sense of adventure, and her academic standing attracted his desire for knowledge. 'If you can help us authenticate parts of the script, we could perhaps even discover that Mary Magdalene may have even pushed the quill over this vellum herself.

As for the vellum, it is as fresh today as it was two thousand years ago. I suppose you could take the body of Bernadette Soubirous in comparison—an example of an incorruptible entity—dead for over a hundred and thirty years and yet still smells sweet as newly cut roses. A hundred and thirty years, and as yet no decomposition, why do you think that is Miss Gammay?'

The Doctor was turning the page upside down and trying all angles of light to scrutinise the epistula. 'Impossible.' She said. 'Can you see here, here, and there, these larger letters appear to be made up of other tiny lettering.' Hastings flicked the page by one of the corners.

'Imagine your scholarly career chums' reactions when they find out that you have deciphered the handwritten work of one of the most famous women that ever existed: Mary Magdalene, a female of the species way up there with Joan of Arc, Helen of Troy, the Queen of Sheba, Mary Queen of Scots and of course Marge and Lisa Simpson from the telly.'

Darlene Gammay gave out an uncontrolled giggle nearly knocking over her latte in the process. 'I don't think I would place the Simpsons on the same pedestal as Mary Queen of Scots Mr Hastings, there are approximately five million Scots men and women who would say otherwise too!' she said, shaking her head. 'So, let us be serious here, this manuscript requires lab testing and an acute detailed analysis should be undertaken.

We will have to conduct gamma correction OCR overlay, there will be classification of text that must be applied, and the biblical studies group will have to assemble to determine the potential political dispute that may arise as to custody. The origin of such a page must be sourced, you know there are eminent boffins who would take to murder just to view this document.'

The Doctor was getting excited again as she ran through the series of processes and protocols that it would take to authenticate this page legally. Kemp Hastings clicked his fingers several times; it had the desired effect and got her undivided attention.

Doctor Gammay was clearly agitated. 'You're rambling Darlene, excuse the fingers, but that is exactly what we do not want to happen. What I mean is this whole thing must remain our secret until such time as we are ready to release this to the world at large. Will you help us or not? Do we have put this piece of historical archive data back inside the Vatican's vault for no one to see until the next millennium?' The challenge was incredible for Darlene Gammay; she had never got this close to any such document, one that carried this amount of biblical importance. Once or twice she had handled a few snippets of manuscript from the older church records, but nothing so colourful or powerful and exquisitely detailed, and of such potential significance.

'Okay,' she said. 'But I need to pay my rent.' Kemp smiled and placed a small brown envelope in her hand and lifted the document.

'Here is my card and some resources for you—money is such a filthy word. Darlene, it has been an emotional pleasure, please call me tomorrow, my number is on the card.' Hastings flicked open his mobile phone and pressed redial.

CHAPTER TWO

REVELATION

Darlene Gammay lay awake on top her bed staring up at the ceiling. She was thinking that the day was going to be an important one for the rest of her whole academic career, and maybe she should call her best pal Susan in case she had got herself into any trouble, trapping herself in a predicament that she could not get out of. What if this whole episode was a prank by some of the students at the University to make her feel better? 'Buggers will suffer if they are behind this,' she said aloud.

No, she would wait and see what the nice smiling Mr Hastings had to offer, she decided, then jumped as the phone rang. She slid the facia panel down and answered.

'Hello, Dr Darlene Gammay.' Darlene waited patiently, trying to work out the strange noises in the background. She instantly thought of a church. 'Miss Gammay some things should be left alone.' The voice at the other end was very low in tone and almost muffled, there was a series of clicks then the voice spoke again. 'Are you the cipher?' She thought about the line of questioning; an odd question to ask.

'I am not sure what you mean by cipher,' she replied. The voice had echoes of heavy breathing and slurring, it was an almost perverted, even deviant, phone call. A shiver ran down her back as she decided enough was enough. 'Get off the phone you creep, don't ever call me back, or I will call the police,' she yelped, slamming the phone down. She realised that this could have been someone calling regarding the not-so-hidden Magdalene manuscript, but had a distinct inclination that it was a group of students from the university, they were always playing games like that.

She dialled the reception at the University and spoke with the administrator. 'No Doctor Gammay, the four students you mention have all departed campus. Charmaine, she has joined her local football club and is doing well apparently, Perry has started his own building company and lives somewhere near London, Middlesex, I think.

Cyrus has joined the Greenpeace movement as a staff consultant or something, and Kerrie has crossed over to Graphic Arts and is currently in Europe, so I don't think any of them can be playing their little old games with you Doctor.' Darlene could not think of any other students who would want to bug her like this. 'Dorothy thank you for your time, can you please tell that arsehole Benedict that I want my final salary this year, and not next year! And thanks again Dot.' She slipped the facia of her mobile phone closed.

As she did so something caught her eye, she could have sworn the screen on her laptop had flashed. She stared at it, it did flash, and then again, three times. She slid her hand across the series of buttons, and it booted up a lot faster than usual. Within eight seconds a grey screen appeared on her screen with the words 'Holy See' in bold blue lettering etched on the display. 'What the fu . . . '

There were two bleeps then the homepage to the Holy Vatican in Rome came online. 'Wow, that's never happened before, how cool is that,' she muttered, clicking a few buttons trying to exit the screenshot. A shot that was obviously from a webcam came online, and the camera started panning towards a glass case. It spun around the inner chamber several times then slowed down; there were a series of other cases in the picture, each display holding different items: trinkets, crosses and golden chains. She checked the date and time—it was current. She did recall hitting a few web pages last week, but she never downloaded any programs, knowing she would be flooded with spam and emails that she just did not want.

The camera suddenly stopped in front of a large and ornate glass case, and she swore something flew by the lens very quickly, a white flash, then she spied other cameras in the vault panning left and right. 'God what is this crap, "Watch With Mother"?' she exclaimed, then cleaned the screen with a tissue and scribbled a few notes. She tried exiting the screen, but it refused to disappear. She tried holding the 'off' button for a full 10 seconds—the laptop remained powered up.

The vault was immaculately clean, the stainless steel walls were reflecting the LEDs that were bouncing off the adjacent surfaces, each green and blue light was pulsing away in sequence. The vault appeared to be a substantial one; Gammay recognised the sensors and the state of the art security systems. She had often been through the Archives and Artefacts Secure Level of the Museum, and had witnessed the lock down process for priceless works of art that were in custody, 'a bit like Fort Knox,' she would tell her friends.

But why was it being shown on her laptop? She tried cancelling again and was repeatedly pressing the escape button, but nothing happened, she disconnected the electric plug, then the battery kicked in, as she removed the laptop battery the computer fell into darkness. 'I hate those bloody computer hackers,' she said, just as the laptop came back online. 'Typical, bloody typical, internal battery that you can't get access to. Bloody Dells.' She continued to watch the screen.

After a few seconds she was able to read the label on the ornate case, 'Tartarus Inferni', then the camera zoomed in and out in a steady motion. To the rear of the display case there were three small boxes, whose label read: 'Pyus pixidis Sancto Tomas'. After a quick Latin recap in her head, she concluded the wording on the case label meant 'Hellfire Sword', and that the small boxes belonged to Saint Thomas. 'St Thomas,' she uttered the words almost instinctively.

In the very centre of the case she could make out what appeared to be a sword stand, similar to the one her dad had sitting on the mantelpiece at home. Or at least it had been, until last year, before her dad almost cut off part of her brother's ear whilst playing samurai warriors, blood everywhere, mum went ballistic. She sniggered at the memory.

The sword stand on the screen display was not made for the commercial market as her dad's was, this one was probably crafted by an 11th century Chinese or Japanese master carpenter, and most likely cost an absolute fortune to replace today. Although it was very ornate, and was supported by an ivory tusk at each end, and mounted onto an ebony platform, with four gold fingers which extended upwards and held the sword in place, it still appeared to be out of place.

'Shit,' she said softly, realising that some of the things she had talked about the day before were linked to this parchment affair. The laptop had shut down and booted up again but this time straight to her Windows system, she tried desperately to relocate the now interesting vault, raking through folders and files.

After a few fruitless minutes she disappeared into the kitchen and returned clasping a cup of hot tea and a chocolate Jaffa Cake. The desktop screensaver had changed to an image of the full colour copy of the illuminated manuscript and was just as striking as the real thing. 'Oh my God,' she breathed, the Jaffa Cake paused

21

a few inches away from her mouth. She began reading the text; it was one hundred percent clearer than she remembered from yesterday. She began to read the concentric lines at the edge of the page. 'Okay Darlene,' she said to herself. 'Get your head into story mode . . . '

The script was written around the squared edge of the work, each few words were interrupted with little Christian crosses strategically placed to punctuate the flow of the script. 'Scotia Ecclesia Doctrina—Scottish Church Doctrine.' It had taken quite a while for her brain to trigger into the Latin-recall filing cabinet deep within her hippocampus. Although Latin was dominant in her daily life, she spent more time within Hebrew or Arabic, the subtle differences did indeed change the meaning of the written word she told herself, and looked around for one of her many dictionaries. She read out each statement loudly and presented herself with an adaption or translation she thought was apt, then interrogated the dictionary.

'"Absconditus, ac adepto admonition angelus". Concealed at the statue in the Abbey within a coffin is the important church letter of Magdalene. The Angel to obtain divine doctrine, I say deceitful warning, sign at the grave is squared. Fear the Church, stand in the highest part, then commit oneself, in silence, this is of great importance. The table of my lineage and testimony of Magdalene. To carry in front of the Tartarus Inferni—Hellfire Sword and deposit in my holy grave.'

The Doctor was intrigued and mesmerised at the same time, confused as to how the screen saver could just do that, turn up on her private desktop like that. And more to the point, she found it very frightening that someone could just log on to her computer's hard drive and remotely install the damn thing. She read the translation out loudly again and again . . .

"'*Arca archa cello cognomen divinus doctrina dolosus Ecclesia epistula huic Carch gravitas. Signum sepulchrum of Quadratus, Inquam templi, sto summa, se astrinjo, meus silens, et. Tantus tabellae progenies Magdala mon testimonium. Praefero prefero tartarus inferni, repono sanctus selpulchrum, Tego texi tectum au.*'"

Darlene was confused. The only logical sense she could deduce was that the parchment was giving instruction to an Angel or lady who was seeking a divine doctrine. "Doctrine" could be a manuscript, Darlene supposed, and the seeker had to be mindful of, or made aware of, deceit. Then the seeker had to commit to a vow of silence or seek a place of silence; that could be in a library or indeed a graveyard. And the sword relation thing, what could that be? The parchment states it is then to buried somewhere in a grave that might belong to Mary Magdalene.

'How bizarre could that be, who would want to hide such relics, who would want . . .' She stopped speaking out loud and closed the curtains to her fair sized flat's living room. It was all too far-fetched; she had no idea what to think. What was she supposed to do—embark on some great quest to find a solution to something that may be just as elusive as the Holy Grail itself?

She placed the power cable back into her laptop and drank her tea.

CHAPTER THREE

HOME STUDY

Hastings had found an old book amongst his extensive library containing inserts and extracts of some very strange findings, events that caught the imagination of the commercial world. It was a great source for investigating occult practices and religious fanatics; people who have been known to tempt death to meet their twisted, satanic ends. He drew on his library, which contained a full series of the old 'Man, Myth and Magic' series of books that were circulated in the early seventies, and he had the complete set neatly presented on his middle shelf for easy access. Kemp quizzed his broad collection of literature. 'Not bad for a non-academic,' he said, then downed his glass of warm brandy.

The top shelf was strictly for pleasure, containing many fantasy and fiction books such as 'Red Dwarf', 'The Hitchhiker's Guide to the Galaxy', 'The Hobbit' and his favourite, 'Blade Runner'; all the works of authors he admired, Tolkien, Adams and P.K. Dick, all waiting to quench his thirst for science and escape.

He spent a fair chunk of his time browsing his own library, knowing full well that he could never browse every page of every book during his lifetime. Still, he would have a go.

He picked up one of his older books and blew the dust away from the cover, the lettering appeared much clearer: 'Incunabula, version one—Writ of Souls'. He flicked through a few pages, and found an insert referring to the methodology of the 5th century. He had been alerted to the existence of a weapon used to send kings, gods, queens, sorcerers, sirens and beasts back into the underworld of Hades.

Hastings had by default read Homer's 'Iliad', a paperback copy of which had been left on the plane on one his long flights across the globe. He recalled Persephone and how desperate she was for revenge, tricking Odysseus and his crew into remaining on the mystical island, just to feed her not-so-endearing children, who were in fact a clutch of darling little demons. Thinking about demons brought him back to Hades, and the Hellfire Sword. A few pages further and he found what he was looking for. The page read:

The Sword Hilt Manuscript

The God killing sword or the 'tartarus inferni' (Hellfire Sword), the haft or hilt is constructed from skin and bone and encased in a shroud of gold. The length of which will extend one arm's length plus one hand span of the intended user. The weight is counterbalanced with a marble or glass pommel, the weight may shift from user to user.

The blade will have been folded six times and overlapped seven times, the quillon will be attached and annealed. The thigh bone of the 'one' is the omnipotent source of power and thus carved into the haft of the Hellfire and shall be encased in gold and silver. The 'tartarus inferni' once constructed was rumoured to have been placed in the fires of eternity to enhance it with hidden properties, its hardness and strength can only be matched with construction methods that only the sciences and techniques of the future will detect.

The new technology in years to follow will discover chemicals such as beryllium, aluminium or magnesium alloys or other such compounds unknown to 5th century swordsmiths, some of which have not yet quite made it to the academic periodic table. The Haft is of hollow construction, and within it is lined with glass, it once contained a single page of hidden esoteric knowledge hidden in a crystal phial, placed in the void by physical intervention. Then the pommel is turned twelve times in anti clockwise direction to the lock position and further annealed. The quillon is made of the purest of gold and cross plated with diamond studs of six. The seamless work will be quenched in the blood of the ox and offered to the 'worthy'. When the time comes, and only when the skies are darkened and the population weak, will the Hellfire be raised to avenge the wrath of the dark side if and when imposed on the human society.

The manuscript itself was well worn and most of the edges were ragged from continual use, there was a light layer of grease that left the fingers moist, years of bacteria having been transferred onto the unsuspecting surface.

The residue was mostly at the left top corner, but for a document that was estimated to be over four hundred years old it was not in too a bad condition. Science was still based on older values and equations with ancient models being referenced as modern day answers, but nothing like what was to unfold in a very short space of time.

The Tartarus Inferni

Hastings had made contact with this Hellfire Sword during a previous investigation; one which had led to some rather inexplicable events. The Fisher Queens had offered the Sword to the Vatican in exchange for access to the hidden vaults that ran the length of the city. The engagement of these two societies in the

21st century solidified their stance against a greater evil that was stalking the globe.

He flicked on his webcam and pressed record, then spoke.

'The unity of the Vatican and the Fisher Kings and Queens would reunite the brotherhoods together in an effort to stabilise this volatile world, a world that both enterprises have been fighting against since the early 3rd century. Science, belief and faith should come together in the 21st century until the time is right to inform the world of the intended Multi Realm Order, a plan that was made by the Super Powers of the planet earth. We must acknowledge the work of the current pope Benedict, who, incidentally, has just left Scotland, leaving the papal imprint of faith on this once ignorant pagan world.

The tyranny and destruction of our planet is still evident and will have to be controlled if we are to exist beyond the 23rd century, and the Hellfire Sword of the gods is just the tool for the job. The power that controls the Sword is the power that controls the people.'

His ramblings were to be included as part of his notes on a new novel he was planning to write. He had embarked on a journey to record how the church was influencing world powers; his plot was to bring the Ecclesiastical Super Powers together for world domination . . . He was just about to take off his headset when he was disturbed.

CHAPTER FOUR

PONTIFICATION

The Swiss Guard officer placed the silver DVD disc from the CCTV camera on the table top of the Internal Affairs Officer's desk. The red leather covering of the table stretched its full length with the single embossed motif denoting the office of the Pope stuck firmly in its centre making it very clear and plain for all to see what this ecclesiastical office represented.

Major Pierre La Rou sat down in front of the panel of three high ranking papal official administrators and crossed his legs. 'Major La Rou, good morning, thank you for coming,' said the Minister of the Interior clasping his hands over the desktop. 'It appears that you have something of great importance to share with us, information regarding the removal of our latest acquisition, the Hellfire Sword of Scotia?

'Yes Minister, it is the CCTV footage I took from the recording machine at 05:33 this morning, the machines as you know run 24/7 and we have instant replay for when visitors or workmen are inside sensitive areas of our beautiful domain, I basically collate them together and store them daily.'

The Minister nodded as ministers do: ministers generally have the attention span of the average goldfish, normally in the range of approximately 7.3 seconds. Although each member of the Vatican's elite team had special qualities, ironically the aged one's held a particular niche for procrastination. This minster was no different and in this particular case probably even less alert than the humble goldfish. The Major did not pass any further comment and just thought this officer was 'apathy on legs' to say the least. The Major straightened his tunic and spoke.

'I ran this recording a full three times, and honestly could not quite believe what I saw.' The Senior High Justice clerk of the Vatican wiped the disk clean, placed it in the machine, then pressed the 'play' button. He waited a few seconds as the vault came into view and then sat down. Major La Rou was the most senior of officials in the Vatican guard, he was respected by his peers, and certainly instrumental in maintaining the Vatican's global integrity and therefore was permitted a fair degree of autonomy in his duties.

A tall gentleman, his suave good looks would win over any female who was seeking good DNA. La Rou was in fact a well-trained soldier and officer, but remained on the quieter side of the organisation; he was too wrapped up in his domain to be bothered with the politics of global warfare, he was dedicated to the Vatican and knew his place.

The Major continued to speak. 'The normal vault screen display was running as expected, and we see that the digital clock is ticking over as normal, and the screen resolution is also set at normal, humidity levels were ambient, runtime and other display control functions are all in good order. That was up until 03:33:33 hours when a thin white mist appeared inside the glass display case number 33, the hermetically sealed case containing the Tartarus Inferni—or Scotia Hellfire Sword.

It was pretty evident from the way the mist was forming that it was not a gas release or condensation build up, no visible lines or pipes were feeding into the case. The glass case filled with the mist to such a volume that nothing was visible for a full 10 seconds, after which the mist just simply vanished.' The Major picked up the remote control and stopped the DVD. All eyes turned towards him. 'Major, do you have something else to say?' prompted the Minister.

'Gentlemen, I have been protecting these walls for twenty six and half years, I have encountered thieves, vandals, anarchists and terrorists, and what you are about to observe is something that I simply cannot comprehend, let alone defend you from.' The Major took a swallow and sat back down on his seat, then pressed the 'play' button on the handheld remote control.

The digital recording machine buzzed a little then screen cleared and the image presented was the digital display that fed the security systems. The gauges on the outside of the glass case clearly showed a visible rise in temperature of 5 degrees, the red coloured digital indicator LED was increasing slowly bringing the heat level to what would be the normal human body temperature. It was then that an apparition became visible as the heat sensors and motion sensors recalibrated themselves against the screen display and showed a sudden temperature drop eventually displaying that the chamber was returning to almost zero.

Although all the heat systems were detecting a physical mass present in the vault, no alarms were triggered; the digital floor sensors gave no reading of weight on any of the external indicators. Although all peripheral proximity sensors displayed the presence of a physical being, a detection expected if a person was actually standing in the vault, on this occasion no person could be visually observed, but one who would weigh 56.5 kilograms exactly was present according to only one sensor within the display cabinet that flashed '56.5, 56.5'.

The mist in the cabinet began to coalesce into the shape of a full human type figure. This apparition was not the common or garden variety, but a mix of mist and obscurity. This, as far as the Papacy was concerned, was the most significant manifestation since the Lady of Lourdes appeared to Bernadette Soubirous more than a hundred and fifty years ago in Nevers, but this time caught on state of the art digital camera and imaging systems. The figure continued to linger around the cabinet, until the case too was enveloped in the mist.

The figure stared directly at the camera and smiled softly, gently even. Then raised its right hand over the case, the left hand appeared to be holding a bouquet of white roses. The apparition then kissed two fingers and presented them to the camera. In doing so it appeared to walk backwards and disappeared into the stainless steel bulkhead that lined the inner vault. The DVD stopped playing.

'What kind of trickery is this?' Demanded Colonel Anjou of the internal affairs security guard. 'This is obviously a hoax; no one could have got into that vault. I have the master digital fortress key and I also carry the only master key to the old door. Sir, it is impossible even for me to gain entry without endorsement and approval or without detection, but this, it can only be trickery.'

The apathetic Minister sat quietly and had obviously been moved by the vision, clearly disturbed by its sheer awesome power. Then he spoke: 'How can a mist or an apparition remove a physical sword weighing 6 to 8 kilograms through a stainless steel barrier, let alone penetrate a hermetically sealed, bullet-proof cabinet, then just disappear into the walls?'

The room was very silent contemplating what the Minister had just said. There was an air of apprehension, almost fear, as the reality of what was on the camera disk sank in. 'We will run this DVD through the science department, let them apply their investigative techniques and provide a rational approach towards this event, until such time as we have a confirmation or denial of its authenticity gentlemen, this matter is of the utmost secrecy, and is not to be discussed outside this room.'

The Minister ordered that every DVD recording system and the hard wiring looms across the Vatican's domain were to be inspected and interrogated for damage or intervention. The Minister for the Interior halted the Major as he was about to leave the room. 'Well done Major La Rou.

I am not sure what I think of all this, but I know you are a man of great substance and that your team are of the highest calibre, just as a domain such as ours would command, but please, make sure that this issue remains within our walls. If this is real, and I think it may well be, then we will have some thought provoking questions for His Eminence and senior conclave next assembly.'

Meanwhile, in the subterranean vault number 33 there was an intensity of activity that amounted to a full forensic crime scene investigation, one which had been underway since the discovery of the mystical theft. The Vatican had pulled all their professional resources from their homes and beds and it was just turning 07:13 hours on Sunday morning. The walls were being thermally scanned, thickness tests were being conducted, adjacent ancient vaults were being identified on schematics, none of which highlighted anything of significance.

The outer vault wall had been cemented to almost six feet in thickness throughout when the vault was originally constructed; it had been reinforced with steel framing to prevent anyone from drilling into the vault. This particular vault was, in fact, designed to protect its contents from a potential nuclear explosion.

There was slight damage to the lock system, but this was dismissed as a slight grazing to the lock which had occurred during the planned cleaning rota. It had been recorded in the installation and maintenance records of cabinet 33 in vault 33, as a slight abrasion and nothing of concern.

Eighteen hours later and it had been a very long day, for both the administrators and the security staff. At 23:33:33 hours lockdown was activated and the Vatican's vaults fell into infra red silence, the security had doubled their manpower and each station was technically in control of the environment with no anomalies to worry about.

CHAPTER FIVE

THE LADY VISITS

Kemp Hastings fell onto his puffy duvet with his laptop just as his email flashed up, having just returned from an excursion to town, a chance meeting with a colleague in the village provided an excellent excuse to chill out and let the day go by without anymore annoyances, and now he was completely coffee'd out. His mobile telephone rang, he flicked open the lid and gave the incoming number the once over the screen displayed 'Number withheld.' He threw the phone down beside him on the soft blanket and stretched out across the bed it was, then that phone rang again. 'Hello, Hastings, very tired and very late at night, how can I help you?'

'Kemp, it's Darlene Gammay, I know this is going to sound crazy but five minutes ago there was a figure or an apparition, not sure which but she was standing in my bath, and earlier on this evening, my computer was being sent pictures of safety vaults and weird apparitions, then my computer would not turn off and when it did turn off, it suddenly came back on again even though I had removed the power source. I know this will sound stupid but the image on the manuscript you showed me well I am positive it was the face from the lady on the vellum, the one you think may be of the red haired Madonna, I just caught a glimpse of her in my bathroom mirror.'

Hastings had dealt with this kind of call before, but not from a rational scientist. He then tried to calm the Doctor down and rationilse what she was saying. 'Calm down Darlene,' he said. 'Has it gone or is it still there?' There was a brief silence followed by a 'Yes.'

'Okay Darlene take it easy, is that a "yes it's gone" or "yes it is still there?"' 'Yes it's gone,' came the reply.

'Listen, you sound a bit stressed out to me, yesterday's chit chat may have just been a bit too much for your overdeveloped brain to handle, make yourself a nice cup of tea or take some drugs, but you must relax.' The phone suddenly went very silent. 'Don't patronise me Mr Hastings, I was just about to run a bath, and as a matter of fact, I do not take drugs and have my life is very much in order thank you, a simple viewing of a 2nd century piece of vellum is not going to send me doolally now isit? Good night.' The phone clicked. Kemp took a deep breath. 'Well that went well,' he thought, kicking himself. He then rolled over, eventually falling asleep.

Three o'clock in the morning came very slowly and Hastings found himself lying on his bed staring up at the ornate plasterwork above his head. Tiny cherubs and angels adorned the cornice, each little figure sculpted in elegant poses and all appeared to be singing and dancing. He smiled as he spied their little wings and Pan's flutes that had been so delicately sculpted into the moulding. And then eeling a bit guilty, he sent a text to Doctor Gammay's phone: 'Sorry, did not mean to patronise, call me!'

He then grabbed a book from his bedside table, 'The Old Road to Damascus' by Darlene Gammay, and began to read. At some point mid-page he fell asleep again. Darlene Gammay in the meantime opened her bathroom door and stared in to the modest sized modern shower and toilet space. All was quiet, no figure of the white lady holding a bouquet of roses for her to accept, no mists forming an apparition to frighten the living daylights out of her, there was just the lingering smell of sweet scented roses.

She ran the bath and stepped into it letting the bubbles absorb her aching, tired, middle-aged muscles. Thinking that Kemp could be right—maybe she was a bit uptight with losing her job at the university and the parchment being one of the best examplse she had ever encountered, and she was just interpreting things differently. As she dozed off she could feel the warm water lapping away at her skin, a million tiny sparkling sensations massaged her into relax mode, it felt as if champagne was being poured all over her, then the sweet smell of coconut and chocolate filled her nostrils.

She took another deep breath then fell into oblivion. Her flight sensation was vivid: she could feel the wind wafting through her hair and the sporadic puffs of warm air passing over her ample breasts. She awoke in a warm haze and could hear her name being called very faintly, it was a rhapsody from the heavens and the soft tones of Angels singing filled her head.

The water around her was suddenly littered with white rose petals; thousands of them lay scattered across the top of the bath water in a white blanket of patchwork petals. She stepped out the bath and opened the plain wooden door that led into her living room. Dr Gammay stood transfixed at the sight before her, unable to move she watched on in awe to what lay before her.

The room had been transformed into the central aisle of the largest of cathedrals in the kingdom of belief, rows upon rows of candles brightened up the house of someone's god. All the candles were fantastic sizes and colours and no expense had been spared on the copious amount of golden candlestick holders and refinements that adorn any modern day cathedral, even if it was in her living space.

She was caught up in a dream state. She wandered towards the four figures that were kneeling before her just a few yards away, and she was floating on an air of warmth and comfort. She stopped and gazed upon them, she knew who they were, she knew their stories and their accounts of the Old Testament and perhaps snippets of the New, she readily identified their task: they had come to her in her dream to confirm her belief in the 'one'. She licked her lips and could taste the sweet scent of roses and grapes as a wisp of wind caught the back of her throat. She spoke.

'Is this heaven?' she asked. 'Have I died in my bath whilst seeking forgiveness for my brash manner and misunderstanding of the Lord's work?' The four white-mantled figures remained silent and motionless. A few moments passed then one figure stood up, followed by the others, each entity was holding a golden chalice with their own names heavily embossed in red lettering on it. 'Mathew, Mark, Luke and John.' She smiled.

Behind the assembled phantom Apostles the apparition appeared again, she still holding her basket of white roses. She was a beautiful woman—her skin whiter than white, her eyes bluer than blue. The mass of flowing red hair matched Darlene's own, reaching down over her shoulders. The apparition then cast her right hand over the four white clad individuals, then spoke very softly.

'These are the storytellers, their words are my words, these prophets are my prophets. And they are now yours, your words will be their words and the Lord will tell all.' The lady stared on as Darlene reached out and covered herself with a silken sheet from the sofa, which was somehow there and yet not there. 'Who are you?' she asked. 'Why have you come here to me?'

The white lady smiled a smile beyond all smiles and blinked those big blue eyes. 'You have been chosen to carry the gospel of the 'one', for I am the Silent Apostle relative to Andrew, and perhaps deemed the Apostles' Apostle,' she said, then melted out of sight, along with the conclave of supporting misty clerics.

Darlene suddenly jumped up from inside her bath sending waves of cold water sweeping across the marble floor and over the taps. 'Shit!' she exclaimed very loudly whilst grabbing the sides of the bath to prevent herself from slipping under the water again. 'That was so vivid.' She cut herself off in mid sentence, because floating on the bath lay a blanket of white petals. She froze momentarily and picked up a single petal—it was real. She carefully stepped out of the bath staring all around her, her slender mature body speckled with white petals, each sticking to her skin as the sweet scent of roses still lingered in the air.

She stood upright and took a step towards the door then froze, very hesitantly she opened it, expecting to hear the toccata being played on an old church organ at a million decibels and the choir sitting on her sofa singing 'Come All Ye Faithful', but it was not the case. Her living room was just as she had left it, untidy with a healthy littering of academic study books and notes from her university days, and the odd Marks and Spencer bag stuffed with shoes or handbags lay in the corner.

She grabbed the white sheet that lay strewn on the sofa and covered herself up, then sat down. She felt quite vibrant considering she had nearly drowned in the bath after an episode of deep sleep, and an encounter with four apostles and what appeared to be the Virgin Mary in her living room.

'Happens to me every day,' she muttered, then made a strong cup of tea. She sat in the quiet flat and began to feel itchy; her clean sheet was irritating her skin as if she had used a dodgy fabric softener during laundering. After a few seconds of scratching she made her way back into the bathroom, appearing quite relaxed on the surface, but was ready to run like the wind if anything else popped up out of the woodwork or her shower cubicle.

Anointing

The blackbird's morning chorus was too much for Hastings to endure; he slowly kicked off his duvet slid out of bed then jumped in the shower. The radio volume was loud enough for him to hear some cleric talking about the Old Testament and biblical life in its numerical layout. Kemp threw the towel, embroidered on the corner with his initials, on the bed. He wanted things that were his to be his, and therefore had most of his worldly belongings embossed or printed with his initials, 'KHRL', in blue. He liked blue, it was a warm royal colour, and the Army brainwashing compelled him to identify his own space. The presenter on the radio continued.

'We see that most of the bible is made up of numbers and references, but what we have failed to do is record all these numbers in their sequence of appearance. For example, let's take Jeremiah from the Old Testament, second major prophet of Christianity, in his work he records the destruction of Solomon's temple in the year 587 BC, so therefore logically our first number is 587.'

The cleric on the radio went on and so forth through the whole of the chapter culminating in a huge list of numbers. Hastings turned off the radio and stared. 'What a saddo,' he said and threw on his glad rags. 'Gospel or Godspell same old conundrum, the good news book, what a storyline,' he thought. 'Ten percent of global sales would be great.'

Hastings continued on his train of thought and muttered out loudly. 'Plus the addition of four new testaments, all about the life of one individual. Now let me think, what was Mathew famed for, five great teachings claiming the Messiah as the King, I bet King David was a bit upset when he heard that one, this new King of the Jews. And of course there was Matthew's role in life, and if he was a taxman, then I bet he was very popular with the masses, not.'

Hastings wandered around his apartment adding some little homely adjustments to his living space as if he was walking through the palaces of the East, taking time to reflect his thoughts whilst reading the parchments. He stopped by a large oval mirror. 'I wonder what inspired him to mention Moses, did Moses pay taxes?' That was going to be his question for the day, who paid the bloody taxman? He walked on. 'Of course writing under the pseudonym of 'Levi' was always a good way to remain incognito.'

The radio buzzed and gave a few bleeps and the radio cleric chap rattled off a few numbers, groups of threes and sevens: there were three gifts, three temptations, seven parables and seven woes, chapters two, four, thirteen and twenty three. Hastings gazed up at the ceiling. 'All too much to remember,' he said tracing his steps back to his book shelf.

He grabbed a small book from the bottom shelf, it read: 'Assisi', he flicked a few pages and studied a few passages. A few moments passed as he stood in his humble abode, then donning a more theatrical pose he began reading out loudly, as if presenting to a much larger audience.

'Hello all ye who have gathered in my presence, my name is Francis my full name is Giovanni Francesco di Bernadone, I lived between the years 1181 and 1226, and led my life as a Catholic Deacon and a Preacher albeit in my time I founded the Priors Minor. I have a great love for animals and I am seen today as one of Catholicism's patron saints. My simple baptism was conducted in the name of St John and provided me with great aspiration to climb the dizzy heights of the church's senior ranking officials to become a dominant religious leader.' Hastings was walking around his flat and casting his hand over all the furniture and blessing all things in his path.

'My father and I moved to the village of Assisi where suddenly he began calling me Francis to accommodate this new culture of

French influence, not sure if I liked it much, the new name well it sort of made a certain sense. I spent some time in the village of Assisi and took to selling cloths and linen in the small marketplace, eventually becoming a well known and a recognisable face in market society, especially when I would drop my prices to sell more items than other traders. I know they must have hated me for it.

After a turbulent time with my father, and having gone to fight a battle for some inane reason, the justification of which really still eludes me, I find myself chained and in captivity, over twelve months now, and I have taken to deep prayer in this desperate time of my life.' Hastings found the mirror again and stared at his reflection and read on. Circa 1204 Francis became very ill, which dragged him into spiritual crisis.

'I am ill, delusional even, and yet I see godly visions. Angels have visited me several times, each messenger of the Lord telling me not to worry as I am not due to be visited by the Reaper too soon.' These angels decreed that I Francis of Assisi should take time with the poor and infirm and look after the many lepers who walked the cold inhospitable streets of the city.

'My father Pietro he is also ill, fuelled with alcohol and rage he has beaten me several times now, I despise his very being, yet I love as any son loves his father, our love is destined to be distant I fear.' Francis turned to god for forgiveness and eventually walked the streets as a beggar.

'My world is greater than this, I have my health today and I have my respect for others.' Hastings was becoming emotional, this account of Assisi's life was not one of money and rich pickings, but one of a man who had been ostracised by his family and left to defend what little self worth he possessed.

'Francis would hear callings, angels singing 'Mary of the Angels' over and over as he slept, he would wake up in the morning in the cold street and head for the church of the same name just outside the city boundary. 1209 was a turning point in his holy life; he had recently heard of Claire of Assisi and asked the Lord, 'Why was it not me, why have you chosen another and not your devout son?' He left Assisi and was soon to be found shipwrecked off the coast of Dalmatia en route for Jerusalem, and then forced to return to Italy.

Francis soon found he wanted to travel to many countries, and he returned to Assisi a wiser and older man. Up until around the year 1220 Francis had been to Egypt and back several times. In 1224 the traumatic event of stigmata happened to Francis in a whirlwind of events. His brother Leo and Francis were enthralled at the awesome power of the Lord; and Francis duly received all the wounds of Christ.'

Hastings was singing aloud and was twirling about in his humble abode, he was singing psalm 141 to his captured audience of one, himself. Francis eventually passed over and had a not so blind date with Mister Death, who just happened to be in the area. It was on October the third 1224.

Kemp stared out the window, it had started to rain and tiny trickles of accumulated water ran in strips over the glass. Kemp turned and pointed across the room. 'How much pain did you actually suffer Mr Francis of Assisi?' he said aloud and closed the book, then continued his speech on the life of Assisi.

'Buried four years after death, why so bloody long Mr Pope? And what was Pope Gregory thinking of waiting so long, mind you he founded the Basilica in the name of Francis, then had his remains interred in a large jar for all to see, must have been air tight as well, and then again I wonder if they used any chemical enhancement products, mummified with a good layer of wax to provide a clean image. After all Francis was a well respected man of the cloth.' All these simple options Kemp allowed to run riot through his head.

'Right! So then what about our lovely Bernadette, why is she still in a state of perfection or non corruptibility, was her body treated any different than any other high profile religious person post death, Francis as a recent example. Apparently not it seems, she too was given great dignity in death.' Hastings searched his extensive library, knowing full well he had a book on Miss Soubirous and her very strange young life.

'Marie Bernada Sobiros, born 7th January 1844 in Lourdes, France' read Hastings from the book's abstract. This 14 year old peasant girl who had little perception of worldly goings on, let alone the standing of the church in the big wide world, why would she choose to take on the might of the world at large with these visions or sightings if they were not true?

'Amazing,' remarked Hastings, picking up on the only coincidence he could find, he concluded that they both shared a few letters of their names, and yet nothing more. Bernada and Bernadone, as an example maybe if one has 'Berna-something' in one's name then one 'art' somehow special . . . Bernadette died on the eighteenth of April 1879 at the age of thirty five years, her body was then entombed a couple of times after death, and of course exhumed a couple of times. Strange that the body had remained supple and still in fairly good condition. Hastings wondered if the soil and the sealed coffin were contributory to this long lasting phenomenon.

'But these visions, she believed she was exposed to some divine visitation by the Holy Mother or indeed the "Immaculate Conception". But what is it that triggered these visits, if they are to be believed, especially over a fifteen day period? And yet the holy waterspring had sprung for the betterment of mankind. Maybe these events are inexplicable, but what were the real circumstances that led to such media coverage? And what about the digging of the holy well, a fountain that is hailed to heal the sick? Is this not fantastic in its own right?'

Kemp was very sceptical, he never hung his hat on trickery or believed in witchcraft, but recently had turned his thoughts towards time, space and science fiction, especially because of his recent encounter with something that still defied his logic. The most recent medical examination of Bernadette revealed that her skeletal frame was intact and in a good state of preservation.

There were sprinklings of salt found on her body, but insufficient amounts to be of any concern. The doctor performing the examination recorded the softness of the inner organs, and stated he was very surprised that the body had not deteriorated as one would have expected.

Hastings was baffled, he had seen many dead bodies in his time in the Armed forces, and had been exposed to a few older carcasses lying in the sun, and he had smelled a few, he knew the aroma of death was not a good one, yet these special people supposedly exhibited a sweeter smell in death. Hastings placed the book back on his library shelving.

CHAPTER SIX

THE REVELATION OF ANDREW

The next day Hastings had agreed to meet with Dr Gammay at Deacon Brodie's, and two o'clock was fast approaching as he sat at the corner table on his lonesome staring at the manuscript. He had agreed to lend the document to science but only under the watchful eye of the Biblical Studies teacher.

He was twisting the manuscript around in his hands when he caught a glimpse of the fiery red-head approaching. 'God,' he thought, 'she looks different today,' watching her curves sway captured in the tight fitting red dress, her soft long hair enhancing her ample womanly attributes. Why had he not noticed her in this attractive guise before? 'You look radiant,' he said standing up and moving the chair for the Doctor to sit down, and took her jacket and placed it over the third chair. 'Thank you, I do feel a bit dynamic today, must have been a good sleep.' Kemp placed his index finger in the air.

'Not the apparition in your bath then.' Darlene stared through him.

'No that episode I have put down to my reflection in the mirror. Kemp knew when to stay quiet and this was one of those times, fiery red haired Scottish women are not to be challenged when they think they are right. 'I have the manuscript with me, the Fisher Queens want your assurance that it will not be physically tampered with in any destructive way, but we understand that you will remove the most minimal of threads, just a few millimetres of fibre, for your sample test in line with current protocols, is that all the tests consist of?'

The waitress appeared again, ironically the same one as before but a little more with it this time. 'What can I get ya?' she offered with a smile, then remembered their last order: 'chocolate with brandy and a latte?' She said with conviction, then stood staring at Darlene Gammay for a full five seconds as her mind wandered.

'Please.' Hastings responded. 'That will be all, thank you.' The waitress disappeared into the back kitchen and returned a few minutes later with the hot drinks. 'So this must be an interesting time for you, Darlene, with your ad hoc lecturing and no pimple-arsed students to fight with, life must be exciting?' Hastings was desperately trying to grab her full attention. 'Darlene?' he said, raising his voice slightly higher.

'Sorry, Kemp I was miles away, drifting away on the aroma of your chocolate and coconut brandy, smells nice.' Kemp took a deep breath. 'You're right there, I can detect a hint of coconut in this, mmm! Darlene then explained the test process in its entirety to Hastings as he sat staring at her beauty and sipping his chocolate drink, giving the Doctor his full attention. Darlene placed a small booklet on the table. 'This describes the complete process, no damage that's guaranteed,' then she slid the brochure towards him.

'OCR or Optical Character Script Recognition software is where we place a known language script on the plate, and scan it many times using or manipulating a neural path technique, the software recognises every miniscule anomaly and matches against other known documents of the same era. We can also identify the handwriting to 98% clarity. Mr Hastings a document is deemed ancient only if it fits certain criteria, and only if it is two hundred years of age or older.

And it must also fit the condition that it is free from suspicion concerning its authenticity, and must have been found or located in a place where writing was likely to be kept, so, if this document came out of an older archive such as the Vatican or a library as an example then it would be a great start point. But these are the federal laws and they must be given due consideration for any document that is likely to raise the blood pressure levels of the Pope or the President of the United States.

Script recognition has been conducted this way for a few years now, and is the assured method employed by most universities. The software, believe it or not, is multilingual and can be set up for 80% of the known languages on our planet, the advent of the Nag Hammadi scrolls for instance has opened new horizons into this world of nanu featuring and script identification practices and these are being developed as we speak.

Believe it or not Mr Hastings we can train the software to recognise classifiers in a language and watch that language migrate across a nation whilst at the same time observing the subtle changes to each written script, the method today is also based on harmonics and voice recognition software, when coupled with the OCR program we can almost pin point every detail we are looking for in order to corroborate our target document. We could argue that other documents allude to the existence of this document but, again, this could be taken as hearsay. The process of documentation authentication is indeed a very complicated one.

Convolutional neural networks on the other hand are enhanced at component level with properties of local receptive fields for weighting. The sharing of spatial sub sampling of text layers is where they capture or learn data of images extracted from the raw data. Data which has been interpreted from the source document, and by the time it is analysed the document is effectively almost bare. In a nutshell Kemp, the document is placed within a pipeline, as it were, and pushed along a long tube from the image process phase to script identification phase, where we end up with a series of overlay documents in colour, each highlighting anomalies and trends. We then try and piece it all together like a jigsaw, and that is the art of science.'

Kemp was bemused. 'So, what you are saying is that you x-ray the document and break it down and print out as pretty pictures of each stage then check it against the handwriting, in a calligraphical type of approach?'

Darlene was almost fuming at his very accurate and succinct analysis of the most tried and tested scientific process, a method that had corroborated most of the important documents in existence today. Suffice to say that Hastings was definitely not a moron but was a silent learned man with a sense of humour that needed taming.

'It's not that simple Kemp, you have to ensure that any chemicals do not deteriorate the paper, or that ambient air temperature is not too high or too low, or moisture is not allowed to ingress into the test cell, they all seem like silly insignificant things but they can destroy illuminated manuscripts in seconds.'

Kemp smiled. 'Remember this thing survived the great fire of bloody London.' Darlene had the inclination to give her shoulder another scratch and reached around, making the excuse that she must have an allergic reaction to the soap powder she was using. Kemp took a drink of his coffee and smiled. 'Love that coconut, don't you?'

She smirked back at him, still giving herself a wee scratch. 'Does that look inflamed to you?' She asked, turning her shoulder towards him. 'It looks a bit a red but nothing dramatic, most of it is hidden by your tattoo,' he said, placing his mug on the beer mat.

Darlene was staring at him, her eyebrows half cocked. 'Very funny, I don't have a tattoo, I don't even like them they tarnish the skin, and look terrible when you are old and wrinkly with bingo wings.' She shrugged her shoulders.

'Well if that is not a tattoo, then you have to explain to me why a rash would take the form of a dove's wing not unlike one of Rossetti's masterpieces, I mean it looks good from here.' Darlene was bemused.

'Mr Hastings-' she cut herself short, grabbed her bag and disappeared to the toilet. Kemp meanwhile caught the waitress's attention and ordered two more hot chocolates with two glasses of neat brandy.

Darlene closed the door to the cubicle and stared at herself in the mirror. 'Right Darlene, a lot of strange shit has been happening the last two days, now if you have a tattoo there will be a perfectly rational reason as to why. 'Now when did you last check your shoulders for a tattoo?' She took an extra deep breath and pulled her T shirt down over her shoulder then flicked the elastic of her bra strap out of the way, then turned to see what she could of her back against the tiny mirror.

Sure enough she could make out the blue-white wing of a dove, then a colourful patch. She stopped and grabbed the wash hand basin. 'What in God's name is happening here?' Then she stripped down as far as she dared for a better look. After a few minutes she returned to the table, almost shell shocked. 'Kemp do you have a digital camera with you?'

He placed his mug down on the table. 'I do in my apartment.' 'Good. You are probably the only person at the moment I think

I can trust, I have no idea how I have managed to get a tattoo on my shoulder, it was not there when I took a recent bath . . .' she stopped herself. 'Anyway it has appeared from somewhere. If those little bastard college students have done this they will suffer.' Kemp leaned forward. 'Okay no problem, do you have a girlfriend you can call and let her know where you are, make things less tense for me.' Darlene rubbed her forehead. 'I have already text a friend your car number plate and she knows your name.'

Kemp pushed the Jaguar just above the speed limits to appease Darlene, a show of understanding given the gravity of the new scenario that neither of them understood. In his flat he found his camera and gave it to the Doctor. 'No, Kemp please take a full picture of my back,' she demanded and disappeared into the small bathroom. Hastings now wished that he had taken a residence with a larger bathroom, one which didn't have the bath actually situated across the corridor. At least there was a mirror. He smirked in embarrassment.

A few seconds later she emerged wearing a standard Kemp Hastings fluffy Royal Hotel bathing gown with embroidered initials and turned her back to him and dropped the top half of the robe. Kemp was fidgeting with the SD card, when he glanced up he was taken by total surprise, what stood before him was not only the beautiful well proportioned body of Darlene Gammay, but a tattoo that covered eighty percent of her back and left shoulder blade.

A work of art with a depiction of what Kemp could only describe as a biblical pre-Raphaelite imprint adorned with words in Latin and some strange symbols, the same wording that was reflected in the manuscript that lay just a few feet away in the hidden drawer in his writing bureau. He took several pictures, three straight on and a couple from the side capturing her ample left breast. 'Darlene,' he said in a very soft calm voice. 'This is a work of art, why would you want to hide it?' She pulled Kemp's robe back over her shoulders. 'Okay then, what on earth is it? Here, let me see.' Kemp pulled the camera away from her.

'Listen. You say you never had a tattoo, before you look at these pictures, just give it a single thought, did you go out with students from the university or get drunk with friends? Because that tattoo must have taken a few sittings, it's a work of art.'

Darlene stood up straight and took the camera off Kemp. 'Listen, I would know if I had a bloody tattoo now wouldn't I?' She flicked the power switch and worked her way through each exposure, slowly beginning to cry with each flick of the forward button. A few moments later she looked up as the reality and the enormity of the tattoo subsumed her natural logical self.

She placed the camera on the Mexican table top and sat on the edge of the sofa. 'How can this happen to me? This is the same as that manuscript, the Latin is quite clear, the woman, that face there.' She pointed to the face on the camera screen. 'She was the apparition from last night, oh my god Kemp, I am being haunted by someone or something unnatural.' Kemp leaned over and offered her an open pair of arms.

She accepted, and cried herself to sleep. Eventually he settled the doctor into his comfortable big bed and took refuge on the sofa. As he downloaded the pictures onto his laptop, Darlene Gammay was very much fast asleep. Kemp trawled the internet then called a few friends, he was desperate to let someone know of this unique event, but knew there would be absolute chaos if any of the media got wind of such a happening.

He decided to read more about the Hellfire Sword, his short exposure to its presence a few months back had left him with a fear of the unknown. His last investigation was placed under a blanket of secrecy by the Fisher Queens and the Ministry of Defence, and he wanted it to stay that way. A couple of hours had passed and

Kemp was sitting near the open fire when he was alerted by a presence in the room.

'What time is it?' A soft voice said, and Hastings jumped out of his skin, and closed the laptop.

'Are you okay, you have been sleeping for hours, shall I make you a cup of tea?' Darlene dragged a hand through her thick red shiny hair. Kemp stared at her for a few seconds then made his way to the kitchen.

'Yes please.' The Doctor leaned on the door frame. 'Thanks for letting me sleep,' she said then sat cross legged in the middle of the floor. 'You are quite welcome to use the sofa,' he murmured passing a mug of tea down to her. As she reached up Kemp was taken aback by the intensity of her piercing blue eyes, they were the bluest he had ever seen with the whitest of white sclera. They pierced his soul and he melted, even her hair was redder than red, did that mean she was more fiery than most red-heads? Probably.

His mind wandered off to another planet; she was not just the plain Jane of biblical studies he had taken her for. She was now an incredible phenomenon with a tattoo the size of an A2 sheet of paper spread across her body, and not just any tattoo this one depicted a biblical scene which had miraculously jumped from a piece of dead animal skin onto the living tissue of Doctor Darlene Gammay.

This woman had obviously been chosen to represent a higher order of something, the only problem was why and how and where and when and so forth. Darlene stood up and said she was going to have another half hour's kip as she was still tired and made her way back into the soft land of Hastings's duvet.

CHAPTER SEVEN

RESEARCH

Kemp flashed up his database and searched some internet links, he could find nothing that even touched on the phenomenon of the Epistula of Magdalene being transferred to a human, it was not even remotely mentioned. He tossed the idea around in his head, now what was stigmata all about, one who is blessed or cursed with the wounds of Christ, one who is devout beyond all comprehension, one who revels in worship. Had the Holy 'one' singled out Darlene Gammay and blessed her with this sign of an unnatural origin? How could an entity manage to tattoo such detail within a few short hours, the detail would take the normal artist 54 hours in its entirety and even then the detail would be bland and not as crisp as this example.

He researched the Veronica veil, then browsed a few web pages for the Shroud of Turin. Although each had significance in the world of Christianity they were coupled with conjecture, stories or testimony from what may well be credible sources. Kemp was searching for terminology in order to get his head around the situation.

He concluded that Mary had been silent for years, her story was originally thrown into obscurity and regarded as non fact, an attempt by the church to discredit the fact that she was perhaps the driver behind Christianity in the first place, but, and it was a very big 'but', she was a woman, and in the eyes of the old world Arabic community not deemed an equal. She had kept silent and portrayed her likeness and her story to the modern day world by visual representation although still in silence.

'Yep!' Thought Kemp, 'very apt, she was to known as the Silent Apostle, whilst speaking volumes in the grand scheme of things.' Darlene Gammay had indeed been marked with a phenomenon that the media press would exploit beyond the normal realms of exploitation. Kemp struggled with his emotions as he watched the good Doctor sleep, although a fiery red head, she was still a female who needed protection from the external society of modern day life. Kemp stared on as she slept. In her dream state she kept drifting in and out of real time and 'dropped off the cliff' more than once as her muscles flinched into spasm.

'Darlene Gammy may well be the first woman to have been singled out and adorned with holy recognition since our Lady of Lourdes,' thought Kemp. He contemplated the real impact that such an advent could have on the Doctor's life, let alone the psychological trauma that she would have to endure if this went public.

Kemp read a few more snippets from the unconfirmed Gospel of the Magdalene. Doctor Gammay had written a comprehensive study of the Apostles and reviewed over 1700 documents in the course of her study. Could her condition be self induced? The phenomenon of stigmata sprung back into his mind. He opened the book at page thirty two and read the top line of the gospel according to the 'one.'

Maybe this is the soul that will overcome the third power, the one which took seven forms; primarily darkness, then desire, followed by ignorance, the blissful one, then death, naturally preceded by human flesh coupled with the wisdom of flesh. Wrathful wisdom was the final conclusion of the seven.

'Well that makes no sense to me at all,' he said flicking the many pages. 'Maybe I should read the whole thing again.' he muttered, and placing his hands over his forehead he began to read. 'The life cycle of nature is where all things formed will return to the ground whence they came, dissolved back to their roots.' He decided to review the cycle of human life from cradle to grave and quizzed his laptop.

He then drank some of his cold chocolate drink whilst opening the link to the Apostles and their worth on the computer. One phrase kept repeating in his mind. The son of man is with you, the daughter of human creation coexists within us all. 'Surely this brainwashing has got to cease somewhere. These comments are after all written or recorded by mere men.'

Why is the lady known as the Magdalene silent? He sat back and let his stress dissipate into his laptop as he punched the keys mapping his way between many pages of available information. After an hour or so he began drifting off into a hazy slumber desperately dragging his memory with him, an effort to trawl up anything that made sense relating to Darlene's condition. He knew there must be a rational explanation for all this, but it seemed to be hovering ten thousand miles away from his grasp. He recalled some of his biblical study periods, casting his mind back to what was known as 'Gospel Week' during his school days.

But what of this hidden gospel? Now that was a subject that was never really discussed, what was it all about though? Had Mary Magdalene actually written this work by her own hand, if so what language would it be in? Certainly not English and not Latin. He contemplated retrieving the parchment from the bureau.

This sample was clearly written in ancient Latin but there were a few odd symbols, Aramaic or Migdalese. If Migdalese still actually existed, it would be the local dialect of the fishing village of Magdal and it was plausible that this Mary could read and write amongst her other many attributes. This would be unusual, bearing in mind that not many of the women of the land were permitted to write, only those of influence.

A woman of influence was nevertheless still a woman in the physical sense, had this Mary actually sinned? Kemp muttered, 'Who cares anyway this is the 21st century it's part of daily life, too much killing and global trauma to worry about a few indiscretions, although back then, things were probably not as easy, and an order of things had to be maintained. The Romans may have even restricted population growth.'

'Taming a red head today would be a task in itself, and not one to be taken lightly,' he thought. 'If a man decides to marry one of these selective bright ladies then it would be at his own peril. These women are decisive, direct, commanding and demanding, yet possess the calmest of loving natures until you piss them off, then you may experience the wrath of hell.' Kemp retrieved the manuscript and sat at the bureau, he flicked open the A4 fly sheet and froze.

Transition

The manuscript lay in front of him, the same cover, the same protective sleeve, and yes, the vellum was still as fresh and rose-smelling as it had always been. If it had not been due the fact that the written gospel had either been erased completely or the sheet had been replaced, things would have been okay. What remained within the folder was a nice new, clean, and very bare, sheet of vellum waiting to be employed, a single sheet of hide presenting itself for use. He turned it over, the back was blank too. Kemp placed his head in his hands.

He stood up and stretched. Taking a few steps towards his bedroom he took a quick glance into the room—his guest was still sleeping. She was face down and naked, the duvet covering her lower body, the work of the unknown author offering its text and message and image for all to see. He tried to make a comparison.

What if somehow this vellum, this unique Epistula Incorruptible of the Magdala Lady, had mysteriously migrated from vellum to human skin, what if it had jumped into Darlene's DNA mapping when she ran her fingers over the vellum not so long ago, surely that's miraculous? What if Darlene was the only woman to have made contact with the physical parchment since its writing, unusual, admittedly strange, almost bizarre, then again there a few things in this world that are inexplicable. 'The supernatural at work,' he thought and closed the door.

Kemp wandered back to the desk. What was it that Sister Roza said about the Gospels? "Do not grieve or mourn this passing for he is not dead?" The message clearly recorded, and Peter may have said: "Mary our Sister we know that the saviour loved you more than other women." Well that just confirms he was a red-blooded male and would have confided in the Magdalene more intimately. Mary's biblical words are perhaps recorded as: "What is hidden from you I will impart to you." 'Must read Matthew 6:21 more clearly,' Kemp thought, then quoted another snippet to himself.

He flicked a few pages of the book. "I saw you in a vision." 'Yep,' thought Kemp, 'past tense not present. What was the translation of James's Bible trying to achieve, did the King think that the masses would be easily converted by one English translation of a work that was fabricated or moulded to suit the times having been bastardised from the original gathering of data?'

Kemp placed himself back a few hundred years in time. 'Imagine trying to exist in the turmoil of Jacobean Scotland and England.' The world at large was not going to fall for an English version of events, especially since Europe was in turmoil, the world was at war with itself and religion was being implemented by the rulers of the day, Kings who had differing perceptions of what was to be the master model. 'Glad I am alive today and not then.' Darlene had done her homework; the book was interesting and informative, but indicated nothing as to what she had been exposed to, no previous data to follow up on, no archive to interrogate.

He appreciated that not many sentences from the gospels according to Andrew, who would seek the opinions of the Apostles, were evident today. And Peter opposed her standing in the group and was said to be often distant towards her, as he thought she was more informed that he was. 'Trouble in the ranks Bombardier,' he muttered closing the book.

Internal Inquiry

The Swiss Guard security team for vault 33 had assembled in the upper gallery. Major La Rou was sitting with a note pad and pen on his knee and was addressing the team. The investigation was to clarify the events leading up to the day for installing the new acquisition. 'So let me get this straight, we took possession of article 333, the 'Tartarus Inferni', two days ago and it was placed and sealed into cabinet thirty three by 15:00 hours on the first day.

It was then installed by Guardsman Vernier and Guardsman Russi, who both locked the cabinet and activated the hermetic sealing. Guardsman Vernier, you activated the passive atmosphere control system, Guardsman Russi you activated the optical imagery and motion sensor equipment, that's fine.' The Major looked up. 'Gentlemen, was there a release of gases, argon, helium or nitrogen or any anomaly after you placed the Sword on the motion sensor array?'

The Guards were crystal clear that the cabinet had been opened and closed as per procedure, and that no indications of uncontrolled releases of gases or vapours had occurred at any time during the installation of the Sword.

The motion sensors were calibrated to the exact weight of the Hellfire Sword and set accordingly, the green LED confirmed that a positive lock was placed on the Sword. They had then retired from the vault. The Major nodded his head and waved a hand at the CCTV camera. He closed his notebook and the door release mechanism clunked open.

'Thank you gentlemen, I am not sure what we are up against here, but please remain vigilant as our lives may depend on it.'

CHAPTER EIGHT

CORROBORATION

Kemp located the Epistula and removed it from the drawer where he had returned it after his initial shock. He opened the cover and almost rubbed his fingers over the vellum, then stopped. 'Darlene, there is something you should see.' He said no more. He knew that trying to explain or provide his meagre interpretation of events to the Doctor was not going to make an ounce of sense to someone of her academic standing in biblical knowledge or with her rational approach to life.

'What is it?' she asked, pulling the robes higher onto her shoulders. He showed her the manuscript, or what was formerly the manuscript, then let himself stare at her. 'What have you done with this vellum Kemp, tell me you have not tried to clean it, have you?' Still staring at her he placed his two arms firmly on her shoulders, looked her straight in the eyes and asked a very odd question?

'Do you believe in divine intervention, because I suddenly do.' She caught on straight away to the unfolding discussion, and her intuition detected the sincere tone in his voice.

'Actually Kemp I do as it happens, ever since I was a young girl I have been praying for miracles like this to happen to me, miracles that would make me different from the rest of the crowd, imagine being able to prove to the world that this gift has been given to me for a divine reason. Surely, I would become a celebrity or even a martyr when I die.

But look at the facts, this affliction does not give me any pain and sadly I cannot view it unless it's through photographs or a mirror, which I would probably stare at all day long if I could. I know it is there, but then again, why is it there? If you can explain that to me Mr Hastings then I would be more than comfortable with this phenomenon. But at the moment I have no choice now do I, I mean it is not every day one is blessed with such a nice affliction.'

Darlene was quite clear that this event was not a curse and accepted that strange things in life do happen, she placed herself in the frame of people who have impacted the course of the Bible in its two thousand year existence, two millennia plus if we stem as far back as the gospels, and Darlene was prepared to get on with her life.

Kemp was a nuts and bolts sort of man who preferred it when things made sense. At the moment nothing added up, especially in light of recent events. That was until he received an odd email from the Vatican via the Fisher Queen's representative in Scotland.

The message explained the Hellfire Sword scenario in Rome and since it was his original discovery he was asked to visit the Vatican to assist the papal team in their attempts to discover how it could have been removed from their now not so secure security vault.

Papal Communications

Twenty four hours later and an email appeared on the desktop computer of His Holiness Pope Benedict as he sat in his papal office, he was planning his pending European visit in the next few days. The travel plan and itinerary of his visit was as he expected apart from one comment written in red ink, 'Sanctos Epistula.' Ecosse.

He then opened the secret sliding drawer in the old papal desk and pulled out a leather covered dossier, the cover of the document was embossed with a single cipher of a rose and a few Latin words spread across its surface. His Holiness opened the book very carefully and found a few scraps of paper that had been tucked in amongst an ancient manuscript marked 'Pius.' The parchment appeared to have been scorched at the edges but was in generally good condition, he found the term he was looking for and gasped.

'The "Sanctos Epistula": a series of letters dedicated to the writing of the Apostles in the 2nd century, they are the earliest recordings of what actions were taken by the early protectors of Christendom to maintain the sanctity of the church, all the credible evidence that shapes the way the Vatican is seen in the modern world depends on the contents of these ritualistic guiding documents.'

Pope Pius had written these few simple words:

We are a special lineage of caretakers and as we transit for but a short time in this mighty role, we must take it upon our shoulders the burden of the Church of Magdalena and Christ, with this burden comes great respect, therefore we must also respect our Lord's armoury, within these weapons of genocide there exists a single sword, this steel is known as the Tartarus Inferni, this weapon is not of this world and must never be housed within our walls, it contains the fires of hell wrapped within its skin, the haft contains the sword hilt manuscript and must never be recited to a living audience, this can only be heard by the ears of Hades.

As with our holiest of Arks this too is armed with man-killing qualities and designed for the use of the pure and not the greedy, those adorned with humility may only act as temporary custodians of the Tartarus, these will be known as the impoverished soldiers of Christ, beware—this is the sword of the whispering swordsman and wielded by Odysseus and is the Hellfire Cross Sword used to slay the siren Persephone, and more importantly was used to decapitate John the Baptist to satisfy the lusts of Salome.

The Pope sat back in his chair and wiped his brow, picking up the second parchment he read the inscription and scrutinised the enclosed drawing, this was of course of the Vatican's latest acquisition. He summoned Major La Rou and the chief acquisition officer to his office. The meeting was very quick and straight forward.

'Major La Rou I would like you undertake a task during my visit to Scotland, I wish you not to physically pursue our Tartarus Inferni sword, but to ensure that when you locate it, that it never returns to our midst, you may use whatever resources we have available. There have been many developments and there are some things that must remain so, please furnish the cabinet with a more desirable artefact, an item that brings colour to our collection. Thank you gentlemen, Dona Nobis Pacem.' The Major and the acquisition officer left the office.

It was not that the Vatican wanted the sword back in their possession—it was their intention to ensure that it never came back at all. Therefore, the papal office wanted the sword placed back in the location it had come from. Somewhere just as secret, safe and secure from papal predators. Major La Rou was to embark on a quest during the extensive Papal visit to the UK and made plans to ensure that it did not make its way back to the Vatican under any circumstances.

CHAPTER NINE

Dei Donum—Epitaph

Kemp smiled another one of his broad smiles. 'History must be repeating itself, there is no doubt about it.' His mobile telephone buzzed and began making its way across the table top. He picked it up, 'Hastings,' he answered. The voice at the other end was not Scottish and it certainly was not German. He pondered for a moment or two longer on the accent: it was Italian.

'Mr Hastings I am Major La Rou from the Vatican in Rome, and was wondering if I may have some of your valuable time, I would like to show you something of biblical importance regarding your Hellfire Sword.' The Major had got Kemp's attention. A few minutes later and the trio sat together and discussed the major's immediate issue with what may have been Constantine's and Charlemagne's sword of destiny.

'But of course Major, where are you?' Major La Rou and Hastings sat quietly on the park bench in the cemetery away from any potential prying eyes or cameras that were secreted in any buildings. La Rou was wearing less than casual attire, Kemp would have dismissed him as a local if it had not been for his suave Italian physical appearance.

'Mr Hastings we thought you should see this, it is a copy of the videolink filmed within vault 33 of the Vatican's secure zone.' Kemp was bemused by the statement—what did he mean, 'the Vatican's secure zone?' And the thing the Major was proffering was an official-looking stolen object.

'This was taken during the removal of the Sword from its display case, our science department are, as you would say 'baffled', they say that the digital interrogation has revealed that this footage is as real as you and I sitting here.'

Kemp was astounded, and flicked his mobile. 'Major, I think one more person should see this video, for reasons I will explain later, it is perhaps our best lead. This person is my colleague she is probably the current global leading authority on this subject and she may have some information to share.'

The Major nodded. 'Mr Hastings, this cannot go beyond our meeting, my employer is very clear about how this will be conducted. But, if this person can help, then I obviously have no choice.' Kemp nodded and flicked the phone fully open and pressed the contacts.

'Hello Darlene, it's Kemp. Can you meet us at the grave of Wishart? This is important, thanks.'

Twenty minutes later and Doctor Gammay appeared at the gates of the old cemetery deep in the heart of the Victorian graveyard. Kemp waved and caught her attention. Darlene introduced herself to the major and viewed the video. She was clearly excited by the fact that she was not alone in her experience of witnessing this particular apparition.

'Kemp this is the same one, the same face the same flowers and now it is corroborated, thank God.'

Kemp scratched his chin then spoke. 'I suppose the timings coincide as well, this confirms one thing. This is an orchestrated form of exposure, someone wants us to know that the hellfire sword is pivotal in this enquiry, but who is this lady?'

Kemp explained to the Major the sequence of events that had ensued since he had taken delivery of the manuscript from the office of the Fisher Queens. The Major was aware that the custodians of the parchment were the Scotia Epistula office of the Fisher Kings. What he was unaware of was the fact that the vellum was now blank and probably on the safest location on the planet. Darlene was staring at the camera.

'Major La Rou does the Vatican know the identity of this image?' The Italian took a deep breath.

'My dear Doctor this image is, as far as we can tell, the holy Madonna, the uncanny image painted by Gabriel Dante Rossetti, in his "Damsel of the Sanct Grael" dated about 1840.

It appears that the painter may have had access to some of the older Vatican archive images, and he really did capture her likeness; by all accounts the literary descriptions are very prescriptive, Dante the artist was a very talented man, and driven by the occult, or at least mythology.'

Kemp and Darlene froze as the Major pressed the forward button on the camera to reveal the painting. Kemp watched on then suddenly spurted out the words 'Shit, it was there all along, remember I said that your tattoo was the white dove with the bluey coloured wings.' He stopped himself from ranting. 'Sorry Darlene, it's not my place to disclose this.'

Darlene smiled and stared at the papal official. 'Major are you a deeply religious man?' she asked. The major quizzed her question in his mind, his facial expression was one of slight amusement and it said it all. 'Doctor I have spent thirty years of my life under the umbrella of the Vatican and twenty six years as the chief security officer in charge, you could say I believe in most things biblical. Are you a believer in faith?' Darlene smiled.

'Not really, I do study, but I don't pray religiously every Sunday if that's what you mean?'

Hastings pulled out the digital camera from his laptop bag and showed the major a series of photographs, each image clearer than clear. La Rou appeared to be almost distressed; he could not understand why someone would have such a tattoo. Darlene clasped her hands. 'Major La Rou this is not a tattoo, this is your Incorruptible Epistula of the Magdal, your so called Madonna, she has adopted my back as a picture frame to show the world her beautiful face . . . '

'I am, for all intents and purposes, the only living image of your Madonna. This image was somehow transferred onto my skin just three days ago after I touched your holy parchment, and what Mr Hastings failed to mention was that the Magdalene manuscript at present is one hundred per cent blank. Now, can the papal office explain any of this, because I will be really interested?'

La Rou was stunned as the reality of his predicament hit home. 'Doctor I will personally guarantee that the Vatican will take care of you, the office of His Holiness will cater for your every need.' Darlene placed a hand on the Major's knee.

'Major La Rou these events are short lived, they usually end up in confusion and as much as I want to be a martyr I do not want to be a dead one.' The Major scratched his head. 'Doctor have you ever heard of the Veil of Veronica?' Darlene nodded her head in response.

'I have read many things about the Shroud of Turin, but the Sadarium is not one aspect I am too familiar with, as I study documents or more literal interpretations, artefacts are more Mr Hastings' expertise.' La Rou clasped his hands together.

'Okay, the Veil of Veronica is a piece of cloth that was used to wipe the sweat of Jesus Christ as he traversed the path to his crucifixion, he was in the Dolrosa en route to Calvary, when a young lady, 'Veronica', breached the masses and wiped his brow. It is documented that the face of Christ was imprinted onto this cloth and is today revered as a relic of the Bible.'

'According to our records Veronica travelled to Rome and presented the cloth to the Emperor Tiberius, and apparently it can cure a varying range of diseases from blindness to something as simple as quenching thirst. These may be metaphorical statements as I have not actually touched the cloth, but naturally, I know where it is located.'

The Major rubbed his fingers together. 'Although the story is only documented to have begun in the Middle Ages, we fear its authenticity may be questionable, but we cannot discount the 'relic' as a piece of Biblical mystery.' The Major's strong Italian overtones had captured Kemp's attention; 'Very Latin,' he thought. Darlene Gammay appeared to be not so convinced.

'Anyway what I am trying to say is that the phenomenon of the Veil could be linked to this manifestation of the 'One' on your skin. It transmitted by your touching the original vellum, untouched by female human hand for a very long time. You could travel to the Basilica to see the Veil, but it was rumoured that Veronica would travel with the cloth as it was paraded across the Christian world—the validity of the veil being corroborated by the one person that was present during the actual event.'

Kemp pointed a finger in the air. 'If I am not mistaken there is great controversy over the Veil of Veronica and that it has in some way been built into religion as an integral part of process? Is it not said that Veronica was in the presence of the papacy during John VII's reign in the early 7th century, and not totally captured or reflected in the many mosaics of the day that were the only real tangible account of the event. Would it not be fair to assume that until now, this was an 11th century insert to history?' The Major was shaking his head.

'I can only say that the cause and effect of something of this extraordinary occurrence must bear a relation to one of previous events, it would only be natural to attribute it to something we can relate to, and Veronica's Veil and the Holy Shroud are the only two such relics that appear to have been impregnated with the Face of Christ, why not work to the supposition that the Sanctos Epistula has acted in the same way? This is only my interpretation Mr Hastings, I can only make some informed assumptions, what do you think?'

Kemp was in agreement, something would have to be targeted in order to add any rationale to the advent of Darlene's new tattoo. The Major leaned forward. 'Darlene, every year on the 5th Sunday of Lent we see the face of Christ appear on the veil we have in our possession, this is what we call "passion Sunday". There are other veils in existence, one such is the Manopello image, perhaps it is a copied image or it has contacted the original in some way, but we, the Vatican, have the original and yes Mr Hastings it is not without its controversy.'

Darlene spoke out. 'Major what about the cloth that Christ's head was wrapped in after the crucifixion, is this not a similar type of mystery that academics struggle to understand, I think they call it the Sadarium of Oviedo, and not this Veronica's veil article.' La Rou was nodding again in unison with Kemp, they had both obviously been concentrating on the Veronica aspect of the event, but as expected Darlene had studied a more direct line and knew of the existence of many veils.

The Major raised his index finger. 'But Miss Gammay, regarding the Magdalene, I do not know of any such ancient images that could actually be significant, or any articles that would provide conclusive evidence about the form of your image, and as I have said, Dante was a modern painter. I have no indications that he had access to the Vatican archives, but obviously his work has many depictions of the Madonna, and this one picture alone is indeed very relevant, as it resembles the many texts and inscriptions that do describe Mary Magdalene.'

'But here we can observe the bird of peace, and a physical chalice, these are metaphorical subject matter, and the Aramaic inscription, well that's very clearly old-world Latin, and a language that is not evident in today's Aramaic society. I suppose you are aware that this painting is known as the Holy Grail?'

Hastings' phone buzzed exactly the same time as the Major's, and they both answered simultaneously. Darlene sat quietly staring at Wishart's epitaph. After a minute Kemp flicked his phone shut, and was about to say something interesting when Darlene said 'They have found the Tartarus Inferni on the Isle of Iona.' Major La Rou was staring back at them, Kemp and La Rou both looking mystified.

Darlene's voice had become lighter in tone and her eyes were firmly closed as she spoke just above whisper. 'Major La Rou,' she said, then continued her monologue in perfect ancient Latin with acute emphasis on the older style syntax with an odd hierarchical structure. 'We will deal with 'Hades' our way. You can inform His Holiness that the Hellfire will not be returned to his house in Rome, but will be secreted by the decree of Pope Pius, but his house must be prepared to receive a token artefact for safekeeping in return.'

The voice died away and Darlene opened her eyes. 'So, Major, we will deal with this my way, I am sure you can appreciate this.'

Darlene was totally oblivious as to what had just transpired, she thanked the Major for his time and explained that he should go back to Rome and await contact from them within the next 48 hours.

Darlene sat patiently in the churchyard, her thoughts were very distant, no one could have contemplated such an event in her life, it had indeed been turned upside down. She was momentarily caught in what she could only describe as an out of body experience and although she was very much awake she experienced a euphoric trip beyond her physical state.

Kemp and Major La Rou were discussing something or other, but she had drifted too far from their conversation to be included. Externally, her aura was pale blue. She stared back at herself sitting there between the two men on the bench, a mirror reflection of her spiritual being. She looked good she thought, very healthy, no ailments, just as she wanted to be. Her eyes were still sparkling bright blue against the sunlight and her skin fresh and free of any blemishes, unusual for a red head, she was normally enshrouded with a freckled blanket that seemed almost like military camouflage, she hated it, even more so at this time of year.

A wisp of warm wind caught her cheek and she raised her hand, pushing a few strands of straggling hair from her face. It was then that she took a very deep breath then went for a free flight in her astral form and was projected through the graveyard. She was not alone, she was very surprised as she spied several other forms hovering around some of the marble gravestones, some figures were ascending high into the sky almost to the roof tops, others just hovered over some smaller headstones, but appeared to be contained within the cemetery's walled boundary.

After a few moments of observation they all suddenly started to descend as if they had been summoned by some internal beacon, each descending down towards the tomb of MM, a single older stone monument located just in front of the angel with Pan's pipes in her hands.

These forms were not what Darlene would class as ghosts or ghouls, but normal people like herself. She was confused by her surroundings but relished the overall fantasy experience of tranquillity and escape. Every now and again a phantom of what she thought was an Apostle could be seen drifting in and out of her consciousness, appearing then disappearing. Darlene however was not sleeping, her body was sitting upright on the park bench, just day dreaming, unless she was disturbed by Hastings or Major La Rou she was going to be there for a fair while.

She watched on as the entities circled the tomb waiting for something amazing to happen, every now and again one would disappear then re-appear. Darlene remained fully present as she watched what she could only describe as a super entity appear from the Mausoleum to her right, she recognised the form instantly as John the Baptist. Why on earth his body would turn up in a Scottish cemetery eluded her sense of biblical understanding, but then again she was in dream state.

Then she suffered an acute moment of epiphany and realised in this dream state that she was not just amongst the Apostles of the bible, but was one of them. 'Wow!' she said loudly, as they all suddenly stopped their swirling and swooping and stared directly back towards her. 'Who is she?' asked the figure of Luke, pulling his hand down the length of his long blackened beard.

'She is the chosen one,' came an answer out of the blue. 'Deemed spiritual enough to assist us in our quest of obtaining the Tartarus Inferni and bringing stability back into Hades.'

The spectre of John the Baptist stood back a few yards placing his hand on the gravestone of Wishart. 'This, my dear child, was the mystical sword that took my life and of course my head. That is why we exist here as a collective today, we are the brotherhood of twelve, we have been honoured in life, bonded together in death to inform the ethereal world of man's wrong doings, that's also why you are here. This is the cold tomb of Salome, she is living a life of servitude, she dwells in Hades for wishing a mortal man dead for her vanity, lust and revenge.

A demand for her own moral standing, wretched woman, but, as a consequence of her woeful ways she suffers in hell as one would say.' The spectre of St Mark hovered forward. 'You look just like her you know, our Mary, young, beautiful and if I may be bold, you are also blessed with the hair of the dragon. Mortal men curse the redness of the hair and fear the strength of women adorned with such.' He pulled his energy back as a larger entity came into view from behind her. The spoke.

'I am Andrew, and over here you see, Simon, Matthew, Thaddeus & Acts. Acts he is shy, even in death he fails to accept the limelight of his achievements. He is perhaps the most sensible of us all, blessed with the power to love and forgive, virtues that we have lost for mortal man, but they remain in him strong enough for us all to share.'

Darlene did not turn around to face the voice, she seemed very comfortable, then Andrew took up a position to her left. 'Our guiding light should be here soon, the sun is almost at its zenith, this is when she appears, even to us in this misty form. We are blessed by her celestial visits.'

The vision of St Andrew spun on his axis and hovered over the footstone of a tiny grave. 'This little mite would have been King if it was not for the cruelty and savagery of this earthly world, lost in time until the next advent,' he said pointing to the small open marble bible adorned with the simple word 'Forgotten'. Darlene drifted higher, just high enough to take a look over the high wall, then caught a glimpse of the 'ethereal world'.

It was covered in a pinky mist and very clean, a glaze of sparkling silver glistened over the people in the street, the horses and carriages. All were in striking poses for any would be artist; this world was stuck in the 1820s, but steeped in glass and elegance.

There was a loud bang and Darlene Gammay hit the deck like a sack of King Edwards, her lifeless body springing to attention as she sat staring into the face of Kemp Hastings. 'Hello dreamer, time to go,' he said as she came to her senses and followed Kemp and the Major out of the cemetery.

CHAPTER TEN

THE COVEN OF 'ARCANA OBSCURA'

Standing at the back of the cemetery in deathly quietness was the veiled bent figure of Grizell Jaffray, her eyes trained on the tall figure of Major La Rou. She was clutching what appeared to be a rolled up painting in her frail grasp. Her haggard old lips tightened and her anger and contempt shot across her sullen face as she realised that pictures from the camera were being shared by strangers. Then she muttered 'Dante, you show the world the beauty of the 'one' yet you know nothing of her tragic world, your earthly world will feel the wrath of the Arcana Obscura and your image will bring terror to those who follow your god.'

Jaffray hailed from a long line of Dei Donum descendants, one of which was barbarically murdered by a mob of city folk just a couple of hundred years earlier, for 'practisin' witchcraft.' Before this act of revenge and deceit, the Jaffrays had been instrumental in a long line of medieval tradition: they had been worshippers of the more darkened arts in their search for health and wealth. They took part in ritual and in the bizarre and hidden pursuit of alchemy. A well-to-do family, who sadly had ruthless enemies.

She stood amongst her family and their resting places and began walking between their graves, letting her cold hands trail and drift across the many stones then stopped at the largest of the group. Its inscription read 'Arcana' followed by an epitaph of the following words:

In death's dark veil I see no life
To this world I leave my wife
The angels sing as I walk their trail
The ghosts and shadows to the STYX we sail

She watched as Kemp and his companions exited the cemetery then made her way to the tomb of the Angel, she stood over the stone and lifted her black veil from her face. 'Don't rest yet pretty, we are not finished with you, we have the Tartarus Inferni and your messenger on earth will not be delivering it to his master.' She kissed her two middle fingers and ran them along the grave stone, the flowers below died instantly and a cold chill ran throughout the cemetery as the wind whistled to tell all in death's garden.

There was an ominous swirl of mist and the cemetery fell into near-dark as night began to fall and cast her blanket of darkness over the city. Somewhere near the city of London the police were reporting the mystery theft of a painting. 'The Damsel of the Sankt Grael' by Gabriel Rossetti, estimated to be worth twelve million pounds, was traversing the globe in what the police reported was a well-orchestrated theft, and they guessed that the masterpiece was probably making its way to the continent.

Something had triggered Grizell Jaffray's moment of silence and in her unworldly dream state her mind was wandering between the fabric of time and space and this certain physical reality. Although she walked among the dead Grizell Jaffray was always caught in a state of limbo, her sort always are. Limbo land is a place where only the select few are chosen to roam the planet, making their way between the river Styx and the mystical afterlife. But this way is not one of personal choice; but a choice made by the power of the Fates for them, a decision to make amends for their untimely departure.

The option was non-negotiable and decided by not having made a conscious decision to die, but by being murdered or killed through an act of unprecedented violence or hatred. Assassinations could be considered, but these would fall under the umbrella of the whispering swordsman. 16th century Scotland had created a window for three hundred and thirty three condemned witches and warlocks to stalk the Earth and take revenge on society as they see fit, a single mechanism to pay society for their eternal sins.

Their eternal prey are the young street urchins who pass over or die prematurely, normally due to illness, and are plucked to walk the path of the un-dead for a hundred years as company for the undelivered souls. It was a cold evening and the moon hadn't quite managed to place its face into full view, Grizell Jaffray was holding what appeared to be a small bundle of swaddling cloth in her arms. The bundle's wrapping was reminiscent of perhaps how a baby would be prepared for burial, a sight which would pull at the heart strings. The urchins would have most likely have died of consumption or the wretched plague that was rife at this time in history in most major cities.

Jaffray's eyes were firmly fixed just beyond the gates of the central HOWFF burial yard, the lenses of evil trained deep within the cemetery's middle ground, those cold optics observing the solemn slow commotion of a funeral in progress. The group had gathered, heads bowed and in deep, deep sorrow. The women cried and the men had no answers for the state of their union. It was not an ordinary funeral by any stretch of the imagination; funerals should be conducted with calm and serenity and modelled to celebrate our lives and our passing, a time to reflect on our impact on life, family and friends.

Jaffray watched with eagerness, momentarily tempted to run amok and create chaos amongst the assembled party, holding back her passion to whistle up the wind and send the flowers spiralling into the air. No great pomp and definitely no great ceremony to interrupt. She held back, deciding that chaos would be reserved for the more arrogant of gatherings.

The small wooden box was a definitive sign of the times, and an indicator that life was very difficult for this particular family. Poverty had grasped their existence and this event was of great importance; the only child stolen from them, such an impact that it rippled waves of sadness and grief through the family. The external world did not care—it was too full of other problems.

These types of funerals were never splendid or over-indulgent shows of wealth. Not an opportunity to splash out all one's cash on the dearly departed, and so show society the family worth. This one was more of a down to grass roots level affair, fuelled by despair, mercy and sadness for the Martin family. The baby was certainly a girl, denoted by the single pink carnation held in the mother's grasp along with a piece of pink cloth, the many tears cascading down over her cheeks and onto her linen cloth shawl.

What few friends the family had, assembled to pay their last respects to the dear departed, each individual casting a small flower or wooden token onto the small coffin top. A single clump of mixed flowers lay spread over the lid, most likely borrowed from a garden en route to the cemetery or in some cases taken from an adjacent grave. The nine roses fanned out to one side of the graveside each glowing against the dark soil. Life was harsh in these volatile times.

The father was standing tall in absolute silence, copious amounts of tears streaming down his sullen face, each drop driven by remorse and coldness of heart, a hatred towards life in general was building up inside him and he was oblivious to the outside world as he contemplated the fact that his family line may stop with him and his loving wife. He worked hard and he prayed well, but failed to comprehend why he was rewarded in such a way by faith. Life had taken his precious diamond, how could he recover from such a tragedy?

Each family member and friend failed to understand why the good Lord to whom they had devoted their lives with so much devotion could suddenly be so cruel in taking away their dream. Jaffray watched on for a moment then smiled whilst pulling the white cloth from the face of the child in her arms. 'Such a beauty,' she thought as the little pair of blue sparkling eyes gazed back at her, then stared towards the cemetery to see the baby's family again. 'Don't worry child, their sorrow will be short lived, for they too will join the worms and the slugs soon, their souls will be cleansed and presented to the Lord for their troubles, sadly just not in this world,' said Jaffray, cuddling the bundle.

The old witch gave the baby an almost loving soft tap on the nose with her wrinkled finger as the baby girl smiled a melting smile and fell asleep. Jaffray slowly made her way towards the great gates and eventually joined the funerary gathering, albeit unseen by all who were not of the world of limbo. She stood very close to the mother at first, then whispered in her ear. 'Hello mama,' said the childish voice. 'I am with a very nice lady, she smells like you do.' The mother stared across the yard as the small voice continued. 'She tells me that I am a very special person and that I have been chosen for greater things, please don't cry for me mama, this is a celebration of my short life with you and dada, and I will cherish every single moment of it.'

The tears on the mother's face increased as she took a huge deep breath then dropped her head, obviously heart stricken with grief, almost feeling and smelling her baby by her side.' Jaffray took an unusual step: she raised the bundle up into the mother's face and blinked her eyes very slowly. In doing so time froze, and the mother was permitted one final gaze upon her departed child. The baby opened her eyes, and smiled.

Her small voice was very clear in the head of the mourning woman. 'You see I am well mama, pray for me as you have always done these past nights, I must leave you now but won't stop thinking of you. I am to make my way to my new world. I was very ill before, and my poor weak body was contaminated with earthly poisons. Now as you can see I am being cared for in a way that allows me to be happy. No more pain mama, my dada will need your strength for the short time until you both join us here in this very special place where we will be a family again, I will wait for you mama, I love you.'

The mother blinked her eyes rapidly as her husband placed an arm around her shoulders providing that essential comforting moment. Jaffray lowered the baby and stepped away from the mother, it was not common practice for witches or warlocks to intervene with real people, especially once a passing has occurred, but this was somehow different, even for a witch. Grizell Jaffray had not lost her female or motherly instinct; even in death she showed compassion for the living. The mother cried out loudly and turning towards her husband pointed across the graveyard to the angel-adorned gravestone.

Thirty feet away a ghostly figure stood and watched on as the father and mother, united in sorrow, waved goodbye to their daughter. Sarah Magdalene Martin was gone as she was lowered into the grave. The funeral continued as most did with the minister asking the parents to cast a few handfuls of sand onto the newly interred. It was at this moment that the sound of horses' hooves rattled on the cobbled roadway, disturbing the moment. The father could not be bothered to be angry or annoyed—nothing was bringing back his daughter.

The black horse-drawn carriage appeared in front of the gates. Two tall black and red plumes waving in the wind could be seen over the high wall, the horses were snorting and shuffling their way into a steady position as the hearse came to a standstill, the glass panels cleaned to perfection permitting a glimpse of what money can do in death.

Another unfortunate family was having to share the same sorrow as the family Martin, but this time with so much pomp and ceremony that the procession was more of a circus than a demonstration of respectful mourning. A day that would perhaps be disrupted for the family by the dark side of Grizell Jaffray. Magdalene Martin grabbed her husband's hand and they both walked slowly out of the eastern gate of the cemetery having said goodbye to their little bundle of happiness. 'She is in a better place now,' she said, cuddling up to her spouse.

'I know,' he replied as they walked hand in hand. Kemp Hastings stood in awe and struggled with what he had just witnessed. He stared at Darlene, he was unsure if it was a vision or if it was real. 'Kemp what is it, you look as though you have just seen a ghost,' she said, clearing a clutch of fiery red hair from her eyes.

'I think I have just seen something very strange, I saw a funeral just there, that grave with the small white stone, a family were saying good bye to their infant daughter. But there was something else, a cold uneasiness, a spine chilling voice, I heard "witch, witch, witch . . . Jaffray, Jaffray Jaffray. Beware, beware". What does that mean Darlene?' Darlene, who hailed from Dundee, knew the city's history better than most. She grabbed his arm, said 'I think we should have a beer or two,' and led Hastings towards the inner city.

'Grizell Jaffray was a so-called witch, and was burned near to the Mercat Cross at the old Wyshart arch towards the east end of the city. There were several burnings in the city but this was the most poignant as she may not have been a witch at all, but a victim of a nasty neighbour who turned the world against her based on back stabbing and general rumour mongering. But, Kemp, I have no idea where she is buried, logic would say that she was buried out of the city and not interred on hallowed ground.'

'Well Darlene I think she has something to do with that cemetery.' Darlene laughed openly. 'What would you say if I told you that I had an out of body experience while you were chatting to Major La Rou?' 'Oh come on Darlene I am not kidding here, this was a real revelation, just as real as we are talking here and now.' Darlene sipped her beer. 'So was mine.'

CHAPTER ELEVEN

FRIDGE MAGNETS

The ministry was in turmoil over the appearance of the Hellfire Sword; the island was suddenly out of bounds to all pilgrims, the administrators were making extensive phone calls to all corners of the world. The Vatican remained silent, knowing full well that any intervention may result in them becoming the custodians of this unearthly artefact again. The heritage trusts were laying claim to ownership of the piece, each department producing copious amounts of fabricated evidence to support their stake on the precious item. What could not be answered with any credibility by any of these so called custodians was the point of sale or purchase of the item. The Cistercians by default had got their 5th century 'god killer' back in their possession and only one person knew what it meant.

The current Pope sat contemplating what Pius had written such a long time ago. He closed the parchment papers and placed them back into safe keeping. It was clear that not one of the establishments could convince the Scottish church one hundred per cent that this was the property of their particular domain. Many envoys were despatched to take possession of the Cerberus killer, writs were produced, legal documents were produced, bills of sale were examined, and yet not one had a credible signature.

For seven days the many petitions flooded into the Vatican from all orders of the ecclesiastical world, each claiming to own the work of god, to the extent that a blanket message had to be sent to say that a custodian of credibility had been found, as if by magic the global cleric feeding frenzy sank into oblivion. This was of course a true statement although the owner had in fact been dead for seven hundred and ninety years and lay in the back of a churchyard on a distant island. The sword had apparently been buried with its rightful owner on Iona.

Hastings was busy searching his home library when he found a phone number scribbled on the cover of one of his many science fiction magazines. The number was an odd one, he thought, dismissing it as irrelevant, momentarily remembering that the magazine was bought whilst he was in a state of drunkenness and confusion with some friends.

Picking up his warm cup of chocolate he sat in the imposed quiet, contemplating current events. This whole Magdalene thing had indeed triggered his sense of inquisitiveness and challenged his consistent approach to rational thinking. If he was to be honest with himself he was absolutely flummoxed and a bit wary to say the least of this supernatural event. Sky News had nothing to report on the discovery of an ancient sword anywhere in the world, Radio One had nothing, Radio Vatican had fallen silent, the email chain had gone quiet, his phone had lost most of its power showing only two bars, and was not receiving a signal.

He was abandoned and very external to the media world, he had been cut off. 'Oh what joys,' he said leaning back in the big wooden chair and mumbled again, 'imagine if it was like this all the time, ah bliss.' Picking up the remote control to the television he flicked the 'on' button. The words 'Channel Select' appeared on the screen. Television X was not his favourite channel but it kept appearing as the menu froze between the History channel and the adult site. 'Bloody Sky, think everyone's a pervert these days,' he muttered then clicked the 'off' button.

'Typical!' he exclaimed, and momentarily had an argument with himself about subscription costs and the choice of new television stations. 'My life is closing down around me, just great I am being alienated from the outside world just as our most . . .' Taking a cursory glance into the kitchen he paused and began staring into the culinary closet, he was caught in mid-speech as he spied his fridge magnets slowly dancing across the surface of the door, each very clearly finding a logical route to what appeared to be magnetic scrabble.

'What the fu . . . My fridge is possessed, or it's an unorthodox new Ouija board, no way this can be happening.' He sat and watched in sheer amazement. The blue, red and yellow bold plastic numbers and letters were spiralling and had certainly caught his attention. For three whole minutes he watched the big yellow 'M' moving up and down, the yellow 'L' was just spinning on its axis waiting to do something else, and the 'P' was sliding from left to right as if something was trying to work out a word.

Then the 'Mary Poppins' moment arrived. The word 'APOZTLE' appeared across the Frigidaire Coolbox door. He silently apologised for having no 'S' on the fridge. Then he smiled at the Rupert the bear and Muppets magnets staring back, each slowly rocking and waving at him. He stood very quietly as the TV found the god channel all by itself, 'a sort of divine intervention,' he thought, but things were getting a bit too scary and Television X became appealing as magazine pages started to flick open and closed and then flipped violently on the spine, then the page with the telephone number sat directly upright balanced on the spine's edge. 'Shit!' he cried looking at the number, it read '555-666-710'.

His mobile had recharged itself; it flashed indicating an incoming text. It was the number on the magazine. He threw the phone down on the sofa and contemplated fleeing the room. 'Stop! he said to himself. 'There's no danger here, maybe just playful poltergeists asking you to phone home, you know like in some of those Randall and Hopkirk programs, but with Churchy people.' He picked up the phone and dialled the number, all went very quiet as he dialled the number into the cell phone, the receiver was quiet for almost 13 seconds then a faint click could heard.

'Hello!' snapped a voice at the other end. Kemp took a gulp before speaking. 'Who is this?' he asked. The line went quiet again and he could swear he heard singing in the background, then the smooth voice of an older man spoke. 'I am the cipher. You took your time, how can I-' The phone went dead as the battery returned back to a state of no charge.

'Cipher, what the hell does mean?' he yelled, shaking the phone. 'Who is he, what is he?' Hastings found comfort in a nice warm drink of chocolate laced with his favourite tipple and did nothing.

Several minutes later he had chilled. He waltzed around the flat taking photographs of his colourful fridge and the colourful word 'APOZTLE' written across the door. And of course Rupert the bear in his tartan scarf waving back at him.

Hastings picked up his dictionary and flicked to the word 'cipher' and read the definition. There was a cipherman, Edward Larsson, who he had used in the past for encoding and decoding some early texts, but nothing of this significance. Darlene would certainly know, but he felt it prudent to give her some space until he was sure how he could assist. Larsson was good for the Runes and such, but what was a cipher, or indeed in this case who is the cipher? He trawled some of his books and magazines. If he could work out what was the key then he could maybe work out who or what the key keeper could be.

The internet was great for everything but the detail he was searching for, after an hour or so he gave up. Then he contemplated polyalphabetic structure, but that maybe way beyond this conundrum. He felt that it was simple; he just could not see it. What about Roman numerals or lettering? He played around with a scrap of paper then wrote a few odd words. He had read about the DM code and that was so simple that no one could crack it, even today the world at large were struggling to decipher the old Shugborough secret. Hastings gave thought to the graves—Thomas and Wishart. Each could be an indicator or a sign but where would the code be?

Then it triggered—he was back to paintings. Poussin, 'Et in Arcadia Ego' or whatever it was, simply a grave that marked a location as in X marks the spot, then of course it was Rossetti we are talking about. Poussin is interred in Rome, and Dante Rossetti, Britain. Hastings soon found that Rossetti's grave was marked by a huge Celtic cross and traced his steps in locating one, he had been in several cemeteries recently, but no great Celtic crosses were evident, unless.

Iona instantly sprang straight to his mind followed by the fact that the Hellfire Sword had just apparently appeared there. The cipher must be a Celtic cross, but now the question was whose it could be. That remained a mystery. Hastings quizzed a few photographs on the Iona web page and scrutinised the largest, which was attributed to Columba or Macbeth, thinking at least their graves should not be dismissed as resting places of significant importance. There were many rumours of cross-capped stones being stolen and turned into relics. It was not uncommon in the 5th century and Hastings dismissed these as irrelevant, but lingered on the notion if what type of purposes a sixty kilogram stone could serve.

He quizzed many articles in Gaelic and Irish folklore, every churchyard had a few Celtic crosses in their cemeteries, but none that would give rise to the correlation between the mysterious and ghostly figure that appeared in the Vatican and the disappearance of the Hellfire Sword. Hastings smiled and wondered if St Patrick in his youth had been mistaken for a female and had somehow entered the modern world by mistake in his monastic attire, he decided that would be too far fetched.

He stared up at the sky and started to analyse deeper as to what had transpired over the last few days, then the sun broke the cloud line sending showers of heated rays onto his face, momentarily reminding him of the significance of the sun in Christian medieval belief. He contemplated the signs of the sun, and the solar cycle or solar wheel symbology as that also related to the Celtic cross sign but in a more defined literal sense.

CHAPTER TWELVE

REPATRIATION

48 Hours Later and the the Vatican's elite security team assembled in the control room and were observing the casket of the Tartarus Inferni clearly displayed on the television's wide screen, each guardsman and their commanding officers waiting for the magical return of the hellfire sword or indeed its replacement.

Major La Rou sat in front of the screen in his office, manipulating one of the four cameras that served the corridor which accessed vault thirty three. The lighting was reduced enough for any chance of over exposure from the radium lighting. The Major's plan was to switch to infra red capture at a convenient point if the image returned in order to interpret its digital signature.

This would also enable the thermal imaging system to trace the steps or pathway of the visitor and hopefully pinpoint the points of access and egress. Major La Rou traced the schematic again, he was convinced that their visitor was not of this world, but internally dared not to discuss the phenomenon with any of his staff or his peers. His timing would have to be exact to confirm that this apparition was either a supernatural event or a very complex deception, one which would eventually expose that a human was behind this unusual theft. Most infra red cameras can be set to capture a specific heat signature, but the Wi-Image 4000 also captured the cold signature if the ambient temperature fell below 0 degrees Celsius.

The papal office had been given a clear indication of the time and date for the return of the sacred artefact, and every effort was made to corroborate the information source which was still being investigated. A single email from somewhere on the planet had been passed direct to the Pope's secretary.

The Vatican treated such events with absolute conviction in their drive looking for consistent credibility. At 03:25 hours His Holiness and one of his most trusted office officials were standing in vault thirty three and were watching the casket very closely. On the direct instructions of the security office the cabinet had been removed from its mountings, inspected and replaced, apart from new galvanised bolts the casket was sitting back on the three foot thick concrete plinth with a few extra four inch long bolts through the heavy base.

At 03:33:33 hours the vault temperature rose by a few degrees as the six camera motors started gearing into motion as each and every sensor interrogated the immaculate chamber. Just as before, the casket started to fill with a bluey haze of mist and a faint humming sound began emanating from within the steel walls. The two men looked at each other and His Holiness approached the casket and laid his left hand upon the crystal casing. He could feel sporadic pulsing vibrations rippling across the cabinet and calmly caressed the crystal facia.

The office official had taken a step back making contact with the stainless steel wall and watched eagerly, witnessing an event that surely would be recorded in the Vatican's rich history. Although a sceptical man by nature, the official was displaying signs of anguish and uncertainty as the sweat trickled over his forehead. Glancing up to eye level the old man of the cloth watched as the apparition began fully forming in front of him, and dared not to stare into the eyes of the entity at this time but lowered his gaze upon the two golden roses that adorned the feet of the visitor. His gut began twisting and churning with excitement, and he could feel his frail heart pumping blood to all extremities, then he gasped as he caught sight of the beautiful radiant woman before him.

The pope had become void of any rational thought, his sublime and inner self were removed from the present and were traversing through the mists of heaven in a state of total euphoria. The distinctive aroma of incense and roses filled the small chamber to almost choking point, the wafting waves of calmness soon becoming addictive, and the two men found themselves breathing heavily consuming and absorbing copious amounts of the rich godly air. His Holiness could not move and was deeply transfixed by the presence of the image before him, his thoughts were nearly in the room as the mists began slowly clearing from within the golden glass casket and the outline of what appeared to be a human skull appeared.

The apparition, as before, cast her hand across the cabinet and smiled the smile of a thousand smiles. It was then that the papal representative felt a sudden sharpness rippling up through his geriatric spine and gave out a single loud cry in response, then the pain was gone. The office official stared on with one hand firmly placed across his mouth and his eyes were painfully dilated to their maximum, he was searching for an escape as his tear ducts began fighting back the intensifying pressure to burst open and send showers of overwhelming anxiety over his face.

The old man had momentarily filled up with tears and clenched the gold and diamond encrusted papal crucifix, the frail old skin ripping and tearing as tiny droplets of blood trickled between his clenched fingers. It took a few more seconds after the entity was gone for the atmosphere in the chamber to return to its normal state, and yet there was still a distinct deadened silence in the room.

The truth of what was displayed before them was an item that was going to require a huge amount of resources to be thrown at it, just to add a level of rationality to the inexplicable situation. The Pope leaned forward on the cabinet and was clearly still weeping, his godly eyes dwelling on the human skull that was sitting neatly on the blue velvet plinth staring back at him.

It had been a full three minutes since the vision appeared, the Pope was captured in emotional turmoil and his weeping had become tears of joy. He had placed his hands on his chest over his heart, leaving small droplets of eminent blood staining the robes and uniform of the papacy. The vision had disappeared exactly as before, had slowly began sliding backwards on a cloud of white mist and eventually melted into the stainless steel bulkhead.

The official at one point had attempted to approach the visitor but he too was void of the physical ability to move or manipulate any of his limbs, he recalled struggling to breathe and had cried out. The mist had cleared totally from the display case, and the skull was sitting neatly on the blue velvet plinth staring back at them. The bone appeared to have been cleaned to a very high standard, almost bleached to a super white colour, a distinctive jawline and a strong forehead presented what could be deemed as good genetics.

The skull sat facing the entrance way. It was sitting with a proud deathly stare as the security door to the vault swung open, another display case could be observed in the adjacent chamber a few feet away. A very ornate gilt lectern adorned with huge eagles, one on each side, supporting the heavy frame upon which sat a single panel of illumination could be seen in the other display case. It was a 1st century Bible page. The colourful panel depicted a very vivid illumination from the Sanctos Epistula and one displaying the beautiful face of the 'one'. Perhaps Rossetti had in fact caught the actual face of Mary Magdalene in his many visions.

The leader of the Vatican took a single long deep breath then collapsed onto the flooring having first landed on his knees with a muffled grunt, still gasping for breath and reaching outwards for the manuscript. The office official grabbed his radio and made a report that the Pope appeared to be suffering from a heart attack.

Meanwhile, 1,260 miles away on the isle of Iona, a lone Monk had removed the Hellfire Sword from its holding case and was busy twisting the haft from the blade. He had turned the handle twelve times clockwise when the sword hilt slowly opened outwards in a telescopic movement extending to almost thirty six inches in length.

The Monk then bent down on one knee and pulled the pommel or apple end of the sword from the blade, the steel blade just touched the top of the altar stairway and chinked against the masonry as it found support. A single gold encased framework containing a crystal phial was drawn from within the handle. The Cistercian removed the glass phial and returned the sword to its natural state.

The Crypt

The inside walls of the cemetery were littered with many stone plaques and brass plates each identifying the ashes of the interred, those which had been laid to rest over the many centuries. The pigeon hole cemetery, as it was known by the locals, and ironically where most of the visitors were indeed birds. The mausoleum on the other hand was a very grand affair; it resembled a very small observatory with a granite roof.

The carefully crafted doorway consisted of two stone slabs which dominated the structure, adding an almost vampiric, Victorian welcome to the structure. To the left of this grand design stood a single 5th century grave stone adorned with an effigy of a single rose and a sword which marked the grave site. The stone was adorned with the face of a very beautiful woman on its façade, and the letters MM appeared to have been carved in the middle of a fish motif. The grave was obscured by a congregation of foliage from the nearby hedge and yew tree as they reached out to capture the stones in their natural growth pathway.

Directly at the front of the grave sat an ornate stone square with the single word 'destiny' carved into its surface. Behind the mausoleum stood a single white marble statue of an angel blowing into a set of Pan's pipes, her wings fully spread out with her eyes staring down over the grave of MM. 'A tune for the dead Pope,' whispered Kemp, locating the old bench. Hastings had wandered through this cemetery at least a dozen times and would often sit directly opposite this old stone on the wooden park bench and never took much notice.

'Imagine, her being the 'one',' he said, then sat silently under the old yew tree. 'After all this time she has been watching this big old world go by.' Hastings was sitting cross legged when his phone buzzed. He read the text 'Tartarus Inferni Dei Donum Wyshart' illuminated on the screen.

Hastings turned and placed a single rose on the grave of Mary Theresa Hastings, and sat quietly listening to the song of the nightingales as they flirted in and out the long branches of the old tree. then whispered.

'Well mum that's another year gone by, met a wonderful girl, you would like her, she is bright as a button and an academic too, and, of course she hates tattoos, but you know that already don't you? Bright beautiful blue eyes, just like yours, and that red hair, well you know how I feel about redheads. I will give her your regards when I see her, might even bring her along to meet you, in fact here she comes now, you can say hello yourself.' Kemp Hastings and Darlene Gammay turned away from the grave stone as the apparition waved good bye and vanished.

CHAPTER THIRTEEN

THE PRIORY WARNINGS

Noun—*'Assignation'—a clandestine—meeting or tryst.*

The squeal and screech of the warm tyres on the warm tarmac was almost unbearable to the ears as the red flash of the Jaguar skidded passed and beyond the wooden gates to the old Scottish graveyard. The huge mass of the machine could be seen sliding easily along the soft tarmac by a good 20 feet as the driver wrestled with the controls as the car skidded from left to right to avoid the man standing in its travel path.

Kemp Hastings had hit the brake pedal with so much force that he could almost feel the pressure of the hydraulic oil travel up his right leg and deep into his unsuspecting groin: an instant reaction of his body in relation to the sudden appearance of someone or something which had quite simply and unceremoniously stepped into the middle of the roadway catching him unawares.

Kemp would normally navigate these leafy lanes like a rally driver on heat as a matter of course and knew every twist and turn on the rural speed track, as this would be his little escape as he battled with rules and regulations imposed upon him for road users in the back drop of rural Scotland.

His escape would be exercised on most occasions as he sped through the back roads and country lanes of Angus, an enriched part of Scotland, whilst releasing his anger and frustrations for a few brief seconds in his protests of heavy costs and very bad automobile service. Of course always, remaining mindful that the odd animal, such as a deer or a sheep, which had, on occasions, wandered on to the roadway. Or on one occasion, a stag had leapt the fencing and surprised him, and may actually surprise him still.

But this event was something entirely different. It wasn't every day that a person wandered deliberately into one's travel path. This vision was certainly not an animal and it was not a clump of grass or a shadow. This unsuspecting figure added a whole new dimension to his physical reaction speed times towards avoiding the apparition which was, as far as Hastings was concerned, that his responses were spot on perfect. And he had hit the brakes within a hundredth of a gnat's bollock nana second on spying the person.

This single event somehow sent a sudden, cold fear propelling up through his shocked, grey matter; momentarily catching his senses totally off guard and unawares, forcing him to make a split second decision—a decision where such lightning-quick reactions to such events had cost and saved many lives in the past.

It was that moment in time where Kemp had taken a very deep breath. Just seconds before the asbestos abrasive coating of the brake pads gripped the stainless steel discs of the ABS braking system, momentarily sending a series of incredible jolts up through the body of the car and deep into Hastings's lower spine.

A strong series of sporadic pulses that had technically brought the crimson beast to an almost controlled mechanical halt as the forward momentum of force began hurling his unsuspecting body forwards into the smooth beige leather seat. Then, simultaneously sending his upper body headlong towards the soft cladding of the steering wheel.

Hastings had been propelled so far forward that he bumped his face against the rim of the steering wheel, cutting his upper lip in the process. That was before being hurled violently backwards in the opposite direction, almost ripping the muscles in the back of his neck apart.

Time had also frozen momentarily as the spiritual and phenomenal detective momentarily sat backwards in the driving seat for the second time, having fought with the padded bulge of the car driver's airbag: the life-saving appliance strategically hidden within the confines of the steering wheel itself.

Having wrestled with the steering wheel for several seconds with all his strength and skills, as any mature driver normally would, he was struggling in order to bring the car to a controlled halt. It was then that the air bag fully popped out of its housing and deployed itself in a haze of fluff and the release of pressurised air—coupled with a high pitch whine and almost smothering him in the process.

Another very deep breath and he gazed into the rear view mirror, still wrestling with the airbag. He was expecting to see a body strewn over the black tarmac roadway, albeit he recalled that he had heard no bumps or thumps, and had been psychologically preparing himself to have witnessed a twelve to fourteen stone person first being struck by the front bumper. Yet, to his astonishment the figure was still standing there, and scarily was staring whilst pointing back at him.

"Shit! This is not good," he exclaimed, softly.

The car itself could have had easily become an insurance write off and things for him, physically, could have been much worse by far if he had not been so alert at the time the stranger had suddenly stepped out of the Chapel gates and on to the roadway.

Never-the-less, he succumbed to the fact that his precious, little red car had suffered extensive damage and his seat belt had perhaps saved his life. And yet, he was somehow supposed to be grateful.

He was correct in his assumption in that he had in fact missed the figure completely. And he was somewhat relieved at the same time, but, not exactly sure what he had expected. Especially during the critical moments prior to contact; then a moment of nothing, followed by a very uneasy, cold fear.

He stopped and paused for thought again. He was half prepared to experience the body of a person being hurled over the bonnet and up onto the windscreen of the car, ending up in a sprawled mass of blood, shit and feathers across the tarmac road—not unlike a deer or fox.

"No way can this happen," he muttered again softly under his breath. Then he began to exit the Jaguar.

Stepping out of the car, he took another glance back up the roadway. Then he stared aimlessly at his handy work, thinking that, potentially, he could have flipped the soft top over completely, which would have been almost fatal. He then thought hard about having to peel the heather and the clumps of wet, green grass and foliage from his mirrors and from inside the cockpit, had he rolled the one and a half ton vehicle over, let alone observe what may still be a dead or very injured person. He was relieved of course that he did not have to. He smirked inwardly, then thought again about what might have been. Shrugging his shoulders, he stood fully upright.

"Ouch! Oh, cack, that's not good!" he cried, then coughed, which was followed by a few more small, muscular cricks and twitches from his spine and lower back. And he reckoned he was in good shape—well in good enough condition—that was whilst considering the force of the impact of the machine as it was rammed up against the stone wall.

Then considering his state of being having observed and acknowledged the amount of damage the car had actually sustained, he gave himself another internal 'well done' for having brought the vehicle to a well-controlled stop under extreme conditions and not killing himself, and he gazed on.

"Well, that's not going to be cheap," he muttered away to himself, and snorted whilst wiping his brow, simultaneously flicking open his mobile telephone and staring back up the roadway to where the figure had been previously standing. He then glanced over toward the churchyard and gazed directly at the tall, tower walls of the medieval keep of the Priory building that dominated the foreground.

The blood on his lip had started to trickle down on to his chin and had already stained his new blue and red chequered countryside 'Fruit of the Loom' shirt, leaving a tiny trickle of DNA for all to see.

It was then, that he momentarily became very uncomfortable and somewhat confused as he could not make head or tail of what he had really just witnessed. The car accident was real enough but the circumstances leading up to the event were pretty much inexplicable as far as he was concerned, even for a man of his educational standing.

He then began walking nearer to where the figure had stood. He was hoping to find some sort of clue to the odd event, although he was consciously glancing to his left and right side as he walked, half expecting to find a deranged druid lurking in the nearby bushes, potentially waiting to jump out from the hedge line and mug him.

After three steps or so he began to talk into the mouthpiece of his cell phone. "Hello, can you hear me? Anybody out there? Hello it's me, Kemp."

He heard nothing apart from incoherent mumblings and ramblings coming from the earpiece on his mobile. He stopped and listened intently trying to decipher what sounded to him like a range of gargles and burbles coming from a three year old child in the background.

Several moments later he dropped the phone down by his side on hearing what he thought was another vehicle approaching from the near distance. It was then that the battery on his mobile telephone decided to die, and it bleeped three times just to let him know that it had had enough activity for the time being.

"Piece of cack! I thought those bloody batteries lasted more than six hours."

Stepping off the roadway and onto the soft grassy verge, he waited and watched with the intention of grabbing the attention of a passing driver and to find an opportunity to ask for assistance. He even considered asking for a lift back to the village, as opposed to just locking the car up and going for a brisk walk to his home.

He also considered asking for a tow to his home just a few miles away, or conversely, if he should just call the police and get a lift home from them. Well, he would call them if his damn phone had retained its bloody charge.

Kicking a stone underfoot, he started making his way back to his car, and he sauntered by the chapel gateway where he stopped and took another long glance at the Priory's tall steeple tower. He thought he had just caught sight of a figure standing in one of the tower's higher windows.

But he dismissed this as an optical illusion because of the weather conditions and a trick of the morning light. His peripheral vision was normally very keen, but he remained mindful that he had just taken a bit of a knock during the incident.

He also knew that to find anyone standing in the tower was clearly impossible as the stairwell up the tall tower was long gone and pretty much destroyed in the tower's volatile history. And primarily due to the fact that he had visited the Priory so often that he, on one occasion, had tried to scale the outer wall himself. But to no avail: apart from scraped fingers and a bruised knee whilst destroying a rather nice pair of chino denim trousers. Any notion of a figure in the window was quite out of the question.

He momentarily spied the underneath of the machine and acknowledged to himself that it was totally mangled. The hydraulic piping appeared to be okay but the plastic and metal cowling that covered in and around the offside light cluster was severely cracked with the lens and housing literally destroyed. He then spied a few droplets of what he thought was hydraulic oil on the greenery.

He was more than pissed off that a long, hairline crack had appeared across the top left wheel arch and the new front alloy wheels had suffered severe damage and scathing. He knew that it would require careful repair or replacement.

But all in all he knew it wasn't going to break the bank completely—after all that's what insurances are for. But still, Jaguars do cost a fortune to maintain, and he reminded himself that his ego had been somewhat tarnished. Although he was still very annoyed with himself but he still managed a smile.

The car was possibly driveable or so he thought. Just as the oncoming car approached the scene of where the black tyre skid marks had started. Kemp could see the four way hazard warning lights had started to flash on the car and that was when he flipped his phone closed and stepped off the grass verge.

The oncoming driver was already alerted to the scene before her, and had taken safety steps and had parked her vehicle nearer the grassy embankment. The car had pulled up against the verge a good ten metres or so away—just as Kemp turned and placed a hand on the bonnet of his damaged sports car. Then he nonchalantly stared into the open green fields that stretched out before him.

He took another glimpse back at the motorist to find, to his further astonishment, that his friend and colleague Dr Darlene Gammay had emerged from the driver's seat and was walking briskly toward him.

"Hello, Kemp, how's tricks?" she said, in an almost smuggish, cynical way.

"Can't say that I am surprised to see you hanging around yet another church yard," she muttered softly, observing the awkward angle of the crashed car, which was propped up hard against the stone curtain wall that ran the length of the boneyard.

"And what an odd way to park your bonnie wee car."

Kemp was obviously annoyed, especially as his ego had been bruised, and only compounded more so by Darlene finding him at his most vulnerable. Hastings blinked his eyes several times, he wiped his face again, shook his head sideways and then responded in a relatively well-controlled manner.

"Not now, Darlene, please. I have just skidded half the length of this bloody road. Right from over there to away down over here, and I am a bit annoyed to say the least . . . Well, you know what I mean, and if I did not possess the reactions of a jet fighter pilot,

I could have easily ended up simply slushed and pulped under the weight of my own car, and that would have ruined my chinos completely," he replied, pointing to the tarmac road as it stretched back to where the signpost was sitting at an odd angle, partially obscured by the overhanging branches of the tree line. He tried simultaneously to raise a smile.

"Mmm, Kemp, not sure being a jet fighter pilot would have saved you from the undergrowth. Though, maybe you would need to be more of a dodgem driver—that skill would best fit. But, really are you okay? You do look a little bit flushed to me," she asked, as a concerned friend.

"You whizzed passed me about five miles back. I tried catching you up, but you took off like a Scouser at a police convention, a certain red bat out of hell. And I see you must have lost it on the corner then?" She leaned forward and turned to look at the front of the car. Meanwhile, Hastings took a good look at Darlene's slender, rear end as she bent over the bonnet of the vehicle to inspect the damage.

It was not the first time he had been distracted by her womanly charms especially when presented with high end clothing attached. It was then that she spied his lecherous, boyish gaze, and smiled back at him. Then as she momentarily stared into his eyes, she flippantly remarked, "I hope it is in better shape than your front end is, Mister Hastings!"

Darlene was clad in a retro 1950's outfit: a black Coco Chanel pinafore dress with matching scarf and gloves. She wore classy and black sensible Jimmy Choo shoes and looked every part the biblical studies Professor that she was.

Hastings momentarily smiled and thought that Jackie Onassis would not look out of place standing next to his new partner, and he inwardly smiled, harbouring the thought that he might himself come to a sticky end. He then motioned her to see if they could, together, free the heavy car from the grappling undergrowth. And, after several minutes of vehicular jostling, both cars were parked up in the small car park nearer to the Priory. Darlene sat next to Kemp in the Jaguar. Then picked her moment to speak, "You look a little pale, Kemp, that jolt might have given you a hidden injury or something."

Hastings coughed and leaned forwards toward the Doctor, then explained what he thought had happened, "Darlene, you are most probably correct. But you must listen to this, there was actually someone standing bang in the middle of the road—I swear it. I know I should have mowed them down like a mouse in a wheat field trying to escape a combine harvester, but I missed them completely or they were just not there. Maybe I was hallucinating, I do not know. The person should have emerged like crinkle cut chips having passed through the cheese grater grill on this machine.

And I know there was nowhere to run, as I was travelling at nearly forty five miles an hour. But, here is the funny thing, I drove straight through him, her or it. I am sure it was the figure of man standing directly in front of my car, and he was positioned right in the middle of the bloody road. Darlene, he materialised from nowhere, and he, she or it, was there for a full three to five seconds before I . . ."

Kemp cut off his dialogue and took a moment to pause for contemplative thought before speaking again. "Darlene, it was a Grey Friar Monk and that much I am pretty certain of. Shit, I have spent more time talking to them recently than I have talking with my own Mum."

Darlene crunched her hair up in a quick bun, and flicked a few curls from her eye line. "Okay, I do believe you, all things being equal and all that poppycock," she replied, having applied her specific kind of logic, and more importantly given her recent biblical experience. She knew she could talk to Hastings about most things—herself having had a bit of experience and authority in the given subject matter.

"These inexplicable things do happen, goodness, and, you have probably had more exposure and seen more than your fair share of odd and inexplicable occurrences, and weird and wonderful experiences than most professionals have," she said, whilst remaining informed about the nature of Kemp's complicated investigative world, just before she posed another question.

"Do you think this might have anything to do with my new tattoo? Or maybe, like me, you're just a little bit stressed because of circumstances at the moment? Kemp, you said yourself these things slowly chip away at you and can just creep up un-noticed and build up to a point, where sphlaaatt you are knackered," she implied then stroked his forehead flicking a few loose strands of his thick head of sandy brown hair back into place.

She then found a tissue and wiped the residue of dried blood from his upper lip and chin. "That's much better; you don't look like a dodgy vampire now. I think you had best get the quack to give you the once over though, you never know with car incidents you may feel okay now, but in a week's time or so you could fall over with a broken rib or ruptured something, and could develop into a far more worse condition. I have taken the liberty and sent a text to a police friend of mine to inform him you clipped the verge and no other person was involved—there is no reason to complicate things anymore than they already are . . ." Hastings glanced over her right shoulder and smirked. "Thanks, I have absolutely no idea," he replied, and turned the ignition key. "Coffee," he muttered. Then he asked Darlene to follow him.

"No wait Kemp, before you go, do you think this is a good idea to drive? And you do have to ask yourself will this nice machine actually make it? I mean, after all, it is only a bloody car, it could have some sort of hidden hydraulic damage—you know, brake pipes, clutch that kind of thing. There is absolutely no sense in tempting fate again, now is there? C'mon, I'll drive you home, how does that sound?" she offered.

Hastings thought for a second then agreed with Darlene's logic and removed the ignition keys. Then grabbing his brown leather satchel from the rear seat, he exited and locked the Jaguar and jumped into the passenger seat of Darlene's Range Rover.

"Cannot drive with an airbag like that anyway," he said.

Darlene smiled back at him, then drove more slowly than she normally would have, especially through the back roads and lanes in that part of the country, where mindless, city dwellers would use the back roads as racing tracks. And, of course, Kemp was testament to that statement, albeit the Range Rover was too big to throw around the tight lanes, too many tractors for Darlene's liking.

She flicked the interior mirror forward then thought about a way to distract him from his recent trauma, then she spoke, "I received a parcel in the post yesterday, and you will never guess in a million years what it was." She posed the question in a more relaxed, jovial kind of way, still trying to keep the subject matter away from the macabre and the recent car accident.

Hastings pursed his lips waited for a second or two then nodded his head slowly from left to right then spoke. "It's not our stolen Dante oil painting by any chance is it?"

Darlene was momentarily dumbstruck and just stared aimlessly straight back at him at first, then, stared way out beyond the passenger window gazing well into the far distant horizon, somehow avoiding to crash the car in the process. "How the hell in God's name did you manage to guess that," she exclaimed, whilst abruptly flicking her mobile phone shut. Then she pressed the blue button on the disk player to play.

"C'mon Darlene, I was only joking, it was a wild, educated guess. Look at things this way: with recent events and your current physical condition it seemed logical to me that who ever had orchestrated this bizarre situation in the first place, was obviously playing us like a couple of puppets on strings. I mean, let's face it, it is not every day that a twenty million dollar work of art is stolen, let alone in such bizarre circumstances either, and removed under some very odd conditions that could be deemed beyond the normal run of things. It also seems logical to assume that we might be getting set up by some international arts thieves or some unscrupulous antique dealers, or even a gang of very clever illusionists.

But, either way we had better keep our wits about us. But, I don't mean that your tattoo is part of it, that in itself is an incredible occurrence, but for the image to be the same face on the oil painting as the Rossetti, well, for me that's far too coincidental.

I am afraid I cannot even begin to provide an answer or a rational explanation for the removal of the Hellfire Sword either, well not yet, anyway. But, in reality you would expect such a masterpiece, if stolen, to be found in a dustbin or discovered in some back street antiques' fair or something. It would not be the first time a priceless antique has been discovered in a sale, now would it? We should check eBay, or visit a local car boot sale to see if it is lurking about there," he said flippantly, and stared back out of the passenger window in desperation as his mind juggled with the information, and jostled it around in his one and only complex little brain cell. "And, I also think this is not the last we have heard of this subject if you ask me. But nice car, Darlene.

I do Like the high up observation position, you get a good view. And, you can see over the bushes into the greenery. I will tell you what has occurred though, Darlene, just recently I have had some very weird telephone calls. Tell me, have you received any odd letters or demands in the post recently?

Or ad hoc telephone calls where no-one has actually spoke on the phone, but just seemed to listen until you place the receiver back down, you know like a crank caller trying to piss you off? Or have you met with any weird or wonderful strangers? People who have asked for assistance in some strange way? What I mean is someone who has suddenly popped up out of the blue and is trying to get back into your life for some reason? You should let me know, as it could be important, I have had some strange things happen, you know like every kind of stuff, but they seem to be just more frequent."

Darlene flicked her hair backwards, thought for a bit, then responded, "As far as any strange and very odd people are concerned, there is only one I can immediately think of, and that is you, only you, Kemp Hastings, only you.'

Darlene turned and smirked, as Hastings smirked back at her and then smiled.

"Nope, just the electricity bill," she answered, then nodded in bemusement, as he shrugged his broad shoulders.

He spoke again, "Just the painting then, and a love letter from those greedy arsed electricity moguls who are just as bloody threatening with their demands for extortionate bills, just as terrorists are, if you ask me. But, then again, can't make tea without electrickery now can you? Those buggers know that. So, you have received no red letter mail offers or death threats or applications to join pyramid schemes on offer then? Well, that's a good start," he said, whilst shaking his head.

"None!" she replied. "I do, however, have Dante's twenty million dollar painting with me in the back of the car. Does that count?

Thought I would bring it along and show you it, before I did anything stupid with it."

Hastings pointed forward and jerked his finger ahead. "Best not look at it here, we might crash another car."

Darlene agreed and drove the Range Rover a little bit faster towards the village of Farnell, just a few miles away from the Restenneth Priory—albeit heading in the opposite direction where the figure had recently appeared.

"You shouldn't drive for a couple of days you know. We will come back and pick up your beloved little car later, or you could contact a car recovery company, best leave it to the professionals." She took another glance at the investigator, and thought that he had probably drifted off to somewhere in dream land as he normally did when caught in deep thought. She drove on.

"So tell me, what are you thinking about at this very moment in time, Kemp? You look a bit lost," she asked, wiping a few strands of red hair from her eye line again.

He slid his head off the window then straightened himself up, sniffed a little, then faced his companion. "Not sure, Darlene. I have an odd feeling that this biblical thing is not quite over yet. You see when we left the cemetery in Dundee, I was 100% absolutely sure that things would just ease off and that your tattoo would simply disappear as with the Sadarium or Veronica's veil, you know after the period of lent, but apparently this is not the case. I am still researching the subject, and may have to travel to Egypt for more answers.

I have a friend in Cairo who has deep knowledge of the bizarre events in biblical history. He is of course a complete and utter pointy headed lunatic, but an amazing source of information. Do you fancy a trip to Cairo?" he asked.

Later that evening and in the quietness of his surroundings, Hastings picked up his little black book and quizzed its contents. Darlene, meanwhile, had made arrangements and was making her way back to the city.

He read the words he had written in his book whilst consuming a few healthy drams of brandy and slowly but surely drifted into a hazy state of happiness.

Rossetti.

Dante Gabriel Rossetti, born London 12th May 1828 and died of 'Bright's disease', 9th April 1882 Kent, London. Rossetti was an active member of the Pre-Raphaelite Brotherhood who changed the course of painting during the Victorian Era of British history.

Dante had painted 'The Damsel of the Holy Grail' in the year 1874 which depicts Mary Magdalene holding the Eucharistic chalice and is overseen by a bird of peace or a white dove.

Mary Magdalene or 'The Apostle's Apostle' travelled with Jesus to Jerusalem and was present at the crucifixion. Luke 8:3. Holy Bible. Mary Magdalene had taken the time write a gnostic gospel of which many fragments have been found scattered across various countries. Several parchments have come to light dating in and around the 5th century.

Just then, he was alerted by the sound of a loud bang. He jumped up, as the book he was holding fell from his grasp. He had momentarily fallen asleep and shuddered as he found his empty glass.

"Ah refill time," he said, then scrambled to his feet, just as a warm wisp of fresh air drifted through the room. Picking up his glass from the table, he negotiated his way back to the drinks' cabinet and stood staring at himself in the long ornate mirror whilst pouring himself another larger than normal size dram of brandy. As he turned back toward the mirror, he stared at his image more intently and was almost amused to find it was not his reflection staring back at him. The drink had obviously taken the right effect he thought, then smiled at himself or whoever it was looking back.

"Who the fuckin' hell are you?" he asked, as the reflection just stared back at him with no indication or signs of life or emotion. Hastings drifted more into a challenging prose. "Ah! Ah! Wait a moment—do not tell me? I know you. I have seen your sad and lonely face just recently, I know who you are! You are whatshisface, the poet, no that sculptor fellow, no the writer. No, oops, shhhh!" he slurred, whilst placing a single finger over his lips.

"Don't tell me. I got it, you now, you are that Rossetti, you are Gabdramelli Dante Rossetti" He spluttered in his drunken verbal attack of the artist.

"You are a jack of all the artistic trades, them all, the painter, the soldier, the sailor but more importantly, le poet and le artiste . . . is that not correct?" he said, in his drunken stupor, still pointing at the reflection as the image shuffled its position and was moving closer towards the mirror. Then the image smiled and nodded as if to acknowledge his remarks.

Hastings had a huge grin on his face as he recognised the artist who was now fully dominating his reflective life.

"So you are responsible for all this shit, are you? Do you know you are putting me through a living hell, and not just me either, but, me and my gal Dashlene, you and your vile laudanum opium sprees along with your acts of acute drunken-ness, your so called active involvement in unearthly pursuits of the black magic. Your high and mighty Victorian shodding values. I can't say I am that impressed, by your antics.

Well, can't say I blame you for actually for getting pissed, but dabbling in the Majick, well, that was bloody stupid, on your part, and your talents as an artiste, damn amazing, absolutely genius, if you ask me. But tell me why all the fuss? What is this shit all about? Why has Darlene been cursed? You tell me that, Mister El Dante," he asked, in his slurred speech attack on Rossetti, and then lifted his drink and saluted the figure in the mirror, as it appeared to gaze back at him.

Then the image spoke. "I am, as you say, Dante Gabriel Rossetti. Yes, I did dabble in hallucinogenic drugs and yes I do obey the darker side of the occult, and all to my sad demise, depending on your outlook of life and death. But you, Mister Kemp Hastings, well, you are a lot closer to me than you will ever actually know.

Your friend, the beautiful Miss Gammay, she has crossed over, she has seen the other side of death, and has been blessed with hindsight and will take time to understand her role as she moves into our glorious ethereal world. She has been chosen by the Magdalena herself."

The image seemed to glow a bright blue as a haze of mist bellowed up from the bottom of its feet. Then the image stabilised as it spoke again, "Your time will come soon but please tell me one thing: what year is it?"

Hastings leaned closer to the mirror and gazed at the dress sense of the reflective image as Rossetti then took a single step backwards for a better view. Then he looked at his watch, it said the 12th May. Then he answered the great Rossetti's question. "It is the 12th of May in the year 2011 in the 21st century. What year did you think it was?"

No answer came as Hastings quizzed the image which was clad in its 18th century, heavy grey trousers and black waistcoat and tunic. The distinguished look of a man of substance, a man with influence and flair, especially on the day that marked his earthly death.

He spied the golden chain that linked the golden time piece attached to its end link, which was clipped to another heavy-linked gold chain running from the middle button hole of Rossetti's waistcoat where the watch itself sat snuggly in in the left side waistcoat pocket. The image was very much how Hastings had remembered what Dante Rossetti looked like on the picture that was neatly tucked into his little black book, along with his footnotes.

Rossetti looked much younger than his photograph depicted. His hair was more well-kept, receding a little but he was never-the-less a good looking man verging on the more mature side of life. He was clean and well-groomed.

The image was holding a black hat and was swaying from side to side, as it spoke softly to the investigator. "I have not died yet; none of us here on this dark plane have died. We live within the ether gases; we move as ghost-like figures and we have rational thoughts and urges, but, we have a balance to maintain, and you have a duty to perform."

Hastings took another drink of his beverage, then he mumbled a few words. "Well, if that is the case, then my duty is to my friends. But tell me Gab, I can call you Gab—yes, no? Doesn't really matter. But please tell me one thing, your Damsel of the Sank Real, is she real? Does that painting really capture her true likeness, and why would you want to inflict such an image on a living person?"

The image moved closer to the mirror as Hastings continued in his ramblings. Hastings heard echoes coming from his bathroom. It was a soft voice and it was very clear.

"This image is real and the events in your life are as real as you want them to be. She is the ultimate earthly entity; she can move in and out of reality just as she wishes. But she must also ensure that faith is maintained. The control of billions of people is important and much is at stake if we get it wrong."

Hastings was nodding abruptly as the strong alcohol was making a more potent and direct hit on his logical senses as he quizzed the entity further. "So, Gabriel, what do you want me to do? Because you and your ethereal friends have virtually thrown my life into turmoil and have ruined Darlene's life completely—what sort of bloody balance is that?"

The image placed the black hat on his balding head and removed the time piece from his waistcoat pocket, then began tapping the face of the watch. Hastings noticed that his lips did not move but the words were clearly heard.

"Look at the painting, Mister Hastings, observe the symbols and absorb the hidden esoterical messages captured within its framework. Read the maths and more importantly think about the woman in question, not the subject matter but the earthly woman. And, if you get time, come visit my graveside and ready my epitaph. We can talk there."

The mirror appeared to have glazed over and resembled what Kemp would describe as a cold front as the icy image started to disappear from view. Hastings hiccupped three times then burped and started waving goodbye to the mirror.

"Nice meeting you too, Mishter Gabriel, please do call again, but try using the door next time," muttered Hastings as he stumbled over the small table that lay in his way, missing the mirror by a few inches as he toppled over in a fit of laughter, then started laughing out loud as he grappled with his drunken state.

Then he was confused as he stared at the base of the mirror. He then reached out and grabbed the black hat that sat adjacent to the lion's claw and ball foot of the mirror stand.

"Thanks." Then he fell asleep on the floor.

CHAPTER FOURTEEN

EPITAPH

The following day Darlene and Kemp had met for lunch and were discussing all the facts that they thought they knew about mythology, folklore and history and the couple spent the complete day together. Yet Hastings had consciously failed to discuss the previous night's events in his drunken stupor with her.

Darlene, had remained overnight in Kemp's bachelor pad, love nest—the two having slept apart for the second time in their somewhat short liaison time frame. Yet they both would both agree a mutual respect for one another, but neither would rule out a bit of 'slap and tickle'.

And, although Kemp liked her a great deal, he didn't want to make any stupid 'amour' advances until he was absolutely certain that Darlene would reciprocate accordingly without leaving him sprawled across his Egyptian rug with his 'family jewels' wrapped around his throat.

Conversely, Darlene would be the first to admit that Hastings was too much like her father and even possessed the same body scent as he did. Her dad had sadly died some eight years earlier from a long illness. He had passed away just as she entered the university as a senior lecturer, but she would swear he was always around her, which often left her thinking if Kemp was related to her and she knew that she sniffed the odour around him far too much.

She would also admit that Kemp had the exact same mannerisms that her dad had possessed, and he even complained about the same things, which again, she found amusing but found herself all too often sitting back in admiration as Hastings explained almost any subject to her. Although there was a strange mental and physical attraction to him.

If Darlene was asked about Kemp Hastings being in her life, she would say that their relationship, for the time being, would be a very platonic one, as they would often sit and discuss the world's problems at great lengths to the wee small hours.

The morning came quick, albeit that Kemp had spent a fairly comfortable night on his large sofa with his aches and pains from his recent road accident, which had miraculously gone—apart from a slight stiffness around his shoulder muscles.

Darlene, on the other hand, had fallen into unconsciousness in the warm duvet of 'Kemp Hastings' land', for the second time and fuelled with a tot or two of brandy, and awoke to the morning chorus of the local rooster, nicknamed Lynford, as he informed the world that he was awake and still very alive much to the dismay of the village's inhabitants.

The name Lynford having been attributed to this huge, male chicken mainly because all attempts by its owner to catch the avian often resulted in the bird's owner coming second in the race of capture, and he had, on occasion, spent hours trying to catch the bird. Kemp had always thought he would get the feathery bastard with the Jag one morning, but the birdie was far too clever for mere humans.

Kemp had just flicked the 'on' switch to the kettle and was about to find the bread for toasting, when there was a loud knock on the downstairs entrance door. He flinched at first and thought that it might be the police checking up on him for leaving the scene of the previous day's accident. He quizzed the clock: it was nearly 08:15 hours.

He then made his way slowly downstairs and opened the door, gingerly at first, but to his delight there was no blue-uniformed officer to confront him, but he was presented with a stockily-built workman, who was instead was clad in grey work overalls covered in a coating of light brown dust.

"Morning guvnor, what a nice day for it . . ." said the young man.

'Mr Hastings is it, can you sign here please?

Kemp nodded his head from within the wooden doorway.

"Delivery for you. Where do you want it left?" asked the delivery man. "It's quite a large item, I can't bring it into the building it's over 25 kg, not allowed to lift that kinda shit, not these days with all that health and safety stuff.'

Kemp motioned the man to leave the package by the outside foyer or near to the gateway and said that he would pick it up later. The grey clad man agreed, and after a short argument with the electronic signature pad, he wandered off.

Kemp returned upstairs and grabbed the kettle, just as Darlene passed by the doorway, and was heading for the shower cubicle, muttering something in the realms of, "Coffee, really black and lots of sugar—I feel like shit." Then she disappeared off into the bathroom.

The delivery man, meanwhile, fired up the winch on the back of his IVECO flat bed truck and clipped on the hook to the lifting bridle. Then, operating the many control levers, he carefully lifted the slab slowly off his truck. He then swung the granite plinth toward the grass verge and laid it neatly in the upright position against the stone gate pillar.

The stone from what could be observed was clearly an old grave stone and was now somehow the possession of Kemp Hastings of the Royal Order. It was then that he took another quick look out of the window having been alerted by the loud noise of the hydraulics of the winch truck. And he stood motionless as he watched the slab being placed in situ.

"What the hell this time?" He smirked and tutted, then returned back to his coffee, just as Darlene emerged from the shower all wrapped up snuggly in a Kemp Hastings' white, fluffy house coat and stood by the doorway.

"Anything interesting?" she asked, whilst grabbing the mug and began to take a sip of the hot, milky brew. Kemp, meanwhile, raised an eye brow and his left hand, then pointed somewhere towards the top of the window in a non-committed type of fashion, as if blaming the Gods for yet another act of ludicrous intervention.

"Nope, just another twist to this bloody crazy conundrum. I think this time someone has decided to send me a half ton grave stone, that's all, nothing normal."

Darlene almost froze in her tracks and smiled, then muttered. "Okay, then why on God's earth would you want to buy a grave stone, Kemp?" she asked, inquisitively then waited for an answer.

Kemp stood and stared at the plinth as it leant it up against the gate post, then he started shaking his head and turned to face her and then responded to the question. "Oh no, Darlene, not purchased, just bloody delivered. I think I may need to find it a new home or donate it to some church somewhere, who knows? Whatever bloody next?."

He then walked across the room to his modest library and extracted a clutch of documents from the middle shelf. His library mainly consisting of a multi-mixed compendium of spiritual, biblical and science fiction books. He had found himself returning to the same reference book time and time again, only this time he actually knew what he was looking for.

He picked up one of his older looking booklets and blew the light coating of dust away from the cover. The lettering appeared much clearer.

It read: ***Incunabula***, version one—'Writ of Souls'.

He flicked through a few pages, then stopped and found an insert referring to the use of biblical weapons and methodology of the 5th century. He skipped the first few pages covering the Ark of the Covenant and the Art of Crucifixion, then he flicked between the Hellfire Cross Sword and the Spear of Destiny pages.

According to his manuscript the two items, the spear and the sword, were once combined together to bring the lands of the pharaohs together in unity. It was a strategic attempt to meld the upper and lower regions of Egypt together. This particular article of faith was to be the Pharaohs' ultimate 'weapon of choice' to control the Gods.

He had also been alerted to the existence of a single weapon that was used to send kings, gods, queens, sorcerers, sirens and beasts back into the underworld of Hades. It was rumoured that this 'spear tipped' sword could keep the Grim Reaper at sword's length and that was obviously a good thing.

Hastings had by default read Homer's 'Iliad': a paperback copy of which had conveniently come into his possession the previous year. He recalled the tail of Persephone and how desperate she was for revenge, tricking Odysseus and his crew into remaining on the mystical island.

A deceptive ploy in order to feed her not-so-endearing children, who were in fact a clutch of darling little demons. Thinking about the demons aspect, instantly brought him back to Hades, and the Hellfire Sword itself.

A few pages further through the book and he found what he was looking for. He had read the passage several times before, but now, it had more significance.

"What a deception plan, good job the Greeks had their wits about them."

He ran his index finger down the page and stopped at page 137 and searched for paragraph 33 and took a deep breath before reading the text out loud as he began moving around his living quarters.

The page read: The Sword Hilt Manuscript

The God killing sword or the 'tartarus inferni' (Hellfire Sword), the haft or hilt is constructed from skin and bone and encased in a shroud of gold. The length of which will extend one arm's length plus one hand span of the intended user.

The weight of which, is counterbalanced with a marble or glass pommel, the weight may shift from user to user. The blade will have been folded six times and overlapped seven times; the quillon will be attached and annealed.

The thigh bone of the 'one' is the omnipotent source of power and thus carved into the haft of the Hellfire and shall be encased in gold and silver.

The 'tartarus inferni' once constructed was rumoured to have been placed in the fires of eternity to enhance it with hidden properties. Its hardness and strength can only be matched with construction methods that only the sciences and techniques of the future will detect.

The Haft is of hollow construction, and within it is lined with glass. It once contained a single page of hidden esoteric knowledge hidden in a crystal phial, placed in the void by physical intervention. Then the pommel is turned twelve times in an anti-clockwise direction to the lock position and further annealed.

The quillon is made of the purest of gold and cross plated with diamond studs of six. The seamless work will be quenched in the blood of an ox and offered to the 'worthy' of the human society.

End of text. Signed, the Cipher.

"Well if that is not modern day Apocrypha then I have no idea what the hell will be. Hey, listen to this, Darlene, this really has some heavy duty esoterical meanings."

Darlene gazed on with a slight bewildered look upon her face. Then challenged his comments. "Kemp, c'mon 'Apocrypha'? In what context do you mean? Secret religious meanings, writings and all that other stuff that never actually made it into the humble bible—that kind of Apocrypha? Now that will be interesting."

She tilted her head then finished drinking her beverage whilst staring at the investigator. Hastings shuffled his feet as he read further through the book and began wandering about his flat like a motivated biblical professor—an unconscious habit that he did at times like this.

Frequently, he would stop reading the text and look back at Darlene as if he was searching for clarity or deeper understanding.

"Is there any other kind? Well, in this context anyway. I mean this is the 21ˢᵗ century, after all, and we have all seen the X-files on the television. For me, well, I still have an inclination of perhaps a pre-human existence on our little planet, or at least an ancient alien relationship that maybe has died away, out of existence through time. If you want to get bi-polar regarding academics and fact.

So, what I think is that we have here is a 'metaphor' of power and control, because I do happen to know that Apocrypha in the Greek language, as an example, basically means, 'those hidden away', and that must mean people or a life form.

You know if we say 'those cups are hidden away', that would not make exact sense, but from an academic standing would you agree life form? Defined in this case by the word 'those' or let us just suppose for one moment that we are actually talking extra-terrestrial life, and that's where I become very, very uneasy and uncomfortable."

Darlene was nodding her head and had been slowly tapping the side of the porcelain mug, using the gold ring as a percussion tool in time with the music in the background.

She shifted her position and pulled her legs up under her buttocks, then leaned over the back of the soft sofa and followed Hastings around the room with her eyes as he narrated verbatim from the informative book.

"Again all dubious wording and could be utter garbage in all their content. But I also understand that Judaism as a further example of Apocrypha, and that could be the ultimate message that is captured within the Dead Sea Scrolls.

But, the problem here is word of mouth, or Chinese whispers as the message through the passage of time has been added with arms and legs and stories of simple, ancient warring skirmishes became great, unprecedented wartime events, and all due to poetic verbal licence.

So what do I have? Not a damn lot. I can only imagine that something more corroborative will pop up?" He turned and smiled as he watched his house guest drape herself over the back of his soft Mexican sofa.

"Ok, Mister Hastings, your secret codes, all this secret information passed through time . . . Are you saying that the Bible is just a big code book? Or are you saying that only specific portions of the Apocrypha or some detailed, esoteric literature was recorded in the Bible and that there is actually another copy of the holy bible somewhere? a book packed with hidden knowledge.

Because, if that is the case, then, you should not dismiss the complete Gnostic gospels of the Saints or the Nag Hammadi Scrolls either, as they are also littered with your apostle's verbal outpourings and maybe even be riddled with fable type conjecture and yet, Kemp, one point six billion Catholics globally hinge their beliefs upon these ideals and more so upon these very documents.

So the esoteric and the Apocrypha messages could be 'the real' message from God, purely because the way they have not only survived, but evolved through the centuries, and have made their way into modern day existence, and that process in itself is very secret, or was controlled with acute precision by a higher Order."

Hastings was nodding his head again, and rubbed the pages with his left hand. "Doctor Gammay, I totally agree, so here is the million dollar question: How many damned aliens are amongst us today, or let us be even clearer: How many Angels of Death or Angels of Mercy co-exist within the complex fabric of our mixed society? All scary stuff. But, let me change the subject just for one second, listen to the radio right now, can you hear that Boney M record?"

Hastings pointed to his iPod that was playing softly in the background—the sound track of early 80's and 90's music was quietly humming away as the couple conversed. Darlene was still tapping away on her mug with her ring to the very tune.

"Well, you will just love this bit: now think 'out of the box' and think about 'ancient psalms'—what if I said that Psalm 137 was behind the very message that this record alludes to? Sounds quite silly unless you actually know or understand history. And of course, my dear Doctor, you do," he said, pointing his index finger straight at his colleague.

"By the rivers of Babylon, we sat and wept, blah, blah, blah. I am sure you have heard it a zillion times. But what does it actually refer to? Not just the psalm itself, but the psalm number 137 itself. And again, this is another example of an esoteric reference or meaning. A number that can be found in many disciplines of either maths, religion, physics and more.

But since we are discussing religion, let's go to Babylon, or Iraq. Zion . . . the Bible gateway to the new world; a place of heaven on Earth. Well, I would certainly challenge that concept today, but it is both an amazing place and an interesting number nevertheless—if you wish to delve that far into the subject.

So, let us suppose that you could interpret it and say it refers to a date—1st March 2007-1007 or AD 7 BC 7, or conversely, 1/3/7. But, it is indeed the 33rd prime number in a given sequence. Or, if we go a bit deeper a Chen Prime. And that is not common in any equation.

Conversely, Darlene, in physics, it could be interpreted as a fine structure content or the number could be broken down to the 'nth' degree and even relate to an integer number, but that is all far too complex for my little brain to work out.

So, I opt for the more esoteric angle, the age of the universe, or its given age when it was first recorded, and could be roughly relative to an example such as '137' (x) times the square of a myriad of years, or cubed to a specific mass of an interstellar planet or heavenly body, a star—pick one, Darlene, there are literally millions to choose from? Let us say Mintaka, within Orion's belt, how could we ever work out its mass and density? Well, esoterics and geophysical tellurics and all that kind of stuff all hang on the 137 numerical notion of mass, and I have no idea where that number actually comes from.

So the other question is: why do I think this is the better option? I hear you cry. Well, my dear lady, it is simply because it will never be proven or disproven. And again, if I was to ask 'why bother to record such detail in the first place?' Especially if it was not relevant, but why record on such important religious documents or scriptures?

My theory would aim toward space travel, all far-fetched stuff but someone thought it important enough to inform future mankind of a simple set of numbers." He pursed his lips and took a very deep breath. "I think I am at the end of my intellectual capacity to work this sword conundrum to any solid conclusion yet."

He then walked out of the room, heading for the kitchen humming the tune 'By the Rivers of Babylon', with his book of hidden knowledge, 'The Incunabula', flapping loosely about in his hand.

Darlene shuffled in the sofa and spoke out loud, in order to catch his ear. "Kemp, you are aware that the Aramaic version of Psalm

137 relates to the daughter of Babel, aren't you, or the heavenly destroyer, and, if you are looking for a metaphor then goodness there is the best one right there.

But the foreign land reference is also clear, but that just means to me that the song of the Lord will hail from another country, having had Babel destroyed. Oh! That is creepy, you know we have just had the Gulf war. And if we were to get esoterical then we would also have to seek out Nostradamus and see what else he had to say five hundred years back, let alone what these writings tell us from as far back as biblical times."

Hastings returned to the room and passed her a big chocolate éclair.

"Okay what's that for?" she asked, abruptly.

Kemp Hastings stood upright and stared at her for several seconds. "To eat, my dear lady, what do you want to do with it?" he said, flippantly, then laughed.

"So, Aramaic the old world biblical language and Psalm 137 answers all our questions, does it? Nice chocolate—don't you think? Very creamy, mmh, think I will have another one," he said, then wiped the cream away from his lower lip. "It takes away the pain of that bloody car crash; I still get little twinges now and again. But you might be right with the Aramaic stuff, we will have to look a bit deeper, not sure how the sword and the psalm relates together but interesting nonetheless."

Hastings sat next to Darlene and opened his laptop.

"Here look I think I have found something, I am in the book of Genesis and it mentions the daughter of Zidon. Well, that's the place, Zion, and the location of Tyre. Now, is that the Tyre, as in William of Tyre, regarding the Knights' Templars and all that, or is it another place entirely? I don't know as yet. This psalm 137 and all its contents refers to 'affections or disagreements' with the truth, basically explaining arguments against what is in place, so, in this case the daughter's references here, are classed as indications or notions.

Well, that does not help us but it does show us that people were giving early warning to what was transpiring. Nope, sadly that's a dead end, but it shows you that a simple bit of music can be riddled with hidden meanings and that is how esoterics works. Anyway, this Incunabula book has answered my questions. All we need to do is find out where the sword is located and we are in good shape."

The Doctor wiped her lips with her tissue leaving a small blob of chocolate éclair on her check. Hastings leaned forward as Darlene closed her eyes. "Messy pup, that you are, one dark chocolate éclair and look at the state of you, choccy drops everywhere." He wiped her cheek then closed the lid of the computer.

CHAPTER FIFTEEN

A BRUSH WITH THE LAW

Later that morning, Darlene had returned to her flat, and spent a couple of hours answering emails and paying her bills online, a certain chore, like most working people, she hated doing, but it was a necessary evil to exist in the modern world.

After a relaxing few hours, she drifted off into a hazy kind of sleep, never really quite getting comfortable and tossed and turned as her mind was playing catch-up with the current events.

She then heard what she thought was a loud bang, and was rudely awoken from her semi-slumbered state. She quizzed the clock; it said twenty past seven. She had been asleep for an hour, or so she had thought.

After taking a few moments to fully wake herself up, she worked out that she had been sleeping for a good ten hours, with yet another strange dream for her to work out.

Her dream recurred in her thoughts—the words in the newspaper headline had said:

'Doctor Darlene Gammay receives finder's fee for stolen Rossetti!'

There was a sudden commotion outside in the narrow street; it was created by the animosity of the local constabulary, as a big, white 4 x 4 police car came to a screeching halt with its blue lights flashing followed by a series of bursts from the multi-tone air horns. The noise of the high pitched sirens making their unwelcomed presence known, not only in the street but probably half of the city.

Outside her apartment's entrance doorway, three policemen stood in anticipation, awaiting orders from their HQ. The radio had buzzed a couple of times then the words 'Go, go, go' echoed in the small hallway.

Another police Range Rover pulled up very slowly in almost silence and headed towards number thirty three, then came to a halt a few yards from the doorway, which was followed by another bout of screaming and shouting orchestrated by police command as mayhem ensued.

Two officers armed with long steel fence posts were running headlong towards the house with their heavy steel post battering rams ready for deployment in order to break down the next difficult door.

Darlene panicked slightly, and hid the masterpiece neatly under her bed—the blue tube clearly sticking out at one end. She slowly moved the curtain to one side and took another peak outside. It was just then that her doorbell rang, she jumped and flinched momentarily catching her breath. She fluffed her hair up and pulled her cardigan down over her bosom, then took several deep breaths.

Walking very slowly towards the door, she took a glance backwards thinking that this could be her last day of freedom having been convicted of receiving stolen goods. Then she placed the security chain across door lock, and opened the door to the limit of the brass chain.

The chain links chinked somewhat apathetically as the door creaked as it came to a stop, and when a quarter open, she peeped gingerly out.

"Morning miss, can I have your signature please?" came the sharp voice of a deliveryman. "I have a registered letter for you." Darlene had been half expecting to meet the dark figures of the local constabulary and was slightly confused and yet very relieved as she grabbed the electronic signature pad from the delivery man as he slid it between the door and the door frame.

She looked up, smiled, then scribbled her name across the small screen. She paused and shook her head, then quizzed the UPS delivery man's attire, acknowledging his big red ID Badge, and the bright green uniform.

She noticed the letters UPS on the upper left pocket then waited for a few seconds more and unlatched the chain and opened the door and returned the electronic device to its owner.

The delivery man handed over the envelope, then spoke. "Looks like number 27 are being raided for drugs, Miss, noisy buggers the police. Did you know that just last week they raided my neighbour's house, and it was the wrong address, completely trashed the front door. They said that the police and the security people are reading all our emails these days—no escape from big brother—slimy buggers," he said, then tipped his hat and made off down the stairway.

Darlene looked out of her door, she glanced to her left and watched as the inhabitants of number 27 were being dragged unceremoniously and thrown into a big, white waiting police van. She estimated that there were at least fifteen officers for two arrests.

"Morons!" she whispered, then she closed the door to her apartment.

She looked carefully at the envelope, and noticed it had various odd postal markings with five international franking stamps from as far away as Malta and Egypt in the top right corner, and another series of franking machine marks that read 'Artefacts and Paintings'—The Gallery, London.

She returned to her living room and threw the envelope on the sofa. She had definitely suffered enough surprises for the time being and she wandered off into her kitchen.

CHAPTER SIXTEEN

CAIRO

Noun—'Assignation' a clandestine meeting or tryst

Cairo was becoming blistering hot, even at seven o'clock in the morning of late August and the dusty city streets were bustling with a hive of activity; the traffic was chaotic and the local inhabitants were busy beavering away in their daily routines, or travelling to and from work.

The hum of twenty million people waking up in modern day Cairo was not a quiet affair by any standards. Hastings had already been disturbed by the 5.25am religious calling, having been blessed with a huge mosque with at least forty loudspeakers attached to it, which was located near to the hotel. It was the daily reminder in order to alert the Muslim world that it was time for prayer; luckily for him it was right opposite his hotel window.

"Ahh, Cairo, what a pain in the arse, what a good morning wake up call, glad I do not live here," he muttered, and headed for the shower knowing full well that the water was going to be cold—it was just an expectation and a fact of life he had become accustomed to whilst visiting the land of the chicken kebab.

The holy ritual of Ramadan had just passed and Eid had recently finished; the many street vendors were out and about touting for new business and the many tourists were being consistently accosted and bombarded by street urchins and the many stall or shop owners who were open for new business.

Two hours later, Kemp Hastings smiled as the taxi driver pulled up against the overly sized pavement and came to a halt. As he opened the door and stepped out, he was hit by the inner city pungent smell and aroma of the over populated Cairo air. Just as the warm humidity wrapped itself around his olfactory nasal senses, he almost choked and sneezed twice.

He threw his black 'North Face' rucksack over his left shoulder sending a shower of warm, wet sweat up his back. As he turned to walk away from the cab, there was another 'toot' from an adjacent car's horn, it was another taxi, and the driver had begun waving his arms.

Kemp laughed, momentarily reminiscing about the almost laughable taxi driver culture in Egypt: the driver's would often watch you arrive at your stop, then as you stepped out from your current taxi you would hear the words "Taxi, Meester?"

Laughing out loud, he closed the door of the car and walked towards the huge gates of the Museum, only pausing for a few seconds to take in the amount of devastation that the old parliament building had suffered, along with the disrupted locality of Tahrir Square. Darlene meanwhile had headed off on an earlier shopping spree with one of her friends, as she probably knew Cairo better than Kemp ever could.

Hastings watched intently as the military arm of the country's dishevelled government assembled itself across what remained of the old inner city square. Each soldier was standing upright to attention, armed with a baton and a shield whilst standing shoulder to shoulder and rubbing up against their counterparts. The troop began deploying in a huge, circular formation.

He watched with interest as the young Officers inspected the troops one by one, only stopping now and again to adjust a baton or reset a hat, here and there, yet their own attire was somehow just as ill fitting. Hastings smiled again and shook his head in amazement.

He quizzed the backdrop of the surrounding area, it was strangely dominated by a huge, singular building; the very structure which overshadowed the beautiful Cairo Museum itself, the now, dormant shell of what once appeared to be a rather substantial construction of dwellings and offices which had been destroyed by fire—a gutted derelict carcass and a stark reminder of change and reform.

The structure had been subject to an arson attack during the chaos that had ensued earlier in the year, and was completely burned out along with several other buildings. A reminder of what the lack of democracy and control could inflict on the local government if they could not keep the electorate happy.

It was now the month of September, and yet not so long ago back in January the square would have been impossible to visit as the revolution had sparked off and gripped Egypt in its violent struggle for democracy.

Kemp thought for a moment as to how the government could even try and gain control of 22 million people, especially so many in one large city—yet so widely dispersed.

"Mmmh!" he smirked, then walked on.

During the short car journey from a local district known as Maadi, the taxi driver had explained that the government motorcade of the newly informal, unelected new government had left a secret location somewhere deep within Cairo's established inner city. And heading through the square en-route to the Egyptian embassy.

The car-cade or cortege then was due to travel onwards to the government offices. It was then that the driver turned the Blaupunkt radio off for one reason or another, and took a few short cuts up some unkempt side streets. The President, who still lay apparently in an induced drug-controlled sleep was in the worst kept secret location in Egypt, known as The Cairo General hospital, with an armed guard patiently waiting outside.

Pending his international court appearance, and was apparently not running the country and the elected committee had worked through as contingency under the new regime for revolutionary change over-shadowed by the Military.

The court case against him for his crimes against the Egyptian people and humanity was imminent, but the people were not happy with the armed services hovering in the political background. It was obvious that the people wanted the President out of the equation and the outcome of an 'in country trial' would most likely result in a very long term prison sentence or the death penalty for the outgoing tyrant.

Democracy was evidently beginning to take its iron fist grip on society as many local women had adopted to dress down for the occasion—each adorned with flip flops and cut down shorts. Hasting's instant thoughts were tourists, but no, he was wrong, these were indeed local girls and women.

He then slowly made his way to the museum's entrance and passed through the huge metal gates having paid his 60 LE, and was ascending the wide stairway into one of the world's greatest museums. Several populated tiers of nothing but granite sarcophagi and huge door lintels that ran across the many wide doorways.

Each chamber was adorned with a range of huge, glass cabinet display cases that littered the ground level where each display case must have weighed at least a metric ton each. 'Just adding to the hundreds of tons of existing masonry,' thought Hastings as he sniffed the scent of a vanilla aroma that filled the air.

In the office to the immediate left of the main entrance hallway, Dr Mohammed Elfeky was sitting quietly absorbing the local paper with his eyes closed. His brown-stained tea cup was resting precariously on the edge of the chair's wooden arm, potentially waiting to be knocked off its perch, and would undoubtedly end up falling and smashing on the stone floor at any second.

Kemp spied his friend then quietly made his way into the middle of the office and stared at the chaos in the small room: it was littered with everything but office equipment. He laughed inwardly laughed and raised his voice towards the sleeping Professor.

"No time for sleeping Elfeky you lazy rag headed bum, get your skinny Egyptian arse off that chair and make a proper cup of tea," barked Hastings, placing his black rucksack bag on the adjacent rickety wooden table top. Mohammed Elfecky suddenly stirred then slid off the chair, momentarily springing to attention just as the porcelain cup hit the floor and bounced twice towards the small statue of Seth that was sitting nearby.

The cup then flipped onto its base and ended up sitting snugly between the feet of the granite statue, the contents of which had spilled onto the stone floor.

Kemp stared for a few seconds and thought that the statue was totally misplaced in the corner of the office as opposed to being on display for Mr Joe Public.

"Wahid, wahid," (one, one) Elfecky shouted, spying the tall figure of Hastings towering over him.

Kemp wiped his own brow with his handkerchief, then addressed the not-so-sleeping Professor of Egyptian Archaeology and artefacts. "Do you still walk like an Egyptian then?" he muttered, offering him a friendly hand up.

"Salaam, salaam, oh what joys! Welcome to Cairo, Mister Hastings, good to see you again. How are you? It has been such a long time? How was your trip from Scotland? And, my apologies for dozing off, I have been working too many hours this week, a quick power nap does one's body clock good things you know. I expected you much later on today," he replied.

Kemp smiled and shook hands with Dr Elfecky. "So I see," he remarked, taking a seat and simultaneously opening up his bulging back pack.

"This is for your good lady hanum . . . (wife)," responded Hastings, passing a brown package across to the Egyptian. "I hope she likes strawberry jam?"

The Professor graciously accepted his gift.

"Ah, Meester Hastings, today it will be for my wives, for I am blessed with two," he said, proudly just as Hastings turned and stared into the eyes of Mohammed.

Then Hastings spoke as a teacher would to a child. "Ah well, there's the penalty and the problem right there Mohammed: two mother in laws to fight with, two witches from Hades to keep you in a reasonable order, oh what joys!" Then laughed out loud. "My colleague Dr Darlene will pop around later, she is off shopping somewhere, she was intent on buying some original oils for relaxation purposes. She said she will be about an hour or so. I am sure you will like her—she is your total opposite in character."

Kemp removed a piece of parchment from his satchel and passed it across the table to Mohammed who had just placed two cups of brown liquid that almost resembled tea on the table top.

Tea that would smell more like ginger or warm almonds than actual tea if Kemp had not known any better. He knew a bit about the many strange herbal teas and remedies that adorned the land of the Pharaohs and knew very well they had medicinal uses, let alone great for cleaning your intestines and insides.

"Your special tea, Mister Hastings," he said, dropping two sugars in the milky white cup.

"Thank you, Mohammed, another opportunity to chill out. Very glad you responded to my emails."

The Egyptian artefacts manager stood up then closed the door to the office and sat down again, then tapped the keyboard of his laptop.

"Yes, it was an unusual correspondence, quite cryptic, no idea what the hell you were asking for, though, but I knew you would venture out here at some point, Kemp, you normally do."

Hastings placed the satchel on the floor next to his seat and looked up, as the professor sat down in the rickety chair. Then the professor spoke, "What is this journey really about this time, Mr Kemp, more coins for selling, or are you searching for those little gold scarab things that you seem to adore, or is it the hidden obelisk of Khufu scenario?" he asked, then tapped his nose as if to acknowledge that all was to be discussed on the quiet.

Hastings scratched the back of his head then spoke. "In total honesty, I am not really sure Mohammed, but I am drawn here again by fate, and that much is for sure, maybe it's because I like the Egyptian sun, because it is certainly not the food, nor the bloody tea, but, it could be the chocolate and the dates though. But luckily for Egypt this is not a wild goose chase this time Mohammed, but a journey of real discovery, a trip with a real purpose, a journey of adventure and mystery that I just simply cannot explain, just yet. You see I have two subjects to get my head around." Hastings paused and tapped his leather satchel.

"I am actually looking for a chalice, the one that is depicted here on this manuscript, here, look, the cartouche is simple, but if you look at what the cartouche actually has written within it, well I am not sure what it actually means." He then pointed to the, now very interested, Egyptian a few symbols that had been written on the vellum.

Elfecky gazed over the document for approximately two minutes then spoke. "Oh, my goodness this is indeed an odd one, and a relatively new subject to me. But, this is not a copy of the holy chalice that you might think you may have in Europe, or conversely, the one that your scholarly lot seem to always go on about, this is quite unique, and something very different indeed, and equally as potent, if not more dangerous."

Kemp scratched his eye brows then asked a few more questions. "Do you know what it is? Or where it may be located then? And can I get my hands on it?" he asked, slurping the warm sample of murky Nile water, that was thinly disguised as herbal tea in the offering.

"Not me, I am afraid, Kemp, this is not my particular subject matter or my niche. But here in Cairo, I will, however, bet you that I know a man who can. Here look at this!"

Mohammed pulled at what appeared to be an old, dusty leather bound book that was stuck amongst some other journals. Kemp caught sight of the front cover as it emerged out from under the column of literature. It read: 'European religious cards' 1800's.

Professor Elfecky skipped a few pages, then stopped at a series of sketches based around drinking vessels and ran his index finger down the page.

"Now, let me tell you about all these chalices or cups, some of them in the past have been made into engravings, mostly copper or thin plate gold articles, and I do mean actually engraved onto a flat plate. I have seen one example hanging in the tomb of St somebody or other somewhere in my travels, but sadly, my memory fails me just at the moment. And, there is another example which is reported to be housed in the museum archive in the holy city of M'dina, Malta. I really can't remember exactly where, but somewhere near the old central Temple Cathedral museum. Have you ever been to Malta, Kemp?"

The investigator nodded his head in acknowledgement and pointed to the sketch book again and answered. "Not for some time, but I could do with a holiday though."

The professor continued in his search. "Now these elegant copper cups are said to be the vessels of the Magi, or the group of clerics who visited the infant Christ when he was born. There were three such chalices originally, but, one of them was destroyed by Caesar in one of his many angry outrages.

And it was rumoured that the chalice had been sliced into many tiny fragments, somewhere along the historical line, and the fragments were eventually gathered together and melted down. After the re-smelting, the cup was then cast or beat into a single thin plate of copper, and an image of which was a holy chalice was impressed upon the plate but interestingly enough it was rumoured that this receptacle was to possess strange chemical properties."

Kemp stroked his chin and smiled. "Your tea is really crap by the way. But go on, Mohammed, this is getting interesting." Hastings removed his hat and placed it on his knee. "What kind of strange properties, magnetic, fluorescent, three dimensional, what?" he asked.

Elfecky then rubbed his chin again then spoke. "'Well, this particular chalice when it is laid flat can be seen as a normal flat plate, but under certain lighting conditions it could be observed to take the form of a physical drinking vessel—a cup that can be used to store fluid. Magnetic it could be, which would explain how the cup could then be returned to its flattened state. Quite odd, don't you think?"

Hastings shrugged his shoulders and contemplated the Professor's explanation of the chalice. He knew that if Mohammed was aware of such things then there was a good chance that it was a true depiction or account regarding these artefacts.

Elfecky was a man with a certain charisma about him and he possessed a strange wealth of knowledge that often left you wondering when his brain was going to burst open. He knew just about anything or everything about Egyptian culture and folklore that was to be had, even more so in his field of study.

Academics world-wide would be humbled as to how one person could be so well-informed about everything. Kemp took the opportunity to pose another line of questioning toward the omniscient Mohammed. "Mohammed, what do you know of the Sanctos Epistula—Magdalena?" Then he waited patiently for an answer.

The Egyptian Professor pondered for a while and closed the book. He then took a very heavy, deep breath.

"Mister Hastings, you know in your field of Christian study that some things in life are just not meant to be touched, they should be left alone and not even discussed, but, my friend, you know this already, and this subject is probably most definitely one of them.

Why do you choose to dabble in such things? I take it she, the 'Sanct Magdalena' our divine lady, has turned up again. I assume no doubt appearing in some obscure mountain village in rural Mauritania or Brazil, or in a church or other place of worship, the same way she has just popped up through the centuries in order to have a look, and to say hello, to the modern world." He posed his synopsis, then left very little time for Hastings to answer.

"She, my friend, is the holiest of holy entities. She is a roaming free spirit, more of a manifestation than an actual solid visitation, normally turning up for a brief period of time then disappearing into obscurity. But, tell me, my friend, why do you ask?"

Kemp spent a few minutes explaining how Dr Darlene Gammay had suffered the blessings of the Magdalene and her visitation; then after her appearance Darlene was inflicted by having a huge tattoo of her holy face emblazoned across her back and shoulder, appearing on her skin without any rational reason or explanation.

Well, that was apart from her being singled out for this curse in her own domestic bathroom, and not discounting the possibility that a visitor could have appeared from outer space and cast this imprint on her body as far as Darlene was concerned. But it was fact that someone's image was imprinted on her skin that frightened her most. An image that was delivered by no physical means and imprinted within a matter of eight hours duration as Darlene apparently slept.

The revelation of what is known as 'an illuminated manuscript' had somehow impacted or was indirectly related to the recent theft and removal of the mythical Tartarus Inferni Hellfire Sword.

The article was removed from what was deemed a very secure Vatican vault in Italy, and conversely, a Rossetti painting of the Magdalene had also been stolen from the national Italian art gallery in Roma.

As Hastings explained the amazing story, Doctor Elfecky appeared to be unmoved by the series of strange events being disclosed, it was as if he was half expectant of the outcomes. Hastings further explained about the sword weighing almost six kilograms, that was observed vanishing from the Vatican and reappearing at the will of whoever or whatever was in control.

Recently, the sword had been moved across the globe from the Vatican to Scotland and then back again, somehow being transported as a solid object by what Kemp could only describe as a free forming floating vapour, orchestrated by a series of entities or ghostly visions which have the ability to physically move solid objects.

Kemp struggled to find the relationship between these events whilst at the same time contemplating why a twenty million dollar painting was removed also by mysterious means, and coincidentally of which resembled the tattoo on Darlene's body. His problem was finding a distinctive connection.

The Professor listened with great interest and nonchalantly drank his cup of Nile water as Kemp delivered the strange turn of events that had led him back into the land of the Pharaohs.

"Mohammed, this is not normal biblical stuff, this is quite scary, you know what I really think, I think that we are being manipulated by an unseen power."

Elfecky sniffed the warm air then spoke. "Unseen power? If you want to witness an unseen power, then you want to walk around this museum at night time, my friend, I will show you an unseen power, the guards here, will only work in pairs, and trust me they can tell you some stories that would make your lovely head of hair turn grey very quickly."

The two discussed the matter further.

CHAPTER SEVENTEEN

'THE DISAPPEARING CHALICE'

After their heavy discussion, Hastings posed a few more questions. "So, do you think I could locate and purchase this chalice from your source Mohammed?" he asked, whilst scribbling some numbers and an address down in his little black note book. The cover of which was embossed with logo that depicted: *'HMSO'*

The Professor stood up and stretched his over indulged and non-athletic frame. "This is Egypt, my friend, the promised land, and the land of the ancient Pharaohs. You can purchase just about anything in this land if the price is right, and of course if you know who to talk to," explained the good Professor. "But first, let me make a few phone calls."

He then drank some of his off-coloured tea. Hastings, meanwhile, opened another book and quizzed its bland pages, then listened as Mohammed spoke. "So, she has emerged again has she? Popped up into the fabric of human existence. The last time she was around was over one hundred and fifty years ago. I think she was last seen somewhere in France. It was an appearance where some peasant girl claims to have conversed with her directly throughout the period of lent, and probably several weeks thereafter."

145

Hastings suddenly found the need to engage the Professor in the subject matter of Mary Magdalene in light of recent events, and shuffled his chair a little closer to perhaps the only man on the planet who could provide a rational explanation of events.

"So, Mohammed, since we are talking about the Apostles, what do you make of the advent of the Nag Hammadi scrolls and their revelations? In particular the lost gospel of Judas. Do you think there is any truth in these parchments from what you can deduce?" Hastings waited patiently as the Professor dropped a piece of lemon in his tea and started to stir it around with his pencil.

He took some time to consider the question before answering. "Mmmh, very interesting and very complicated question to ask, Kemp. You see we have several institutions and ideals at work here. Firstly, I know for a fact that the carbon 14 dating test on the Dead Sea Scrolls and some of the Nag Hammadi are consistent in their actual composition and have been dated precisely within less than a hundred years of Jesus's life on the planet.

The conundrum is, who actually wrote them in the first place, because the lost gospel scroll, well, the newly found gospel scroll of Escariot, was most likely written by a cleric with very opposing views to what was being actually communicated to the masses, regarding the role of Judas Escariot in the Bible. Or conversely, and more along my lines of thought that they were written by a cleric who belonged to the family 'Escariot' and perhaps wanted to twist the biblical story toward making Judas out to be more of a devout disciple working under the premise of openly identifying Jesus's physical body to the Romans, and perhaps for specific purposes, which may have even been orchestrated by Jesus himself.

And, not to be seen as the traitor that he was depicted as, but nevertheless a man who still sealed his own fate by his negative actions. You see, Kemp, when you look at the actual text, it is very controversial, but it does not make it false in its content, it just provides an opposing account of events written by a credible source.

I am of the opinion, and this is my opinion only, Mister Hastings, that perhaps there was a secret pact by Jesus and Judas, a pact of mutual trust. I mean who really knows, as there were so many strange events occurring at that time. During this turbulent time there was such a flurry of activity that even the scribes themselves had difficulty keeping up with biblical facts and events."

Mohammed stopped talking for a few moments and was nodding his head as he gazed into the black residue in his cup. Kemp had an inclination that the Professor was an active Gnostic who knew a great deal about esoterics than he was letting on about.

He also knew that Egyptian Gnostics possessed a hidden or very secret understanding of the mystical side of the church as he had attended a closed conclave with some very strange people in St Paul's Cathedral in London not so long ago.

"You see, Kemp, if the church accepted the lost gospel of Judas, then they would as an institution would have to not only re-write biblical history, but change the way we view the positive and negative aspects of our religious beliefs in general, so the powers that be, deemed it a fake. These Egyptian desert monks who preserved such detail, they refused to destroy the gospels in their possession. I mean this is the four main gospels of Matthew, Mark, Luke and John, maybe not written by them in their own hand, but a detailed account documented by their followers, you could interrogate the Qumran Essenes.

The gospels were seen as very antagonistic and the Bishop of Alexandria wanted them out of the way, he wanted them destroyed, as they added distraction to his master plan of keeping order in the church. Does that make any sense to you?" asked the Professor, whilst clasping his hands together.

Hastings leaned forward slightly in his chair, then offered a response. "Yes, it does make sense to me. But are you saying that for obvious control reasons they were left out or never referenced by those clerics who wanted their version of the Bible in the public domain, or the winners version of events." The Professor was still nodding as he drank his lemon tea. Hastings smiled and continued. "So, let me tell you what I think, and I am no academic as you know Mohammed, but, in the year 1945 these so called lost gospels came to light after being discovered by a farmer near to Nag Hammadi, the discovery which led to a series of scrolls written by several of the Apostles or their followers at some point in their lifetimes.

I am personally more interested in the lost gospel of Mary Magdalene that was discovered in 1896, and other texts of this so called other Mary gospel, which also came to light as being written nearer to the 5th century.

And I understand that other portions of the texts had been dated to around the 2nd or 3rd century. I really do not know, but I would love to get my hands on them, and so would Darlene. I also understand that some of the detail verges on Gnostic mysticism and Jesus may have disclosed information to Mary that would take us away up into the heavens, and that's where my interest in heavenly bodies takes a whole new angle. Imagine for one minute that Mary Magdalene who was a serious inner circle contender, and who literally challenged all conventions relating to Christian belief in a man's world.

Maybe because she knew that there was another world that took the journey of the 'soul' through the Styx and into the realms of both angels and demons. If Mary was part of the GMSC or the 'Gnostics Mystical Select Circle' who were perhaps influential in every aspect of Bible culture, then we see another dimension completely. The results which could lead to a journey to and from the afterlife. Now tell me, Mohammed, where does that put the church? But more so, does it confirm the belief of the ancient Pharaohs and their ascension to the stars, but the question is, who told the Pharaohs of this secret pathway to the stars?"

Elfecky responded. "Kemp, these episodes only last for a few of weeks, but who knows, I wasn't there, however, since we are talking about things that suddenly turn up, let me show you our new exciting exhibit—it's our new and very exciting sarcophagus."

The Professor was very uneasy as he sat facing Hastings; he too had an inclination that Hastings had obviously conducted some heavy duty research and was almost knocking on the door to the GMSC for clarity.

"Mister Hastings, I believe you may have to meet some people I know, they will perhaps bring a bit of greater clarity to your line of questioning. It is an amazing subject, Kemp, a world within a world, or a world out with a world, let's discuss this later."

Meanwhile, Kemp had stood up and leaned up against the statue of Seth, and drank his tea and watched as the Professor quizzed some paperwork then dragged him across to his new exhibit.

After about fifteen minutes, Mohammed's mobile phone danced across the sarcophagus top and buzzed a series of Arabic noises. Mohammed flipped the phone open and smiled as he read the text message. "Looks like you are in luck my friend, someone, somewhere, somehow knows where the—your Magi chalice plate is actually located. It is near to a place called, Saqqara, that's the step pyramids not too far away, the owner says he would sell it to me for LE 1500—but, to me only. That's about one hundred and fifty pounds sterling, Mr Hastings. The owner says there is great responsibility for the custodian of this article of faith and if the museum wants to take custody of the chalice, then he would be happy to part with it."

Kemp dropped his head in disappointment, the look on his face said it all. He knew that the Egyptian high commission kept strict controls of their archaeological history and getting an uncontrolled piece or artefact through customs and out of the country would be near damn impossible.

"Don't worry, Kemp, I will purchase it, and then present it to your Order as a gift. How does that sound? Now if you have the LE 1500 leave it with me, and I will ensure that you receive your new acquisition, and the documents to clear customs."

Hastings smiled a very broad smile, exposing his very white set of gnashers, and quizzed the Professor further. Although he trusted him completely, he did not trust any outsiders, nor could he understand how such a strange an important artefact can be so readily available and located so quickly.

He surmised it was a case of just 'who you know' as opposed to what you think you know, and agreed to the transaction. Just then Kemp's mobile also flashed up, the word DARLENE indicated an incoming call. He clicked the green button and listened. "'Kemp, can you hear me? Bloody, phones; bloody Egyptians! Anyway, I am on my way, will be with you shortly.

And tell me, why does every damn taxi driver toot their bloody horns every five seconds at me? Even the ones going the wrong way, morons that they are. I will see you in about fifteen minutes, unless I get taxi-jacked."

Kemp closed the phone and watched the great Professor Mohammed Elfecky at work. The Professor was running his fingers across every inch of the granite coffin lid. Kemp giggled as he watched Mohammed jump inside and outside the new sarcophagus, then inspect the sides of the casing as one would if purchasing a new car. Hastings smiled again.

"Moh! That thing is a couple of thousand years old, that's a lot of miles on the proverbial time clock, it is bound to have a few scratches!'

Twenty-five minutes later and Darlene arrived at the museum and introduced herself to Professor Elfecky. Hastings appeared to be excited again. He felt somehow responsible for Darlene's strange affliction and was never more than happy than when she was close by. Let alone being her chaperone in the land of sand and camel droppings, but not just on this trip, but in her life in general, but he was unsure exactly where their relationship was heading.

"What a nice looking woman," remarked Elfecky, who winked and made off into one of his many cupboards, searching for another book or artefact.

Kemp gave Darlene a huge smile. "Darlene, Mohammed has located the chalice for me, how efficient is that?" She turned to the statue of Seth and smiled. "That's good news," she replied, then shook her head and wandered off out in the hallways and then casually made her way upstairs toward the gold jewellery and the gallery rooms.

"Take your time my dear, there is much to see, I will stay open just for you!" shouted Mohammed, closing the closet door.

"Hey you, slow down—you have two wives already; three would just put you in a sarcophagus like the rest of your friends."

There was another moment of humour and the two concluded their business and finished their drinks in a hail of laughter and jovial amusement. They were each remarking on one of their previous escapades together. An adventure and an encounter being one that almost had them both incarcerated for being too drunk to walk home and had somehow tried bribing the duty police officer to drive them both to the museum. In their drunken state they both fell asleep in the temporary tomb exhibit of Seti the III and were nearly entombed as the exhibit was being prepared for transit.

Hastings endured another cup of Nile residue and paid the good Professor for his assistance in acquiring the 'magi chalice' and made out a receipt—in the name of the museum—then handed over the agreed LE 1500.

"Deal done, my friend," exclaimed Mohammed, who placed the money in the Museum's safe.

CHAPTER EIGHTEEN

THE ASSIGNATION OF WORLDS

Twenty-five minutes earlier and three hundred shops later, Darlene had arrived at Tahrir square and then walked through the upper galleries of the Cairo museum. It was quieter than quiet and the warm air wafted through the many sarcophagi and caught her olfactory senses unaware, causing her to take many deep breaths, almost becoming light headed at one point.

"Wow, the jasmine is very strong, and the vanilla very sweet," she muttered, as she entered the papyri room and walked on through the alley and in to the gold room, stopping momentarily to view the row of sarcophagi that stretched the length the chamber.

Darlene, took quite a bit of time and quizzed the many marble or granite tombs' inscriptions; the ancient coffins standing in their capacity as testament to the ancient trade of masons and stone workers, let alone undertakers and the embalmers, each having left their many marks as specialist tradesmen, in the art of death. They were the elite, those who applied their secret skills toward death and its very complicated Egyptian ritual subject matter. There was a sudden clatter that resonated through the museum. She flinched and jumped as the heavy wooden shutters downstairs were closed and echoed a series of clunks across the open void spaces of the chamber. Each security shutter was being closed by the night wardens.

It was the heavy clunking of the matt shuttering surfaces coming together that had startled her momentarily. Hastings, meanwhile, was beginning to make his way up the heavy marbled stairway and was en route to take another look at the mask of the greatest golden face in human history: the great young boy King, Tutankhamen, and to take an opportunity to talk and walk with his assistant.

The boy King waited patiently in his glass case and still maintained his superiority and status of his Kingship, even in death after almost four thousand years in the waiting, as the face that was never to be forgotten. But at this special moment in time, he waited for the arrival of Kemp Hastings to gaze upon his golden shroud.

There was another series of 'clunks' then the vocal mumblings of the duty guards echoed across the museum as they set the heavy steel locks into place, and confirmed with the words 'maya, maya'.

Darlene stopped and thought for a moment, acknowledging that there was no imminent hurry, there were no races within these walls, there were no time scales to be adhered to, and she observed that neither of the four men appeared to be over eager to complete the task in any record timescale.

Darlene had halted her walk about on the second level and was busy staring into the face of an ancient 'el Greco' Grecian mummy, whose beautiful face had been painstakingly hand painted onto the flat surface of the mummified bandages.

It was an attempt to show the unsuspecting modern world of the future, what the interred lady actually looked like, and could be a true resemblance. Darlene thought about the painstaking detail in order to preserve the image of life in death.

She stared for quite some time as she quizzed the eyes of the adjacent mummy; something about the face was intriguing, and comforting, although she knew they lived four thousand years apart. The interred mummified lady had good strong features, clean fresh eyes, a strong jawline, an unblemished skin tone and very fine red hair, but Darlene could not quite place the face she was staring at. She recognised it, and struggled to place exactly where she had seen the woman before, especially in her capacity as a historical studies scholar, and she remained cognisant and understanding—knowing full well that this mummy was perhaps well over three thousand years old.

Another loud 'clunk' rang throughout the halls of the museum as the lower shutters of the remaining windows were fully locked and in place. Professor Mohammed Elfecky had cleared his desk and was busy signing off the staff rota sheet for the weekend—having made his investigation of the new acquisition.

It was going to be another record attendance this weekend as the museum had recently procured these new artefacts from lower Saqqara and two new mummies for public display. The management team were expecting a VIP visit from the good Doctor Hawas himself and the team were very excited.

Darlene, meanwhile, moved to the next display case and ran her fingers slowly across the front panel of the glass case. The cabinet sat adjacent to the case that contained the painted faced mummy which contained the remains of what was thought to be another Greek Queen, and, paused for reflection thinking as to what her own appearance would look like if portrayed in this manner.

She pondered on what would her image look like if she were to be embalmed or had been subjected to cryogenic storage in death, and how modern technology would preserve her body and more importantly her stunning looks. It was then that her fertile mind started to wander off again and run amok into the world of embalming. The room temperature had suddenly changed from being moderately warm to actually getting very warm, just as Darlene slipped into a trance and experienced a 'dream from hell'.

It was several minutes later when Hastings found Darlene standing in the upright position and she was still gripping both sides of the crystal glass case, holding herself in place. She appeared to be clearly frozen or traumatised and was still staring directly into the 'el Greco' inhabited display case.

Hastings gingerly touched her shoulder; she was absolutely rigid solid to the touch. He flinched, and momentarily pulled his hand back. It was as if her muscles had gone into some sort of acute spasm. He then stepped to one side of the glass case and observed Darlene's face from an opposing angle. He flinched again and felt very uneasy as he stared directly into her beautiful green eyes—they were fully dilated and very dull. He then reached out again and touched her hand, her skin was pallid.

If Kemp was to place a bet, he would say that Darlene was in a state of shock and that her body fluid had stopped circulating, but was somehow still stabilised. Reaching up, he placed his hand over her forehead and flinched as the motionless fingers were as cold and as solid as her torso was.

"Oh shit, shit, shit and shit!" he exclaimed, whilst rapidly making his way across to the central main balcony, immediately above the regal entrance of the museum, and shouted over the top of the marble post at the top of his voice in order to grab Dr Elfecky's attention.

Mohammed had instantly appeared from his office and was staring up at Hastings from the centre point on the ground floor, almost standing in the middle of the great circular motif that dominated the lower rotunda granite flooring, where the concentric balcony reached around and towered well above him in mirrored image above.

"What is it Meester Hastings?" he shouted, whilst simultaneously grabbing and placing his black rimmed glasses back on the bridge of his nose. He recalled how Kemp had christened the heavy rimmed optics earlier in the year as 'NHS' glasses.

He had almost forgotten how Hastings had commented on the thickness of the lenses so long ago, which somehow for Mohammed made him feel more like a British academic as opposed to an Egyptian one. But he revelled in the 'learned' change of his appearance, and how he was being perceived by others as an eminent boffin.

"One moment please, Mister Kemp, I am just adjusting my 'bottle bottoms'. I cannot see without them you know," he said, and continued to stare up at the balcony.

Kemp responded in an even louder voice. "Hurry, please, get up here, jaaldi jaaldi (hurry) it is Darlene she is, well she is . . . I do not bloody know, something very strange—just get up here!"

A few moments later the very tired and panting Doctor Elfecky found an almost distressed Kemp Hastings staring at the motionless, upright body of Dr Darlene Gammay from very close quarters.

"Well, what do think of this, situation?" asked Kemp, wiping his chin, which had somehow become splattered in tiny droplets of saliva. Mohammed took some time to look Darlene over then shook his head. Kemp gave him a very odd gaze as if he suspected something was not quite right with the Professor, his mannerisms had seemed to have changed. Hastings dismissed this is a thing of the moment—given the nature of their encounter.

"Well, Mister Kemp, I am absolutely buggered if I could explain her current mental condition, but her physical condition, well it appears to me as if she is in a stasis or a limbo condition." The Doctor took a deliberate pause then delivered his thoughts as an academic. "Kemp, she appears to be comatosed or in a very deep sleep."

Hastings drew his left hand threw his hair and grimaced. "I can see that, but how the hell on God's earth did she become to get in such a state. Have you been spraying some sort of sleep drug or pesticide in here, she could be suffering from some sort allergic reaction?"

Elfecky suddenly turned left and took flight, disappearing into one of the adjacent chambers and began scanning the many papyri documents that were encased in the ancient documents section of the room. Each dossier had been placed in order of date and precedence, some of which were segmented into categories, of ritual and afterlife, and just one of the 130,000 articles that the museum boasted. The huge library of papyri had been chronologically placed in sequence and readily identified, according to the many dynasties in succession, and of which was easy for anyone wishing to find a particular language or script in time to locate and view.

Kemp could actually do nothing at all, but decided to just stand and stare at Darlene from his standpoint, whilst simultaneously watching Professor Elfecky who was now very cautiously walking between the many display cases whilst running his fingers and his mature well-seasoned analytical eyes over the many scripts.

After about three minutes he stopped, then extracted a set of old, brown, rusty, tarnished keys from his pocket, then began shuffling a single key in the lock to the cabinet. Kemp meanwhile, smirked, almost smiling as he observed the Mickey Mouse key fob dangling downwards from the small chain, just as the cabinet sprung open.

It was then that the Doctor turned and faced Hastings his eyes were almost dilated to full glare and he appeared to be very excited. "'I have it, I have found it, I knew it was here, look, look come see," he exclaimed, holding the parchment high up in the air.

"Have what? You mad, deranged, Egyptian scientist," responded Kemp, almost sprinting forwards to grab the papyrus and absorb the secret information. Of course, knowing full well it would be absolutely futile as his knowledge of Arabic was somewhat basic, and he would simply be lost amongst its text.

He often had to rely on his peers such as Mohammed to explain what was written upon ancient documents, and now this old parchment, of which he was desperate to understand and assist Darlene in her moment of need, and presently could do absolutely nothing to help her.

"This, my friend, is the secret Gnostics Mystical ritual of 'live' embalming,' responded the Doctor.

"What?" exclaimed Kemp, almost shuddering in disbelief on hearing Elfecky's comments.

"Live embalming!" he exclaimed again.

"Are you off your archaeological rocking trolley Mohammed? How in God's name could you have come to make such an arsehole assumption as that?" quizzed Kemp, who was almost clenching his fists in total anger and frustration as he reached out to grab the manuscript.

"Oh, that's quite simple, Mr Hastings, we have it documented in the Mystical Circle's paperwork," answered the good the Doctor as he clasped the septum of his nose, then pointed to several incision marks that had appeared on Darlene's pale skin. Each mark appearing as a single red scar at her neckline and ear lines.

Andrew David Doyle

These incision marks were indicators that were very evident on Darlene's motionless upper torso, as she remained standing in the upright position whilst traversing the lands of limbo in her mind, and yet she was still grasping the side panels of the glass cabinet, albeit frozen in the moment of time.

Doctor Elfecky pulled out his pencil and pointed to specific areas of the body whilst explaining that if these areas on the body were cut with surgical precision, then they could stimulate the human brain responses, and in essence telling the brain to shut down into a state of limbo. A physical process, when executed correctly, would increase the levels of melatonin in the body having induced the body's natural defence mechanism to function, therefore, actually tricking the unsuspecting brain to close down and go to sleep.

Professor Elfecky went on to explain similar actions that were common place actions today in some surgical techniques. "As one does when twisting a horse's nose or rubbing and caressing the underside of a salmon—a process used in order to momentarily make beasties vulnerable," explained the Doctor in greater detail, whilst still pointing out the incision marks on Darlene's skin. Hastings was flummoxed, astounded even, as he glanced at the parchment and then back at Darlene.

Dr Elfecky began explaining the ritualistic mechanics of the embalming procedure. "'In essence, Kemp, to preserve a body in preparation for the afterlife which can be a long and arduous process for the embalmers—normally a group of skilled tradesmen will take forty days and nights to prepare a single corpse for ascending into the heavens.

It was in the latter period of ancient times that we, as a nation, had started to inter our dead in coffins, as it was soon discovered during sand burials that the remains were often dug up and eaten by the animals of the desert. But as time progressed the many coffins became more and more complicated depending on the

160

wealth that a family was prepared to spend on the remembrance process. Even then, the many bodies which had been placed in coffins also decayed, that was even if they were not exposed to the hot, dry arid sands of our deserts.

It took several centuries before nomads who hailed from the village of Mumy had found and practised the art of preservation, where the dead remained almost life like even after some time in death. The process was almost described as pickling a corpse, but using special oil recipes and linen strips thinly applied to build up a layer after layer of protection, as opposed to just applying vinegar. But where many layers were cut thin enough to keep the features of the face clear and intact, as you know this is what we deem mummification or embalming."

Hastings interjected. "Yes, but Moh, you said 'live' embalming—surely that sounds like more of a macabre type of ancient torture rather than a process of preservation?"

The Doctor smiled. "Indeed, Kemp, but that only depends on how you view your particular religion. Surely don't you think that receiving the wounds of Christ is equally as disturbing as being embalmed, alive or otherwise, as no-one is quite sure of the outcome, often as not . . . in other rituals, the recipient eventually dies."

Kemp took an over dramatised deep breath whilst running both hands through his hair again. "Okay? Then what does that parchment say about our current state of affairs concerning Darlene. Does it explain how to bring her out of this state of mind or what?" he said, pointing directly at the manuscript and wiggling his finger.

The Professor scrunched up his face and huffed a little, he was contemplating what to do next, and clearly caught up in either the confusion of the moment, or he had a plan of action. Hastings convinced himself not to hold his breath for any decisive actions, as this was after all Egypt.

"Well, if my assertions and understandings are correct, Darlene has been chosen, or singled out to either receive a 'calling' which can be indicated by receiving 'non-incorruptibility' or corruptibility status. Basically meaning that when she dies she will either be preserved or she will not, but only when she is in her deathly state. Or conversely, which is more my train of thought is that she is actually handing something back to its original owner."

Kemp was instantly thinking that Darlene's tattoo was the obvious choice. Kemp nodded in agreement and started to explain how Darlene had received her biblical tattoo 13 days ago and that a strange series of events had ensued since that day. He explained the advent of the 'Sanctos Epistula' or holy parchment again, that was rumoured to have been written and illuminated by Mary Magdalene herself, and the incredible journey the manuscript had endured up through the ages into modern times, and had indeed survived the great fire of London in 1666.

Where the world around its colourful page had been simply incinerated. Hastings also explained the series of inexplicable events regarding the Hell Fire Sword itself, and the theft of Dante's painting of the Sank Real, and not forgetting that the Pope himself had endured the visions and visitations that Darlene had received prior to him having suffered a fatal heart attack in vault 33 of the Vatican's secret museum.

Elfecky was mesmerised, even he thought that this event was somewhat unbelievable but had heard of similar accounts elsewhere and commented earlier during their discussion, a revisit of the same event, and yet only having occurred as recently as the 19th century in France, Ethiopia and India.

The Professor sneezed, three distinct sneezes and wiped his face then started to explain how the process of the afterlife was conducted. "Alright, Kemp, let me explain the open ritual of mummification in quick mode. The corpse is re-located to a subterranean chamber under what we will call a pyramid. Prior to this, the body is laid out in state in a simple tent called an 'IBU' this is basically a cleaning and purification station, where oils and palm wines are used to smooth the body and keep it smelling nice, having been rinsed with the waters of the Nile.

Remember earlier we talked about cuts and precise incisions, well this is when the embalmers will cut down the left side of the corpse and remove the internal organs. But this is where Darlene's condition differs. Come look here," he said, pointing to the detail on the papyrus. "According to this GMSC inscription, or what I can see, is a direct reference to the book of the Dead. Darlene is in an actual condition or 'dream state'. She is enduring non-physical or hypothetical surgery."

Kemp raised his hands in total disbelief. "Stop, stop, stop, you are rambling, Moh!" he exclaimed again. "Are you saying Darlene is enduring surgery in some sort of magic happy 'hippy' trip in this ethereal plane, place?"

Mohammed turned the papyrus over and pointed to a few sketches which displayed a small hieroglyph that depicted the process being conducted by several heavily gold clad ornate priests and priestesses. It was clear that no physical metal tools or surgical instruments were being used, but clearly a range of smaller flowers, lotus leaves and various other foliage and fruits had being substituted for things like surgical scalpels, PM 4O precision cutting tools, knives and needles, normally used in the modern day by specialist morticians as post mortem technical instruments.

Elfecky continued with his explanation and passed the parchment to Hastings for further scrutiny. "The organs decay first, so quite naturally they are first to be removed. But did you know, Meester Hastings, that each organ has a custodian in the afterlife? A deity or notional person who is accountable for the lungs, liver, guts, and even the small and large intestines are washed then repacked in a mixture of natron and oils—this stage of embalming will dry the organs out thoroughly. However, at this stage our physical heart remains in situ to the very end of the process as it is deemed our 'centre of intelligence'."

Just then, Kemp started thwarting a couple of flies that were intent on making his life a living beastie hell, and just would not give up on their unrelenting attacking efforts to give him a bite or three. It was a situation of Egyptian life where he had no choice but to endure the beasts and keep swiping the little blighters away, and had continued to swipe them since his arrival in the land of the Pharaohs; the land where flies are Kings and ever present.

Mohammed waited patiently until he had settled down—having mortally wounded a single fly in his swatting efforts. Then the Professor continued in his lesson. "Of course we as a living entity require our hearts in the afterlife and that's why this special organ is the last one to be disturbed, because, during the ritual of afterlife preparation we must keep the two close together as long a practically possible."

Kemp was wholly amused and could not stop glancing back and forth at Darlene, wondering what she was actually witnessing or feeling in the rather bizarre and complicated unseen process she was captured within.

Clasping his hands and momentarily pursing his lips Mohammed took a few seconds and quizzed the frozen Doctor again. "She will not feel discomfort or any pain, just as the ritual text here explains, but, then again, I am only reading this straight extract from the document itself. It appears that from the perspective in the mind of the receiver, the complete process is over in a flash or moment in time."

Kemp began to squirm a little as Elfecky explained the use of the 'hooking' instrument that was used to 'mish-mash' the brain up into an intellectual mushy pulp. He absorbed in his mind's eye as the residue of off-white, milky warm cauliflower was splashing around deep up inside the cranial vaulted, bony cavity of his head. He shivered a little, as the Professor continued.

"Then, the pulpy CSF—cerebra spinal fluid—is mixed with what is left from the intellectual DNA—deoxyribonucleic acid, or thin blood—which is then forcefully extracted through the nostril cavities using a small set of ice-cream type scoops or spoons.

"Ouch!" exclaimed Kemp, almost falling over as he comprehended the actions of the skilled undertakers scooping the brains out of the head like smooth ice-cream from a solid tub.

"Steady, Kemp," retorted Mohammed, placing a hand on his shoulder—a quick catch in order to stabilise him from falling over. You think too deeply my friend, don't let your emotions get the better of you. Darlene is not feeling any pain or discomfort, to her it will be as if she can see everything but not feel the pains of the incisions or any organ removal.

You can think of it as that she has been given a one hundred percent huge epidural to stem any feeling, a type of astral anaesthetic injection for the brain, but her visions will be clear as day."

Kemp raised his hands again and spluttered out a few words. "How can you be so calm when you know that she is going through such hell and all this in her head Mohammed? Even in her mind's eye she will be traumatised."

The Doctor responded. "Yes, she will, but only for a glimpse into the afterlife, but she will also have been blessed with the gift of foresight as a result of this amazing process. I think what we are actually witnessing here is the complex process of an actual ancient and esoterical 'Assignation'.

Kemp, this is what the Apocrypha is all about; these are things you don't read about in the Bible or on any religious documentation. A process and passing over of a very mysterious transitional custody process of something that reaches well beyond your biblical proportions. Kemp, I really cannot answer any of your questions entirely one hundred per cent, because, this is only the second time this phenomenon has occurred. Well, that is according to this parchment, which incidentally dates well before the days of Christ and reaches back approximately 4,000 years, and I have no idea, of course, who wrote it.

But what I do know is that it is one hundred per cent authentic and most likely written by a High Priest under the watchful eye of the ancient Pharaoh at the time of the first Assignation. And, in case you are wondering, Mister Hastings, it's not entirely scripted in the Egyptian language either; there are odd symbols here and there, symbols that I am deciphering as either Aramaic or Hebrew." The Professor responded whilst drawing his fingers over the rippled, tanned surface of the document again, "Then again it could be written ancient Assyrian or pseudo Babel as the two languages do look very familiar."

The Doctor paused and took time to view the document again then continued his lesson in embalming. "So, Kemp, let us continue with our whistle-stop overview and tour of embalming. Once the body is completely dried out, it is then washed again, and bathed in more oils. But this time the oily coating physically lubricates the skin which then remains like an elastic membrane. Now, before you say it, and this is the important bit, if this process was executed in middle of Europe, the body would be immortalised or have been made almost incorruptible, but without the art of the embalmer it is almost inconceivable, and that is the real quandary that your church faith leaders must consider very carefully before announcing that the human remains of a deeply religious person is canonised or beatified in death.

Unless the bodies of the deceased are physically embalmed in Egypt then moved to a cooler climate then that transition could enhance the anointed properties. If it is a colder climate where the remains would be interred, then it stands to reason the process could be sustained indefinitely, but you know as well as I do, it is only the last couple of hundred years that this anomaly has come to light in Europe.

Anyway, once all the organs are removed they are then wrapped in a soft linen ball and normally placed back into the body, which by this stage had also been stuffed with leaves or sawdust and long soft linen pads, which were then coated with more sweet smelling oil or 'the oils of death'. Then finally wrapped completely with an outer shroud of linen.

If you take time to review the complete process, Mr Hastings, you will find that over the many years our embedded Egyptian religious beliefs have changed toward the afterlife and the understanding of heavenly travel. Our ideals and thinking towards death has evolved—and now, we find that the organs are placed in canopic jars once removed from their host. These jars or cups were normally made of wood, but more commonly we see alabaster or thin clay jugs are used—it is all dependent on how rich your family actually were.

But, we do find, in some cases, that the organs have been placed back into the body and the canopic jars remained in the shrine as a symbolic container for viscera, these are containers for afterlife protection. And finally, Mr Kemp, our organs: the liver, heart lungs, etc., all important elements for existence in the after world, must be kept together.

Take the liver as an example, an important organ for the afterlife the designated god 'Imsety', or the human headed god, is the liver's custodian, and we also have 'Hapy', the baboon headed god, and of which the air that we breathe belongs to him and, so do our lungs. Whilst last, but not least, Qebehsenuef or the falcon headed god, has custody of our intestines.

And that, Mr Kemp, is in reality the physical side to the very complicated art of embalming. How do you feel now? You do not look well at all," asked Elfecky, removing his glasses and giving them a wipe with his well-used handkerchief.

Kemp was nodding nonchalantly and would be the first to have said: 'I am fine, I can deal with trauma, blood, shit, feathers and gore.' But Hastings knew his olfactory senses were telling him otherwise; he was overcome by the sweet smell of almonds and warm blood. He looked up, just as his head started swirling inside, he was consciously nauseous and dizzy, and he could feel himself losing the sensation in his legs and he started swaying again.

Mohammed, meanwhile, had caught the attention of one of the guards and was shouting. "Maya, maya—barraka, maya minfadluk!"

One of the guards ran off into an anti-chamber in an effort to get some water A few moments later and Ashraf, the door guard, had brought back a bottle of sparkling water which Kemp suddenly grabbed out of his hands and consumed in three straight gulps, then apologised for his hasty and unprecedented actions. "Shukran, shukran, thank you," he repeated.

Mohammed, in the meantime, had been simultaneously aware that Doctor Darlene had twitched a couple of times in response to something or other in her Assignation journey to and from the netherworld. This was combined with the fact that a few tears had formed at the corner of her eyes and were slowly running down her pale white cheeks. It was clear to the Professor that she was emerging from her psychological unearthly trip.

Doctor Elfecky continued to observe her condition and had correctly anticipated Darlene falling backwards on to the cold stone floor as she returned to what may have seemed normality from her induced sleepy state. Mohammed had been quick to respond and did indeed judge his timing precisely as he caught the Doctor as she toppled backwards still in the upright posture as her body failed to defy gravity and was pulled to the floor.

Her organs had started to vibrate and come back to normal working condition and were responding to the blood as it started to course and pulse back through her heart and into her veins and around the remainder of her body. Her circulatory system was in overdrive. A single squeal and she had begun writhing around on the floor like someone having an acute fit and a few jerks of her legs then she appeared to shake and shiver with cold.

Kemp was motionless. He knew how to deal with diabetics in the straight who were craving insulin or their chocolate craving, but he had no idea how to react as Darlene twitched and jerked in a very sporadic, un-uniformed manner.

A full minute of hysteria and things had suddenly settled. Darlene had stopped shaking, then out of the blue she shot bolt upright, still in the sitting position and started ripping at her shirt, screaming that her back and shoulders were burning or were on fire. Kemp placed both hands on her shoulders and started to massage her neckline. In response, the Doctor ripped half of her blouse clean off, leaving the remnants of cloth to cover up her right breast and what was left of her bra strap as she continued to struggle with her clothing.

Doctor Elfecky had momentarily turned up again. Kemp had not noticed he had disappeared during the bout of confusion, but had brought back some water and his little black bag of tricks. His bag contained quite a myriad of pots and a range of coloured bottles and little jars that contained just what the Doctor had not ordered: a fine opium extract.

A quick injection and Darlene had been subdued to a manageable state. Kemp continued to keep Darlene warm and comfortable and had noticed that her tattoo had in fact completely disappeared and that the majority of her back was inflamed with acute red or inflamed bruising but he remained mindful that Darlene had not been physically harmed. He certainly could not apply the same diagnosis to her psychological state of mind.

Within an hour or so, the three were sitting in Doctor Elfecky's home discussing the day's very odd events. Darlene was now fully bright as a button and back to her normal active, humorous state as if nothing had happened and was engaged in healthy conversation. Kemp and Mohammed remained very sceptical but remained interested and monitored her condition should she suffer a relapse.

Kemp placed a warm cup of caramel and chocolate coffee in front of her, then asked her about her time in the museum. "So, Darlene, this is going to sound a bit odd, but we thought you had died there and then in the upright position. If it was not for Dr Elfecky's quick witted thinking I would have had you in an ambulance and away to Cairo Central Hospital for treatment in a jiffy."

Darlene placed both hands on her cup and gingerly sipped her drink. "Kemp," she said, softly. "I had the weirdest dream of unworldly sensations. It was just after I thought I had bumped my head against the glass panel of the display case but, huh, that was just the beginning. From what I could gather, I was actually frozen as I watched the 'Anubis' the Egyptian god of embalming, who had begun making some sort of ceremonial preparations. After a few minutes, I was trapped somehow immobilised. Then I could feel my body slowly tighten up all over.

Then I started to struggle and pant for breath and I mean really struggle for breath, I was literally choking. My mouth felt as though it was being prised open against my will, and my lungs felt as though they were being ripped out. Then I took another single, very deep, and I mean deep breath, when I suddenly found myself lying on my back facing upwards. I was laid out flat on a cold, solid bed. I could feel a raffia work frame work of matting with a single ridge that ran the length of my spine digging into my back, and it seemed to arch upwards near to the nape of my neck, then two pads were placed under my buttocks and it was bloody uncomfortable, not painful, just a discomfort.

I could actually see many people walking around me, lots of individuals moving in and around my body carrying jars and bottles and funny instruments, they were Egyptians I think, they dressed like Egyptians but I could not be quite sure, and there were also a few older men amongst them, I have no doubt about that, as they all had donned blue and gold ceremonial headgear and possessed very wrinkly faces. Several of them were walking around the room singing and chanting whilst casting some sort of white powder all over my body.

I definitely felt six warm patches at my ear line and my neckline, and I felt as though my ankles and wrists had been, well, what I can only describe as being cut or slashed. But no pain was evident, just a warmth as I slipped from consciousness into a mellow chilled kind of lazy state, but I remember thinking that I was being drained of blood. I know this all sounds bizarre but to me it really happened. I then noticed directly above me was a single woman, she was leaning over me and smiling, a very beautiful women with red hair, and, oh, Kemp, not too unlike the face on my tattoo. That much I do remember in fact almost the same facial structure.

But her hair was more cropped, and her eyes were more piercing, what I do recall was that above her head, painted on the vaulted roof, was a line of fishes, like the ones you find in reference to your Fisher Kings—you know, the one before religion actually took its iron fist grip, the fish and the letters 'IR' next to it, that 'Jesus' Rex' inscription, just sort of running in a freeze around the room. God that was weird."

Darlene stopped talking and paused for a moment, then crunched up part of her blouse and showed Kemp the top muscle of her left shoulder. "Is it still there?" she asked, expectant of an answer that would ease her many fears. Her worst thoughts being that perhaps she had accumulated yet another unwanted holy gift from the Lord above.

Kemp pulled the desk lamp nearer to the seat and started nodding. "Oh, Darlene, it looks as if it has gone, thank God," he exclaimed. "Looks like it's only very slight bruising now, but there is no huge tattoo. It's definitely gone, Darlene, but there is a small black cartouche at the nape of your neck."

Darlene took a very big deep breath and let out a sigh of relief. Kemp, meanwhile, had grabbed his Blackberry and took a quick snapshot, and then showed the digital image to her. She gazed at it then closed her eyes again.

Doctor Elfecky, on the other hand, was sitting across the room watching the couple with the keenest of interest, quietly absorbing the strange circumstances he had found himself inextricably linked within. Then he spoke out, "You two would make quite a perfect item. Although I know that you are not together biblically—you know what I mean? Yet you both seem to trust each other implicitly, and that's very nice to see." He stood up and opened up the little, octagonal cupboard in the corner. "Brandy anyone?" He then smiled a huge Egyptian smile.

Hastings smirked. "You bet, yer big, bulbous, Egyptian arse Mohammed—brandy is always good."

Darlene almost started to cry and Kemp struggled to fight back his relief that the Doctor had not been struck down dead by some mishap or some strange ungodly act—let alone from a strange God. Darlene momentarily opened her eyes and continued to recite her experience in a mix of emotional burble and whimper.

Kemp leaned over and handed her his handkerchief, then she continued in her explanation of her experience. "After the woman appeared, it was then that something I observed really frightened the crap out of me, and I felt myself being both nauseous but not to the point of vomiting. The instrument that was raised at my eye line was a long silver blade, it looked clean almost hygienic. But when my eyes fully focussed, I could see that she had held up a large, long knife with a pin point hook at one end. It was sort of like an Ankh shape but a lot more open at the hook end, between a shepherd's hook and a long Ankh.

It was then that I could feel my nose streaming fluid and my ears had gone numb with what felt like pins being slowly pushed in to my inner ear, and my eyes were watering, and I mean watery, but there was no sense of acute discomfort or pain, more like having your body numbed and being moved around like a dead pig. It was then that I was aware that my hands were being tied, clasped together and linen strips wrapped around the wrists very tightly.

Then followed by each finger being pulled and fully extended with linen finger wraps placed on each digit and my toes. I had begun to panic as it suddenly struck me that I was being embalmed and there was nothing I could do, and clearly in mind I was still alive. I could hear my heart beat louder and louder almost drum like and, then it suddenly fell silent.

Then I saw my lungs, my liver and what I thought were my intestines being removed, each organ held up in front of my eyes to bear witness to—it was horrible. My arms and legs by this time had been wrapped separately and I could see trinkets being placed across my face, my stomach and my naval, I clearly heard the words: "The Isis knot" being spoken, as the woman conducting the ceremony seemed to chastise someone for not having it ready.

The Isis knot being a protective amulet, and the plummet amulet being the piece that keeps the balance of life and death in the afterlife. It was at this point I swore my eyes and ears seeped blood and my hair appeared to grow in mass quantities. I could see it slowly growing over my face then it went totally dark. Then instantly bright again, as if the lights had just been switched back on.

The woman was joined by what I could only think was a High Priest. He carried a large Ankh and waived a blue, long tailed flail with all other bits and pieces of trinkets and amulets over my eye line, as if I was supposed to acknowledge what he was doing. He had red eyes and was bald with a single band of gold that ran around his head like a crown. He was murmuring incantations from the book of the dead and had done throughout the complete process as I could hear the dull tones of his voice in the background, but, then I could see his face.

The Priest had tucked a single papyrus scroll between my hands and I could feel each letter of the hieroglyphs as if they were being literally burnt into my back and shoulders. There was a moment where my back and shoulders felt as if they were literally on fire, and absolutely scalding hot and burning, as if the skin was being peeled back off the muscle and bone by a heat gun, not unlike peeling wallpaper from the walls of a house with a domestic blow torch. I could feel all the bandages really tighten up when they poured syrup or oil on to the linen strips."

Doctor Elfecky interjected. "It was resin and palm oil. The resin protects and bonds the linen together, whereas the palm oil keeps the smell of death and decay at bay."

Darlene cast Elfecky a snide and an unwelcome grimace. "Well, Mohammed, that may be so, but with the utmost of respect, you can stuff that straight up where the Heliopolis sun does not shine. I was being painted and trussed up like a chicken for Christmas dinner and I was totally aware of what was going on, and that I was not dead. Albeit I was somehow being mummified, and you can trust me, I am not going to be forgetting that too quickly, that much I can assure you of. It was bloody frightening.

That was of course up until the lady leaned over and kissed my lips, and that is not something I am accustomed to, and you can trust me on that, and then I drifted off into a deeper sleep, "she said, then lowered her eyes away from Kemp in almost embarrassment who was still clasping her hand whilst listening intently to her story.

The Egyptian Doctor acted as if he had taken no offence at all. He then stood up and asked if he could translate the cartouche on Darlene's neck. Darlene agreed and pulled her long, red hair to one side. The Doctor took a couple of seconds then opened his hands in almost praise.

"Oh, in the name of Allah!" He was almost shouting out in shear excitement. "This is the cartouche of the Great God Isis and complimented with Osiris—this is not common as they are combined together, written as one entity."

Darlene flicked her hair back over her neck line and drunk more of the cold brandy. "Yum, anymore?" she asked. "So what does that mean? This cartouche that contains both names?"

Elfecky smiled then spoke. "Basically, Darlene, it indicates one partnership two gods." As the trio conversed, Doctor Elfecky's email and phone had flashed and bleeped in unison. After a quick review of the incoming mail, he sat down with his laptop and showed the screen to Doctor Gammay.

"Darlene, when you were in the museum you appeared to be somehow mentally removed from reality and attached to this one mummy. The one that sits adjacent to the Grecian Queen. But do you remember what the actual face looked like before you placed in this trance?"

Darlene answered almost spontaneously. "There was no image on that particular mummy. I remember saying to myself: 'How can you tell who is who under death's dark veil'." Darlene wiped her brow and leaned forward, then carried on in her explanation. "But, the next cabinet down from that one, well, that mummy had a very distinctive face and was clearly painted in the same style as the El Greco one, and it was a female. It was painted in a sort of Pre-Raphaelite Romanesque style—you know Rossetti, Caravaggio or Preti, that kind of painting.

I think I mean an El Greco painted face, and the third cabinet down, that was certainly a man's face that much I am certainly sure of, and when I think about it more, it could have even been the face of that High Priest I saw. I cannot be a million per cent sure, but it was close. I know this sounds very bizarre but if you had been through what I have endured, bizarre is acceptable—trust me."

Doctor Elfecky was nodding in agreement as he quizzed Darlene's facial expressions, and was trying his hand at interpreting her body language and even applied a few odd suggestion techniques. He was unsettled in his mind as Darlene portrayed every idiosyncrasy as if she was telling the truth, and he would agree with any professional that Darlene Gammay firmly believed that she had lived through the embalming process.

"Well, Miss Gammay, I fear you may have been part of something that we thought was always an ancient spiritual gnostic myth of rumour, you see we, as Egyptians, feel that although we believe that we can ascend into the heavens and stars, we do not think that we could actually return back to earth, you know like a return ticket to meet the Gods, or indeed let alone, pass on one's earthly image.

Therefore, the actual ritual process of passing on one's earthly image from death to life is what we deem, or more over, what is only known by a select few members of a very esoteric and inner circle of informed scientists, this is called the process of '**Assignation**'.

This is a journey to and from the afterlife; which is indeed a serious conundrum for us to consider. And I can assure you, Doctor Gammay, that 'we' as a relics and religious study group have no real examples of what this process entails or what it is really all about—apart from a few snippets of information which appears to have been hastily written on a few loose pieces of papyri that basically dwells on the notion that the transition is somehow real.

Of course that is until now, and you are now something of an enigma, not only to me, but to the collective 'the GMSC' institution. Apart from your own recent experience to compare with, this crossing over of human identities or this ethereal relationship between two worlds, I mean, it's just like passing on physical DNA.

The difference being one person is post physical birth and the other in death. The mummy that you were face-to-face with in the museum, the one you were drawn to, we actually have very little detail or indeed know very little about her. But it was known to be just the body a woman, and speculation was that she was perhaps a lesser princess or a high priestess in her own right.

We cannot confirm nor corroborate any identity because she could be a princess, albeit she could also be a simple lay person, so without her worldy riches with her, we could not identify her. But, what we have is a mummy who appears to have had 'no name' or at least our records show that there was no name offered or given to this particular mummy when she was first discovered, and, was thus, simply recorded with the next sequential number on the inventory list, and she is now known as number '33'. However, just recently we think we have found a parchment that you may be referring to.

A parchment that gives an indication that the mummy was relocated from nearer middle Egypt, but what is really interesting, is that we think she may have been named Miriam, Migda or Magidal, or a combination of both, but clearly written in the simple an older Aramaic script. Now, if you wish to speculate and apply any informed opinion, that particular translation could be translated loosely into the European language name for Mary, Marie, Magdalena or Mary Magdalene and of course you also mention the papyrus scroll that was wrapped up in your hypothetical embalming.

But, please remain mindful, many girls of the ancient world were named Miriam. Well, the upshot is that the illuminated manuscript that plays a crucial role in identifying who she is, which is at this very moment in time is being hastily translated, and this is why I am not confirming anything because I am waiting on an email from a close academic friend.

Because, the piece of papyrus that was held by your so-called non-faced mummy was available when she was discovered, we were sceptical of its authenticity. Although we had a single clue, but it was deemed out of place as it was a much older than normal papyrus pages and was subsequently removed. The papyrus, along with the amulet, was placed in one of her accompanying canopic jars, and yes, that is also not quite normal practice. So, we are treading carefully before we tell the international community who she really could be

But firstly, let me explain this email, by looking at these digital photographs it seems this mummy has also taken on a brand new face! This is the same mummy you were with up until two hours ago that had no face on her coffin effigy. What is more frightening is that she may have acquired her old face back, we are unsure, we just don't know! I mean how on God's earth would you explain that to society in the modern day?"

Darlene and Kemp stared at each other for a good few seconds as Mohammed explained the context of his electronic mail. Kemp explained what he thought he had just heard Mohammed say. "Mohammed, step back a phrase or three, will you. Are you actually saying to us that the face that now appears on the mummy in question, by whatever means you wish to class it as, or by any stretch of the imagination, 'unusual' as it is as somehow been re-instated or painted back on the mummy? Placed there by some inexplicable, unnatural phenomenon or inexplicable process that could be deemed 'a miracle of science', and believe it or not, now also appears to be the very same face that was reflected by Darlene's tattoo?"

"Yes, Kemp, that is exactly what I am saying."

The Professor spun around on his chair with a huge smile on his educated face. Then spun the laptop around for Darlene and Kemp to view the new image on the screen. Displayed, in full colour glory, on the laptop's wide screen it was clear that the same mummy was still lying offset in her upright open sarcophagus, and still encased in her glass display cabinet, and had taken on the facial appearance of Darlene's tattoo—if not the actual tattoo it was a very distinct likeness. And it possessed a quality of skin tone that was extremely detailed. Darlene pursed her lips and coughed, then mentally acknowledged the bright red hair of the mummy, then started to cry.

Kemp meanwhile was thinking about the humidity levels within the glass case and the different temperature changes that could have possibly dried out the bandages and some sort of paint reaction had occurred and perhaps the face had been there all along, but had been distorted by light. Or conversely he was thinking camera tricks. Nevertheless, Darlene was unconvinced about any other theory apart from the fact that she had carried this image on her skin and had passed it on.

Mohammed interrupted their conversation and continued. "Here look, and if this is correct, then it basically means that you have been identified as a custodian or assignee. She, this princess, could also have pre-written this scripture in her own hand. But, this is of course is just speculation because the mummy was discovered and recovered in the lower border's region near to the Gaza strip, and may have even been transported there after the fall of Jacob's Ford by the old world Knights' Templar from Jordan. Probably in the era leading up into the 11th or 12th century.

This mummy was moved there deliberately, along with some of the other golden trinkets and regalia that we now house in our museum, and, she was moved there for safety reasons. Darlene, you also mentioned that your mouth was forced open, this is indeed a holy ritual and permits the deceased to consume food and water in the afterlife. There are also occasions when the eyes are removed or are fixed open so that the soul can negotiate its way within the darkened pyramid structure as it's ascends the great gateway to the heavens."

Mohammed became somewhat very passionate in his recital and recollection of the recent acquisition and seemed to ponder on certain aspects in their moments of clarity. Kemp again listened with great interest and Darlene was traversing the room but listening very intently, only stopping now and again only to view the Professor's copious amounts of artefacts and to sip her brandy. She recalled thinking that the Professor's house was probably more of a museum than the actual museum was. His life revolved around Egyptian history and he had become known as the alternate historian, as he preserved the cultural history of ancient Egypt.

Mohammed stood up and shook the parchment in the air like a fly swatter, then spoke. "The scroll, however, is of particular interest to us, as it was not uncommon to bury or entomb the dead with their worldly belongings and the scroll in reality was their actual letter 'Will and Testament' and is often used to today to decide who owns what items—a bit like the Rosetta stone but in parchment form. So, after all that embalming and concerted effort, we find that the body is ready for its journey through death or in your case, Doctor Gammay, life.

But, I do really feel you have been blessed with something more than just a simple coloured tattoo or this new cartouche signature. You see, in our belief system this process would be known as the '**Assignation**', a mark of acceptance that would propel one into an almost sainthood category, and, which may still await you, who knows."

There was a very painful moment of incredible silence that resounded around the small living space. Then Kemp spoke out. "Well, Darlene, let's face it, you are now something of an enigma and that issue we should not hurry and tell the world about too quickly. Life is far too short to have this event told to the outside world, or they, 'the establishment', would have you hidden away in some nunnery. Or a sanatorium or other such place where the hands and heads of some strange and very inquisitive biblical scientists will only want to take blood and samples of everything else from your hair to your urine, and that's not happening."

Darlene and Mohammed were nodding in agreement at each other. Then the professor spoke out. "Oh, and by the way, Kemp, I forgot to mention your chalice will be delivered by a Mister Ahmed Mohammed, El Ahmed, he says sometime Wednesday, I shall buy the artefact as agreed."

Kemp had totally forgotten about the Chalice in his efforts towards these new revelations that would have implications for his relationship with Darlene; it seemed somehow so insignificant with current affairs and he thanked the professor for his assistance.

Doctor Gammay held her glass up and asked Mohammed to refill it, then she dropped another bombshell. "Well, what about the huge black and ginger cats then? There were literally thousands of them running about this hypothetical chamber and one cat even sat on my chest, and I would swear that it spoke to me."

Elfecky stood frozen in his tracks still holding the crystal brandy decanter that was now hovering in mid pour. "Cats, what sort of cats, Miss Gammay?" he asked, whilst tilting his head upwards.

"Cats. Bloody big ones, you know, Felis silvestris catus, moggey mau, mouse catchers, that sort of cat!" She almost spurted at the line of questioning. "I don't really know, Moh, black, tortoiseshell and ginger but very large and I mean extreme. And they were immaculate; each was well groomed, not them all, but specific ones and were very clean, larger than normal sized eyes though, and others appeared to be totally untamed . . . but the big ones, they appeared to have significant standing in this environment."

Elfecky responded with an odd expression as Darlene continued talking. "I do know that cats keep vermin down and keep harvests in good order, but I reckon a thousand cats ran through the chamber as I began to feel a cold wind run through my legs and arms, and that was when you seemed to have stuck something in me."

Kemp spoke out. "We used drugs, sorry, but we had to do something. It was a mild opium extract, Darlene. We used it to ease the pain and stabilise you when we thought you were suffering an epileptic fit or something."

Darlene started to disagree. "No way, Kemp, I was not having any kind of mental fit. I was day dreaming for two minutes maximum, no longer."

Hastings tapped his black jewelled Rado watch. "Darlene, it was easy a full thirty-five minutes when you stood opposite that glass case. I know cus I timed it. I remember distinctly looking at my watch; it was roughly sixteen forty-five when you went up stairs as I recall, cus I was watching yo . . ." he cut himself short, then spoke again. "Anyway, I was just finishing my dialogue with Mohammed here, and by the time I had massaged your shoulders, I momentarily spied my watch face and it was just after the quarter past the hour when you started to return to our time, if that's the correct words to use."

Darlene smirked another 'not interested' type of female smug. Then spoke. "Cobra snakes! The cats were carrying cobras in their mouths, every single cat had a snake in its mouth, just thousands of them, they were not graceful or easy going, as some of these cats were, these ones were just biting the heads off and playing with the writhing torsos."

Professor Mohammed Elfecky rubbed the side of his head and removed his NHS glasses. Then interjected in order to vent his thoughts. "Darlene, snakes as you are probably aware also play a significant role in our society and even today as you have already stated cats still keep the vermin levels down. In Egyptian culture we have a goddess called Mafdet, she is the deification of justice and execution and symbolised as a lion-headed goddess. But she could be interpreted as to controlling these cats which in essence are or were controlling the serpents, or the loose interpretation as the Gods controlling the unruly people, by discipline.

Not just controlling them but simply killing them as well by biting their heads off. The bigger cats themselves, well, they are slightly different, the Cat Goddess 'Bast' or 'Bastet' was her original name, and of which, through time was eventually replaced by the name Mafdet and this is the name we know her by today. But, again, her image was softened over time and is now the deity for protection, fertility and motherhood."

Darlene smiled. "Shit, Mohammed, I could have told you that! But why has the bitch picked on me to leave her mark on society? Your 'Bastet', your bloody deity, she has singled me out to conduct her quick Assignation with, I must admit this shit has seriously been sending me to crazy land, and you can be rest assured, I will not be stepping another foot back in your museum ever again. And if you really want to know something scary, and then listen to this, there are twenty three other mummies up there in your museum that are able to see through and beyond their bandages and their glass display cases, and I do not want to be introduced to them ever again."

Darlene stood up and stared directly at Mohammed Elfecky who had been stunned by her strange revelations, and was sitting back in his chair almost pinned by Doctor Gammay's direct approach and strong dialogue as she continued in her moment of anger.

"They can hear, see, smell and if you listen hard enough you will hear their violent screams—demanding silence, or you will shudder when you hear their relentless pleas to be returned back to the sands of their ancestors. Mohammed, even in death your Kings and Queens cannot sleep."

Doctor Elfecky was totally displaced, and found it very difficult to comprehend what Darlene was saying. His eyes kept widening and his mouth dropped as each new revelation was conveyed by Darlene to his unsuspecting ears.

"And if you listen, you will hear those cats calling in the dark recesses of your museum, and they are not quiet either, the eighty five thousand or so that were embalmed then dispatched into the afterlife along with their masters. Well, they squeal twice as loud as their masters do, and you can trust me when I say that they are twice as big as they are on earth.

These cats are almost the size of mountain lions, and the mummies, well, from what I have just seen they are twice their earthly size as well. And you have an example of a wooden sarcophagus up in that museum, the one that is massive, well, that's about the right size in height, but only on the other side of your gateway to the afterlife, and thank goodness it's only 'ethereal.'

So, professor, doctor, mister museum curator or whatever it is you are, I do seem to have also travelled to yet another place in your Pharaonic lands, this place was definitely, called 'Beni Hasan', and if I am not mistaken it was known by the Gods of the day as the Land of the Feline or Cat City? Of course, I am only recalling these sound bites or distant echoes from my mind, but am pretty sure Cat City is correct. Mind you, I was somehow tripping the light fantastic at the time, so, how do you explain that Mohammed?" she implied, with a degree of control, then began throwing her arms up in the air like a two year old child frustrated by some newfangled toy.

"From what I can recall, I saw many, many cats all lined up in neat little rows, each one sitting next to each other and waiting to be fed, as if they knew they were to be fed by the Lords of the afterlife as a matter of course. It was as if each little animal knew its role in the afterlife, expectant of being looked after. Does that make sense to you? Each cat just waited patiently, then once it was fed, was then consumed by the sands of the desert.

It may be that these cats do re-appear after forty days and nights or later as with whatever ritual, and again, I suppose just waiting to be fed. Sounds like a cat's life to me. But, what was really interesting is that they spoke to each other in multi-tongue, not meow type cat speak tongue as you and I know it, but more phonetically; this was very clearly a structured language and something very different."

Professor Elfecky stood with his mouth slightly open and was mesmerised as the overwhelming level detail of the experience flowed from Darlene's recollection, just as if she had rehearsed the whole thing as an actor would their lines. He was not only confused but was intrigued as his scholastic and historical knowledge was not only being challenged but also corroborated at the same time.

He poured himself another strong brandy and sat down on the leather seat again and gazed through Darlene and beyond into the expanse of downtown Cairo. Outside the hustle and bustle was kept at bay, the Doctor had ensured that his home was both secure and free from unwanted noise pollution and had fitted double glazing in his doors which had heavy rubber seals. He had also taken time to ensure that he had installed controlled lighting, which was both electronic and natural, and he had taken great pains to ensure his own papyri collection was not subjected to any unwanted pollutants.

Darlene recognised bits and pieces of Mohammed's collection—mainly small, alabaster statues and some of the highly elaborate, gold leafed jewelry. She knew his collection would amount to quite a substantial sum of money if they were placed on the open antiquities' market, but in his defense Mohammed chose to keep his country's artifacts and gems in their rightful place of origin.

After a brief stay in Cairo, Kemp and Darlene along with their new 'magi chalice' were en route to visit the Grand Masters' Lodgings administrator and the museum's curator to review early Templar records regarding the role of the Magi during the birth of Christ.

CHAPTER NINETEEN

Malta—unplanned field trip

Kemp and Darlene stepped down from the airbus 320 aircraft and took a slow pace down the aluminum stairway. The sun was almost blinding and the heat was stifling. Kemp shielded his eyes from the rays as he stepped off the bottom step and grabbed Darlene's hand in order to stable her as she stepped from the last tread.

They both then made their way to the airport terminal and passed through passport control. Soon, thereafter, they were booked in their hotel and were making plans for the next three days of fact finding. Kemp had arranged to meet the curator of the Cathedral Museum at M'dina and Darlene had arranged to do some serious shopping.

Two o'clock in the afternoon next day came quickly and Hastings soon found himself standing outside the museum of the Grand Order of the Knights' Templar, M'dina, and was waiting on his contact who happened to be the island's representative for the Fisher Queens in the United Kingdom.

He instantly recognised his contact as the red Porsche Carrera parked up in the designated car park space. Hastings finished eating his chocolate éclair and placed the wrapper in his pocket, then made his way to meet Graham Pinto De Souza of the Royal Order.

"Hey, Graham, nice to see you again. Thanks for making time for me this afternoon—really appreciate it."

De Souza, as far as Hastings was concerned, was something of an enigma in his own right. He represented what Kemp would call the inner sanctum of the Order and yet he possessed the intellect of a mad scientist. His broad shoulders and stature resembled Kemp's own size, height and weight, yet his maturity and stature was clearly established on a well-heeled and groomed individual.

"So, you asked about paintings of Caravaggio that carried any intimation towards a chalice or holy cup. But let us be quite clear here, Kemp, not the Holy Grail, just tell me you are not on some wild goose chase to see if we have it wrapped up in swaddling in our museum archives somewhere?"

Hastings gave out an uncontrolled bout of laughter as De Souza swiped his all areas electronic security pass. "No, I have tried that line already, but do we?"

The electronic gate swung open and Hastings and De Souza passed through. Unknown to him, his life's social and commercial details were flashing up on some hi-tech security database some three thousand miles away, and quizzed by one of its highly trained and technical operators.

Hastings was alerted by another presence in the hallway as a security guard pinned an 'Electronic 'Tag on his jacket's lapel.

"Okay," remarked De Souza. "Level two, here we come. Tell me, how long do you have here in Malta? We must do lunch whilst you are on the island, there is a really good restaurant in front of St

John's co-cathedral, they do a great pizza.' He then turned left into an alleyway and ascended the marble stairwell.

"I am not sure if we have what you are looking for, Mr Hastings, have you tried reviewing Dante's collection in London? Dante was much more attuned to the works of the older masters and their hidden symbols, cups, vessels and the like, probably more than most contemporary artists of his day, artists who basically just copied the given subject matter. But Preti on the other hand, he has indeed left his mark on the face of the Temple across the globe.

He was indeed a visionary and far excelled the expectations of our progenitors. But Caravaggio, well, I must fall prostrate at his feet and indulge myself in his greatness of his artistic talents. As for Caravaggio he was a troubled genius, if you judge him by his account on canvas of the beheading of John the Baptist, you get the feeling that he actually could have been there as a witness. The illicit, graphic detail sends chills up and down my spine every time I gaze upon it."

Kemp smirked and followed De Souza up the circular stairway, every now and again touching the highly cleaned and polished brass handrail for support.

"You know Caravaggio was obsessed with Saint John and his turbulent life; spent all his years in acute study of the man and Saint, and had become an eminent boffin by all accounts, and a talented paint artiste, as well as you know. The skull downstairs is painted or reflected in one of his many paintings as it does in several temple masterpieces. All you have to do, Mr Hastings, is decide who the skull belongs to." De Souza smiled and touched his nose.

CHAPTER TWENTY

A DATE WITH DEATH

The driver of the oncoming car sat bolt upright. His gaze was wide eyed and wholly fixed and concentrated one hundred per cent on the red haired woman who had just emerged into the quiet lane, and was about to step onto the roadway. She had been busy purchasing some gold from 'The Crown' jeweler's shop.

The driver, meanwhile, had waited patiently and watched until she had come back into his line of sight, then slowly picked up the momentum of the vehicle intent on striking the lady. He steered the heavy Range Rover directly toward Darlene Gammay just as she had taken her first step onto the roadway and began accelerating.

The red haired woman was instantly alerted by the sudden moment of something nearby and was cognisant of the car's sudden revving high engine noise and rapid movement. She had momentarily frozen and had somehow decided to ignore the oncoming machine.

The driver glanced in his rear view mirror then gripped the steering wheel with all his strength as he applied the full weight of his right foot down on the accelerator. He spied his own reflection looking back at him, he looked ill, indeed he was sick, a concoction of alcohol and drugs fuelled his suicidal attack on the unsuspecting shopper. He gazed over his forehead and hairline and then stared into his deep inset eyes.

Both of his eyes were littered with oversized blood capillaries, they were almost fully blood shot, and he smirked spying the once striking blue colour that had all but disappeared, dissipated into a heady mix of tiredness drugs and illness and hatred for the follower of Christ. But this was of no concern for him now—he was too intent on ridding the world of one example of the walking dead, and his mission was now almost complete.

The driver's bony hands were gripping the leather wheel and were now a real time, white knuckle ride where the indents of his phalanges and damaged skin began ripping as he grew tense and very impatient. As he gripped the wheel tighter, the ripped strips of skin on his hands became tarnished with copious speckles of blood droplets, each leaving long smears of red on the beige covering of the leather as he manipulated the wheel to straighten the car up for final impact.

His oily, rugged, tufty hair was ruffled and very unkempt. He knew he smelled bad and had not washed in a few days. But Ahmed Hasan Kabbal of the Grand Lodge of Cairo was not too concerned.

Darlene had spun towards her left side and caught sight of the oncoming driver and gave out a loud, high pitched squeal of surprise, spying the car coming toward her, dropping her pink hand bag in the process.

The driver had swerved again in order to strike the Doctor straight on, and, it was just then that a grey figure emerged from nowhere and grabbed Darlene Gammay's torso in a concentrated rugby dive sending them both hurling over the cobble stones and the cold slabbed walkway, in the process missing the steel bollard uprights by a mere few inches.

The Range Rover had simultaneously ripped through an adjacent steel bollard and veered off to the left hand side of the lane, and had started to descend the narrow stairway, smashing off the masonry and the many shop's front facades, sending fragments of chairs, plaster and glass flying into the air in the process.

The car had continued down over an intersecting street, luckily missing other traffic by inches and cascaded down over yet another set of stairs, then collided with a small curtain wall that gave way under the impact.

The last thing Darlene Gammay remembered was watching the number plate and the underside of the machine disappearing over the edge of the wall followed a loud clatter and a cloud of black smoke which bellowed up between the adjacent buildings.

Kemp brushed himself down then offered her a hand of help. "Really, can't leave you alone anywhere can I?" Came the welcome tones to Darlene's ears. Hastings had been her hero of the day, her man of the moment, her saviour. She was very confused and appeared to be very displaced by the event.

"I had just bought you this nice chain with a gold Maltese Cross on it as a present, when I . . ." she stopped. "Oh, my God, Kemp, that maniac just tried to kill me. Why would someone want to kill me?" she asked.

Having got to her feet they then followed the trail and destructive path of the Range Rover and soon found themselves descending to the narrow street below to view the carnage left behind by the mass of twisted metal.

Once they reached the flattened wreckage of the car, it was just as the flames had erupted into full glory as sparks and flame reached high into the sky and the aroma of petrol lingered heavily in the air which caught their olfactory senses. It was obvious that the car had flipped over and landed on its roof, then burst into flames.

He also noticed that the driver's seat was empty and stared around the immediate area for any signs of the previous occupant; no-one that remotely resembled anyone who could have been the driver was in the locality.

Everything in the open area was in normal order, apart from an old lady pointing her finger in the air and blurbing something about the darkened 'rains from heaven above' in half gargled Italian, and of course a one and half ton Range Rover sitting in a hail of fire and devastation in the middle of the small square.

"C'mon we need to get out of here and lie low for a little bit. How is your ankle, by the way?" asked Kemp, as Dr Gammay took a long deep breath.

"I will live, but I need new stockings."

They both smiled at each other and made their way back the hotel.

It was not long before there was a sudden knock on the apartment door which startled them both; it was a knock that was loud enough to wake the very dead.

Hastings instantly jumped up and peeped out of the 'spyhole' in the door whilst trying to remain calm. He was amazed to find standing at the other side was his long time Egyptian friend, Dr Mohammed Elfecky; he was standing and looking somewhat perplexed.

Kemp quickly opened the door allowing the Doctor to enter. Then spoke. "Mohammed, what the hell are you doing here? I thought you were supposed to be making preparations for your Doctor Hawas in Cairo, for this week's visit or something, and the how the hell did you know we were here?"

Elfecky clasped his hands and greeted Darlene. "Indeed, I should have contacted you, Kemp, but you are in grave danger. I had to escape Cairo for a few days while my friends take care of some domestic business," he remarked, then explained that an ancient Order of Cairo had somehow heard about the strange goings on in the museum and were convinced that Darlene was some sort of 'living dead' entity and needed to be terminated.

Elfecky explained that the Grand Lodge of Cairo were amongst the Temple's greatest enemies, and had thought their existence expired a long, long, time ago.

"Well, that was up until after you guys left Cairo and I was paid a visit by one Ahmed El Kabbal, of the GloC. He is a very odd sort of man. He even looks quite evil if you ask me, dead from the neck upwards, and hails to represent the afterlife. He is clearly convinced that a time lock had been activated and that Darlene was somehow possessed by an ancient entity from the other side. But to my real surprise, he had accused me of devil dealings and worshipping Satan, which is absolutely preposterous. He also claims that I was instrumental in this Assignation ritual."

The Professor was clearly upset as Hastings sat him down and provided him with a nice cup of warm Lipton's tea. "Sorry, Mohammed, this is all I can do. Hotels don't cater for everyone's taste I am afraid."

Kemp walked to the window and stared out, then spoke again. "I think we have just met one of the Grand Lodge of Cairo's members, or at least one of their active members. They have just tried to assassinate Darlene, by trying to run her over in broad daylight."

Mohammed stood up and placed a golden amulet in Darlene's hand. "Here, take this amulet, Darlene, this is the lucky eye of RA. It once belonged to the Queen of Sheba, and the Magdalene or your Assignation mummy, or so I am told. I don't think she will mind now that you have been blessed with the 'Assignation' of the Magdala. It is symbolic of eternal life here on Earth, and should protect you. If you turn it over you will see that it has the same cartouche inscription as your small tattoo on the nape of your neck. I did not want to say too much until I was absolutely clear on what we were dealing with."

Darlene was mesmerised as she took time to contemplate what the good Professor had just said, then took a good long look at the golden jeweled amulet. She then stood up and wiped her face with both hands as she mumbled. "A walking zombie, is that what you have just said to me Mohammed, that these morons of the GLOC think I am some sort of half-life?"

Hastings interrupted her and the Professor. "So what the hell do we do now?" he asked, tapping his finger against the glass pane of the window?

Mohammed sniffed the air then took a drink of his tea. "I don't think their activists could have followed me here, as I travelled under my twin brother's passport. I do that sometimes, so the authorities may think I am still in Cairo, but it won't take long for them to discover I am not at the museum. Darlene needs to travel to this address here in Malta. She must show the Cipher her tattoo, and no-one else. Then we have to wait.

The Cipher originally was known as the unique sword maker from the ancient after world, and possesses the power of scrying, or soothsaying and of which is rumoured in some circles that Ciphers can actually see deep into the future. I am not sure how accurate this information is but I have only one other offering and you certainly won't like it."

Hastings turned and glared his eyes at Mohammed. "If it means hurting Darlene in any shape or form then you can forget it, Moh, as long as I have breath in my body she will be protected."

"Oh, no! My dearest Kemp, you misunderstand, it is the other way round, it's not Darlene that will need protecting, she will most likely end up protecting you," came the odd reply.

"Darlene has the Assignation, remember, she has touched the afterworld, she has been blessed with greatness, she has journey beyond the realms of astral life. The Grand Lodge will not stop trying to kill her until they are assured that she is no longer a threat or until they have her locked away in some dark dungeon somewhere. Or in the worst case scenario send her back into the afterlife with her progenitors where she does not belong."

Hasting's mouth dropped open, and then he muttered the word 'progenitor' over and over. "Are you saying Darlene is actually part of some ancient Royal family lineage? Because if you are, then I think you are so wrong. It was I who chose Darlene to authenticate the 'Sanctos Epistula'. It was me who brought her into this charade in the first place. And now you are saying that I have been manipulated by someone who now wants Darlene dead?"

"Oh, yes!" remarked the Professor quite flippantly, whilst staring at Darlene. "You see the powers of the afterlife move across vast regions indiscriminately. They don't settle in any one part of the cosmos for any length of time. They roam the ethereal plane as astral nomads, and stalk the living to pass on their odd legacy of existence. It's just the way of things.

I would wager that our Darlene here was first removed from her job at the university in a trumped up scenario that left her very vulnerable, and you my friend were activated by the Fisher Kings to find someone with relevant expertise in order to quickly to authenticate the Magdala Epistula before lent. And were perhaps redirected by misdirection or manipulated to obtain Darlene's whereabouts and her availability, then recruit her, of course which you did."

Hastings clenched his fist. "Carter, that little, twisted shit! I will wring his little, fat neck, when I get my hands on him," he muttered, whilst staring again at Darlene. Then rubbed his face. "Darlene, when did Carter actually first contact you?" he asked, flicking his mobile phone open.

She thought for a moment then answered. "Actually, he didn't. It was you who contacted me Kemp, when you first came to my presentation, I did not know who Carter was before then."

Kemp grimaced. "He must have orchestrated this bloody whole thing. Mohammed, where do we find the Cipher? Because if my hunch is correct Darlene may not have much time; the Cipher may be our only hope."

Hastings grabbed his laptop and searched a few web sites, then sent a few emails to some serious people in his working life. The Professor was scribbling a few notes into his notebook, as Hastings planned his next move.

"Mohammed you had better accompany us to Scotland. I think we need to take a break somewhere safe where we cannot be intercepted. We will leave in the morning."

The Professor tapped his gold pen on the note book top. "Sounds like a plan. I need to make some calls."

CHAPTER TWENTY ONE

EMOTIONS

The church bells at the nearby cathedral, opposite the hotel had started to sing their song to the Lord above. A clutch of white pigeons had taken flight, sending a flutter of white feathers drifting down from the belfry onto the piazza below.

Darlene had lit fourteen candles and set them around the rim of the rustic cast iron bath tub. The tub itself had been built into a huge, oval shaped marble pedestal resembling what Darlene would describe as a Roman dipping pond, but with hot water.

She paused and sniffed the vanilla aroma whilst simultaneously allowing the hot steam to envelop her face. She gazed as the many flames flickered and danced across the water's top. "Mmmmh!" she muttered.

She had littered the top of the water with a range of rose flower petals that had begun displacing themselves almost covering every inch of the surface. The arrangement of colour was white, blue, red and green leaves and left the bath with an aura of brightly lit water and perhaps one of the most welcoming baths she had taken for a while.

Letting her dressing gown slip off her shoulders and fall onto the floor, Darlene stepped into the warm water and immersed herself into her aquatic, heavenly indulgence.

She slowly smoothed lavender soap over her buxom breasts and shoulders then crunched her hair up, just tucking it up enough to clear her neckline. She then smiled as she simply relaxed and lay back into the mass of petals.

Meanwhile, the latch on the front door had clicked several times then fell silent. Across the open living quarters the bathroom door lay ajar, making it possible for Darlene to observe the complete living space. She knew the door had been tried yet she did not stir, she was mindful that the door was unlocked and yet it still never opened, despite having just been tried.

Kemp Hastings had found a new experience in his turbulent life, an experience that he did know how to control or respond to. Although he was a worldly experienced man, he did not know how to react to Darlene at the best of times. His head spun every time she was around him. She made him feel both awkward and strong and yet her vulnerability gave him a sort of responsibility having brought her into this mess.

He tried the door again. Then it opened. On entering the flat, he gazed directly through the room and straight at Darlene who had slid down deeper into the marble Victorian-styled bathing tub.

"Beautiful," he murmured under his breath, taking a lot longer to avert his eyes from her voluptuous body, even more so now that it was covered in fresh bubbles and coloured petals.

He thought for a few moments remembering Dante's Sank Real oil painting that was pivotal in this conundrum. She was as every bit as stunning as Rossetti had imagined. Yet he, the artist would have never observed his model in the modern world, with these complicated Egyptian inflictions or have been bestowed on such a fine female specimen.

Darlene remained silent and still as Kemp's mind wandered off into the heavens contemplating many ways of approaching her, especially now that she was in her naked and perhaps most vulnerable state. He stared again praying that Darlene would not wake, or turn and catch him in his lecherous state of mind, thus preventing any chance of a physical union with this stunning, flaming-red haired lady.

She momentarily sniffed then gave out an almost erotic long sigh. The groan that sent Kemp's blood level racing high up into the red zone of any heart thumping measuring device. He needed to do something quickly; the timing for him was perfect, but how would she respond? Then suddenly, he found himself talking out loud.

"Is there enough room in that tub for two?" he asked. Somehow the words had uncontrollably had made themselves present in the room. He thought he had said those words. But did he? Had he imagined it? Did he actually say those simple words? Had he actually thought them out loud? No, he could not have done so, it was not like him, he was brave but not that brave, or was he far more sensitive than he thought? And besides, he preferred the woman to play first base.

If Darlene had led him on, then he would have been certainly loyal as a puppy dog and remain at her every beg and call, but still, he would not have given it a second thought, nor given in to her womanly charms too easily. But, as far as Darlene was concerned, he would walk over hot coals for her. He just did not know how to tell her.

The water lapped up against the side of the marble ledge sending a single wave rippling over the base of the candles. Darlene's eyes had opened and she was staring back at him. Her mouth was slightly open, her flaming-red hair hung over her shoulders and down onto her left, heaving bosom.

Kemp stared uncontrollably again. Darlene could feel her nipples becoming stiff as she was becoming aroused; the warm waters and the moment had done their trick and had trapped her womanly make up and desires. The moment of emotions had wrapped them up into a single raging ball of pulsating heat.

She knew she had blushed, and she could feel her body starting to pulse away, her heart rate increased and had gone into over load and she turned her gaze ever so slightly in the water to evade further eye contact, but luckily for her it was too late and she smiled.

Kemp had already taken a seat on the edge of the bath and had started to remove the loose, red strands of hair from her neckline.

"I could spend the rest of my life in there with you," he said, staring into her eyes and smiling. Darlene had melted; she had already succumbed to his charms at least five days ago.

She paused trying to control her emotions then spoke. "Well, if you stay out there, you will leave me lonely for the rest of my life."

She reached out and grabbed his arm, then rubbed her lips slowly over the skin. A single kiss on his hairy wrist followed by a slow tug on his arm and Kemp ended up in the water fully clothed. Neither caring, they were just both intent on satisfying both their lust and desire.

Kemp suddenly leaned forward and grabbed her delicate face with both hands then slowly kissed her lips, she responded by groaning slightly then began gripping his arms as the heat inside her stomach erupted and intensified sending showers of shivers of pulsing warm pleasure through her writhing body.

Her tongue had already found his soft warm lips and was sending tiny sparkles of delight over his face. They both froze in each other's arms enjoying the moment. Darlene had already started to melt like a huge candle under extreme heat; her hands were sweating and jittering uncontrollably as the excitement built up in her womanhood.

Her skin had tightened and her stomach felt as though it was having a great day on a roller coaster at the carnival with a few million butterflies flying in and around in her womb, and yet she was somehow floating in complete ecstasy.

She knew she was panting and she was loving it. Then she moaned again as another shower of warm pulses flashed through her breasts and groin, sending Hastings into a frenzy of kissing and soft dribbling.

Darlene had been overcome by his soft manly charms and good looks. His body aroma was now playing a major role in driving her lustful desires. No matter what Kemp asked her to do, she knew she would openly obey without hesitation. She was captured in his web of 'maledom'

He removed his shirt, and then slid comfortably next to her in the warm waters taking time to caress her bosom at first, and then he slowly let his tongue drift over her erect nipples on their way down to her pierced belly button. She gave out another warm whimper.

Then she moaned louder as he grabbed her face again and kissed her intently on the soft lips as a man should. She, meanwhile, traced his belly and breast hairs with her long finger nails sending ripples of passion sensations over his chest. He smiled and shuddered but let her continue; she fumbled a bit then gasped as she found his manhood.

She knew now he was not the smallest of men on the planet and the rule or notion that a hand's span and width measured up to the length of a man's penis, supposedly equal to one another which now the theory was confirmed as the myth had just been blown out of the water.

"Mmmm, you must have that thing been on steroids," she whispered. Then shifted uneasily in the duvet cover at the thought of his manhood tearing at her soft vulnerable skin.

Throughout the course of the evening they lay coupled together in each other's arms, slowly making love several times in all conceivable positions—putting the Karma Sutra into shame as a few new hidden realms of bodily contortions were tried out, especially now as each new change of position was bonding them together as an intimate loving couple.

After two hours, Darlene was abruptly awoken as Hastings could be heard shouting from behind the locked door to the apartment. She soon realised that she had fallen asleep in her bath, and awoke only to acknowledge she had just had one of the best dreams of her life, and yet the man she wanted so much to be with was locked outside the flat trying to get in.

She donned her house coat and let the private investigator back into the hotel room.

"Well, that will have to become a reality," she whispered softly and headed back to the bathing room.

CHAPTER TWENTY TWO

THE GRAND LODGE OF CAIRO (GLoC)

High on the concrete pedestal, the sign of 'Sophia' stood elegant and proud, a sign that Baphomet was still an entity being worshipped by the anti-Knights' Templar group—the GloC or The Grand Lodge of Cairo.

To the left of the masonic symbol, sat four etched engravings written in the 'Atbash' Cipher text, a reverse image of what one would conceive as normal Arabic scripture

Above the apex of the doorway, the reverse logo of mixed symbols was clearly sending an unholy message to those who walked the paths of the dead, and would acknowledge the presence and a definitive indicator of this unholy order was in their midst.

Baphomet, or Sophia, was the dominant name of a well-known Greek Goddess which adorns the main hallway entrance and was a reminder of the Order's struggle against the Holy Order of The Knights' Templar.

Hastings had crossed proverbial swords with this group several times before but they had never tried to kill him or any of his friends before; well, that was up until they had struck out at

Darlene recently. If the 'Magdalene' had chosen Darlene as her window of entrance into the 21st century then the GloC was her archetypical glazier; a fanatical society who would be on a mission to smash her existence into a million tiny shards of glass.

The anger from the Goddess of the Gnostics was not one to be taken lightly and every step would have to be carefully thought out and calibrated to exacting detail if they were to survive this potential spate of attacks. And where would Professor Elfecky fit into all this—how could he protect the group?

The GloC or the Sophians would often make reference to their prize possession of which was not disputed by the Templar Order in any shape or form. The argument was to the effect that their most treasured possession was that of an ancient skull, in which they pray and observe devout allegiance to. The Order was convinced that this token was not the head of John the Baptist, but the Sophians believed otherwise.

Hastings thought for a few seconds and gathered his ramblings into one train of thinking: he had received three telephone calls asking if he was the cipher. Could it be that his relationship with the Fisher Kings had crossed paths and meanings, and that they had somehow logged his cell phone somewhere in the wrong domain, and someone was using the signal to locate his whereabouts?

He gazed up and caught an extract that had been cast in stone on the entrance wall:

- Plain: אבגדהוזחטיכלמנסעפצקרשת
- Cipher: תשרקצפעסנמלכיטחזוהדגבא

Hastings quizzed the simple text. He could not make head nor tail of what he was looking at, but he knew Darlene could crack the code very quickly. He closed his jacket and made his way into the dark doorway and waited.

Not before long a red Porsche Carrera had parked across the street. He recognised the car immediately. His hunch had been correct, somehow he knew the curator at the Temple at M'dina appeared to be a little aloof and was not too helpful when asked some very simple questions, but Kemp had expected such.

The powers that be were apparently being manipulated by an informal team of dwellers who were not of the direct Knights' Templar Order and were somehow working the Order from within its own ranks. Hastings had his suspicions but would not dare confront the Order head on; he knew that would indeed be literal suicide.

He quizzed his address book in his mobile telephone and clicked a fast call number. "Good afternoon, Major, I need your help. Do you have ten minutes? I wish to discuss the Hellfire Cross Sword with you again."

The Major at the other end of the phone coughed a little, then the phone went suddenly quiet. Then he spoke softly. "Mister Hastings, listen to me very carefully you are in grave danger you need to get out of Cairo soonest. I hear that the Grand Council of Cairo want to seize Darlene, please, Mr Hastings, find somewhere quickly and lie very low. This is a situation of life and death. His holiness the Pope is in the office as we speak.

He is making some ad hoc plans to review our security. It appears that we have found some rather highly technical equipment that can create a 3D super hologram image. We think it was used to project the image of the Hell Fire Sword within display our case number 33. And he said, only this morning, that there is some unholy ripplings in the fabric of our society.

He then asked me to re-open the case of the Sanctus Epistula. We have been very much compromised. We have intercepted a new group who have designs on the Vatican's archive. It has come to light that a small knot of information technology buffs have created a hybrid software package called 'The Archimedes Construct'. It consists of a series of high powered 3D CGI or computer generated images which were used to beam the image of the painting from Rossetti on the wall of the sealed chamber in the gallery.

The other side of the coin is that our own domestic situation here is of grave concern as we have seven Swiss Guard soldiers under lock and key for their deception in the plot to steal the actual Hell Fire Cross Sword. They had created this Archimedes Construct digital imaging software in its mature state and was designed as a military program which projects a make human images known as a 3D-GPL parametric humanoid, normally to project a human form but in our case was used in the 'still program' with no video or motion distortion.

Our Vatican IT specialists say that the program is a multi-layered model using a 'Houdini profile'—whatever that means. So in essence, Mister Hastings, I am all confused with newfangled digital things. But, I do understand that they did not use any software or metadata 3D Modeling programs to create the image of the 'Holy one'. The apparition that had appeared to his Holiness the Pope, as far as we can make out, well, Mister Hastings, this is a bit of a conundrum, she was real!

As far as we can tell. And we have no explanation to say otherwise. The Swiss Guard Officers also say that they encountered a grey, phantom monk who was walking within the sealed archive and was looking for the Holy parchment and that he, this 'ghost', had relieved the guards of the real Hellfire Sword, they also say that he just simply disappeared along with it.

That is why I have sent you some complex emails. But beware, my friend, do not trust anyone. And, whatever you do, don't, answer to anyone called the Cipher. This Cipher appears to be this monk.

He may be an Arch Angel of Death, Mister Hastings, or he may an Angel of Mercy—we do not know for sure. If the GLoC call you, please check your incoming numbers. They will find you simply by your mobile telephone signal, and let us know soonest if you are contacted, Mister Hastings, the Vatican is at your disposal. May the Lord above be with you."

Hastings had responded by sending a simple text back to Major La Rue at the Vatican. It read: MALTA.

The phone went dead and Hastings could swear that he heard a double tap on the line. He waited and listened: nothing. He then turned off his phone completely, and made his way back the hotel.

Darlene was already in the foyer waiting for the desk clerk to appear, when Kemp suddenly pushed her through the glass door.

"Ah, Darlene, there you are. We need to move out of here. I have booked us on a flight to Scotland. We need to get as far away from here and Cairo as we possibly can. Major La Rue thinks that the Vatican security systems have been tampered with and that the case containing the sword was also a 3D hologram image to deceive the actual cameras.

Darlene smiled. "Did they not check all the electrical equipment after the first breach of their security? I recall the Major saying that the only thing that was inconclusive was the image of the entity, and I am sure that was real enough, because there was no way they could beam an image like that into my head let alone into my bathroom, Kemp. Absolutely preposterous to think otherwise."

Kemp looked bewildered, then spoke, still harboring the notion that events were one hundred per cent created by man, and yet somehow the advent of this entity troubled him. "No, but if they could make an image look solid in an art gallery, then perhaps they could even make an image appear real anywhere else. And what I mean by that is Dante's Sank Real oil painting, they made it appear as a real canvas painting, although it was already gone, or more likely stolen."

Hastings presented some thoughts. "What if the painting had been replaced some time ago? Disappeared along with the sword after they took possession of it? That would take more than just a handful of specialists to achieve this level of deception, this sounds very much like a huge cover up. The Major says, that the cameras in the Vatican can be overridden electronically, but to impose an actual 3D picture on a single unit is impossible as several cameras are in each vault.

Well, that's what he thinks. But he did say they have several Swiss Guard soldiers in prison due to their involvement. Anyway all these events would still take some really careful long term planning." Kemp paused for a few seconds then smiled again. "I know that the Rossetti was housed in a sealed case on the wall, and I bet you that some new security system was recently installed, or as recently as six weeks to seven ago. I would wager my next set of car tyres on it."

Darlene looked confused. "Are you saying that these cases are designed to project 3D images onto surfaces within the display cases and could be used to trick the human eye?"

Kemp pursed his lips then spoke. "Not the cases but state of the art micro image projectors that can over-ride or trick the security systems, and these images were projected across the whole Vatican with a range of highly detailed photographs, not just the archive chambers but everywhere, gates, doorways, hallways, kitchens, car parks and even the admin offices themselves. The complete system was replicated, and here is the scary bit: the software was less than 500 bucks to buy off the internet. Not beyond rational thought, eh! Don't you think there is some very clever electrickery at work here."

Just then the desk clerk appeared. Hastings turned and gazed over the car park, then suddenly grabbed Darlene and huddled her into the emergency stairway. "Darlene sssh, just trust me, we need to go and I mean now, hurry back to the room and pack what you need, we might have about ten minutes if we are lucky. I have just seen what I think are the black Knights of Cairo. Three of them sitting in the blue BMW across the car park, they were at the square and at M'dina earlier today. That means they are most likely watching us."

Hastings called the front desk to organise a taxi to the airport, and Darlene packed what little clothing she had, and never asked any more questions. She trusted Kemp with her life and he knew he was taking responsibility for her. She would let him take the lead for now and play along with his mad charade campaign.

Hastings then contacted Mohammed and let him know of their intentions. One hour and forty minutes later the Al Italia plane took off for London Heathrow with the two investigators and one Professor of Egyptian archaeology on board.

CHAPTER TWENTY THREE

THE VATICAN RESPONDS

Major La Rue sat at his desk and viewed the electronic schematic of the Vatican's entire radiotelephony and internet network. His laptop had been beeping almost non-stop over the past hour as email upon email was sent in response to his one hundred and three requests for answers from the internal IT-Wi-Fi-division of the 'Holy See'.

La Rue was perplexed, he was struggling with the notion that twelve members of his trusted Swiss Guard had turned renegade and had been systematically stripping the Vatican of its many riches and he, as a devout soldier and custodian, was hell bent on returning the Vatican back to its absolute status of control.

The interior papal administrator had since been removed from office and was now under investigation from the Vatican's serious fraud squad and had been charged with allegations of perverting the course of justice and actual theft. Major La Rue remained mindful that the administrator may not even make it to the court rooms alive—if caught up in the 'murky' politics of Vatican life.

The internal protocols and procedures of the Holy See's internal process was based on a very old and simple principle; it hails from the time of Alexandria the Great, where if a man or woman can muster up more than three persons to corroborate their side of a case or charge, then they are automatically acquitted, or conversely if three or more persons submit the same charge then the perpetrator is automatically dead.

The process today has been made somewhat more complex as any charges raised of wrong doing are managed under the Templar rule of logic. A rule based on fact and truth.

CHAPTER TWENTY FOUR

WOMANLY CHARMS

After arriving in Scotland, Hastings had planned a further excursion to the island of Iona to escape the GloC-Grand Lodge of Cairo, and had spontaneously arranged a few days rest on the small island known as the Isle of Mull, in order to visit an old friend and cleric Dr Colm Cille McDuff.

As he drove to the Chapel at 'Reilig', along with the Professor and his assistant, the trio took time to absorb the beautiful views on display. Scotland's highlands and islands in the north certainly can put other so called country sites of interest to shame. And, as far as Scotland was concerned, her natural ruggedness and unbridled weather was complimentary and a must for any overseas visitor.

McDuff was the strangest cleric Kemp had ever met. His family hailed from all parts of Scotland and he chose to live the life of a recluse not too far from what he says was his family ancestral home on the wee island.

If McDuff was to be believed he would say that he was a direct descendant of St Columba himself. Or his lineage belonged to one of his many close family of followers that remained as a clutch of protectors through the centuries.

Suffice to say the cleric was an absolute fruitcake but, luckily for Kemp, one of the best sources of island knowledge alcohol could buy. After a couple of hours, they arrived at the wee village and found their host. Darlene and the Professor had taken the decision to leave Kemp to his own devices and walked along the sea shoreline, then ventured into the graveyard as Hastings engaged the cleric.

As the cold wind rushed between the grave stones, Mohammed and Darlene Gammay quizzed a few epitaphs looking for the ancient marker graves. Darlene drew her hand along one of the larger stones and stopped.

"Doctor, do you think Kemp is coping well with all this GloC and Vatican stuff?"

The Professor paused for thought then answered. "Miss Gammay, Kemp Hastings is the most capable investigator I have ever had the honour to know. In certain subjects, he can run rings around any scholar, he is a very learned man, but he won't admit it.

He likes things to be simple and can apply a rational answer to most things he challenges. But you can trust me when I say that you are probably his biggest challenge, Darlene, he does not know how to act around you, he somehow feels responsible for you. And yet you are highly capable of looking after yourself, maybe you should tell him how you feel, but be gentle, his emotions are on the boil at the moment."

After his lengthy discussion with the cleric, Darlene and Hastings walked through the old village then for Darlene it was back into the old St Columba chapel. They reverently wandered between the grave stones.

"Kemp, I think I really need to change my appearance, before we go back to the city. I was thinking of making my hair really blonde and my eyes a piercing blue and cut my hair into a bob style. What do you think?"

Kemp stopped and stared at her for a few moments. "I think you look fine the way you are Darlene. You are everything and more any man could wish for. I mean look at you, you're intelligent, you're sexy, you possess a good chunk of demure and certainly wilder with the outgoing pursuits than any other woman I have ever encountered. Any man would be overwhelmed by your high morals and integrity and certainly displaced by your intellect." He suddenly cut himself short, and just knew he had just committed himself to Darlene's armoury of assets as far as men were concerned, but in his case he wanted her to know that he liked her.

"So are you saying you fancy me, after our tete-a-tete?" Then she suddenly realized that their tete-a-tete was not a real physical one, but one her fantasy dream. She realised her emotions were running riot, touching on her fantasy base and of which were now appearing at surface.

Kemp was suddenly in very unfamiliar territory. His heart started pounding again, he could not help staring at her, Darlene still remained hesitant of an answer.

"I suppose what I am saying Darlene is that you are quite beautiful and you could have any man on the planet as your soul mate. I mean just look at you, simply gorgeous."

Darlene blushed then smiled. "Well then, it's a good job you are here with me then for protection. My knight in shining armour to protect me from whatever it is we are actually dealing with. All you need is your Excalibur; I will be your Guinevere," she exclaimed, just as Kemp pushed by and stood in front of her.

Standing at the door of the entrance to the church stood a single monk, clad in an all-grey habit, holding in his hand what Kemp knew was the Vatican's Hellfire Cross Sword. There was no question about it.

"Stay still and do not move, Darlene, this is the creep from the car accident at Restenneth, and if my suspicions are correct he may have also visited the Vatican."

The monk looked up then beckoned the two to follow him back into the small cloister area of the church. Both Darlene and Kemp knew that this was no dream nor any figment of their collective imaginations and they followed the grey-clad cleric into the chapel.

This monk was real enough and what frightened the investigators most was that he knew who they both were. They slowly and very cautiously entered the chapel. Just as they entered, the door closed without any assistance, then locked itself.

The monk removed his hood exposing his 'nosure' the lack of hair around the central point of his head made Hastings take a moment to acknowledge that he was in the presence of a real time ancient cleric of Christ.

As he leaned forward, the Monk spoke. "I see you have met McDuff, then? I keep him here as a deterrent to keep the nosey few out of my affairs."

The monk then walked behind the altar and knelt down. There was a shuffling sound for a few moments then it was very quiet. He then re-appeared and engaged the couple.

"Mister Hastings you are not aware of it yet, but McDuff has had to deal with your Professor friend; do not worry it was quick and very painless, McDuff is excellent with a blade. Your Professor is not who you think he is, he is not Professor Mohammed Elfecky of the University of Egypt, he is or was, Doctor Rashid Abbas Elfecky from the Grand Lodge of Cairo. He was the identical twin brother of your friend Mohammed who passed away seven months ago, your friend died from a chronic ulcer in his lower intestine.

He was however, very instrumental in keeping this sword in safe keeping. Sadly the sword should have never have been returned to the Vatican under any circumstances. But the GloC they had taken some strange steps to upset the balance of things.

They had hypnotized your good Dr Mohammed Elfecky and had migrated his working thoughts to their pseudo Dr Elfecky, as far you are concerned Rashid and his brother Mohammed were one of the same person. The hidden power of these archaic mind-melding techniques are very much still used more frequently as you would like to think, Mister Hastings. The GloC knew that an 'Assignation' was due and they had orchestrated many events to try and capture assignees as they pass to and from the afterlife.

Luckily, for your Miss Gammay, I was there to keep the under-Lords at the other side of the gateway using the Hellfire Cross Sword, but that was only for a limited time, but let us discuss something that neither of you would have contemplated in any detail, and that is your joint role in your Assignations to the ethereal plane."

Hastings stepped forward and stood directly in front of Darlene. "I will not let you harm a single hair on her head, and I don't care where you are from, we have been through a virtual hell and if you think you can frighten us then think again. Cleric."

Hastings was slowly moving toward the monk who smiled and observed Hastings anger coming to surface.

"My friends. Am I here to harm you? No. Am I here to employ you? Yes. I have travelled here to your planet to arm you with great wisdom and knowledge. You see, you are my succession, you each possess qualities that we of the afterlife require, you are both assignees." The monk stopped rambling and returned behind the alter then bent down.

CHAPTER TWENTY FIVE

TARTARUS INFERNI

Just as the huge oak door closed behind Kemp and Darlene, outside in the bone yard a blue, greyish mist had appeared and swirled up across a single gravestone; an epitaph marker stone that was situated centrally in the marble clad aisle, embedded amongst the myriad of testaments of existence to the dear and departed, albeit, this stone had no writing, just an effigy or carving of the infamous and legendary 'Green Man'.

This mist was however no ordinary run-of-the-mill spectre, this entity was something entirely different, this was the mother of all demons, this visitor was Death himself.

After a few minutes the mist in the bone yard had cleared and standing fully upright at 7 foot 2 inches in height, clad in a mix of black and deep burgundy coloured robes, stood the 'Grimmest of Reapers' in all his deathly glory.

His sullen gaze was scanning death's body park, the bony remains of the interred quietly lying at rest, each calcium corpse peaceful in demise. Death's odd gaze scanned the cemetery. It was as if he was looking for a specific, offending corpse or a lost soul in particular.

He was searching for an entity that may have fallen off the hard beaten path into the river Styx.

"Mmmmmm!" rang a deep, single tone as it resonated across the churchyard causing each chunk of stone to vibrate slightly in its foundations; each epitaph having been struck by the un-heavenly voice of demise. High above and touching the skies, the huge, metal cruciform of the cross was sitting on top of the apex of the high spire and rang out a single 'C' sharp note as it vibrated in unison with the cruet set as it sat laid out for all to see on the altar top down below.

Death was searching for something important; he knew not what exactly! Nor exactly where it was! But he was aware that a single article of faith was somewhere in his domain, and he was to say the least very concerned as to its whereabouts, and its earthly custodian.

Meanwhile, in the small Abbey the Cistercian Monk stood next to the granite altar stone and laid the heavy, golden sword reverently onto the altar top, with its long silver and very sharp blade pointing to the east. He dropped his hood then spoke. 'Sit, please and don't make a single sound. As long as we have this Hellfire Cross Sword here with us, Death will stay at arm's length, but he has very keen hearing," he said, pointing to the doorway at the far end of the chapel.

"We are under the protection of a particular God, one could say, your God actually Miss Gammay but not your God, Mr Hastings, you have a very different path to follow." Hastings was amused by the strange comment. "I am the Cipher, some call me 'The Dream Weaver' others call me 'Intrusive', but I like to think of myself as the provider of knowledge, and I can assure you both my intentions are always for good purpose. And as they say, one cannot make an omelet without slaughtering a few potential

221

chickens in the process, and that's the difficult bit, keeping the balance of right and wrong.

My name is Kyle Wishart and as you may have already deduced I do not belong to this world. I am a free roaming entity with perhaps more of a substantial physical presence, unlike the other entities you have been exposed to recently, they are simple apparitions, they are figments of fragments of time pulses, not really harmful or fully developed, but can play with the human psyche and heart strings on occasions. I am however very different. I am a traveler in time."

The Cipher stopped talking and stared into Darlene Gammay's eyes, then smirked.

"And you, Miss Gammay, are also certainly very different. Although you are not aware of the consequences completely as yet, but you have had a valuable insight into the magical afterlife, a glimpse into a world that mortal man does not exist, nor can.

You have seen and witnessed more than any other mortal living soul on this planet ever has. You, my dear lady, have been very unlucky or lucky depending on your outlook as you have been singled out by the most unusual of circumstances, followed by some 'momentous events' that are even very far-fetched for normal 21st century thinking. But, when we delve back in time several thousand years or so, you are placed right deep in the thick of it all.

But recently some things on the elemental level have changed since your last visit, and that is why I am here. I am the current custodian of the Hellfire Cross Sword, or the 'Tartarus Inferni'. It's awesome, destructive power must be harnessed at all times, and that's why the 'Grimmest of Reapers' will not dare step foot in this holy place. He dare not—whilst this article of faith remains in this domain. This God killing sword is the last instrument of protection for your humankind on this planet. The blade wields potency so powerful that even the grand masters of the heavens don't dare intervene with its existence.

They are all far too afraid to get involved or wrapped up in astral politics, as this sword has brought down many ancient gods and goddesses in its life time. And, I have a duty to pass on custody of such an unearthly weapon to a worthy custodian.

Just then, Darlene's eyes lit up with something that resembled almost pain or pleasure, she was not quite sure which it was, but squirmed on the pew as she adjusted her seating position thinking about the concept of possessing such a weapon. Kemp, meanwhile, sat quietly with his head slightly lowered almost in prayer, and was listening intently. The monk took a single step down from the altar staging as Kemp looked up.

Brother Hastings permit me to explain a few things to you: it was I, who stood in front of your car near the Priory, it was I, who sent the curator from the museum to Malta to warn you of the Grand Lodge of Cairo, It is I who protect the bones and relics of the holy one, and it was I, who brought the 'Sanctos Epistula' manuscript into existence on behalf of my keeper.

But trust me, when I say that these are all real time events, and there still exists some very real threats to both of your lives. The last Custodian of the Magdalena manuscript was indeed the artist, Gabriel Dante Rossetti. It was given to him in the early 19th century by my predecessor, and Dante, the fool that he was, went to extraordinary lengths to uncover its true and potent dark secret powers and did indeed capture the actual face of the Magdalena in his abilities to paint, as did other artists, but not as clearly as Rossetti did.

But, Rossetti a genius by any description, and through his social awareness and understanding of illicit drugs and alcohol had managed to penetrate time and space whilst being consumed in his unique world driven by a heady mixture of Victorian hallucinogenic drugs. This concoction provided him with an unearthly stimulation to his fertile mind, and, he was able to set his mind and soul totally free. And, he did, on several occasions, but he also managed somehow to look into the world that mortal man should fear, or a place where angels fear to tread.

But sadly contributed greatly to his own demise, he sketched his magnificent portrait of the Magdalena onto a beautifully clean and unblemished church blessed canvas. His artistry in this and its subject matter was painted to such perfection that the real image was spiritually exported from the ancient vellum manuscript onto this new living modern platform, or your skin miss Gammay, and, ultimately transported from the face of the mummy, housed in the Cairo museum of antiquities.

This is not the first time either. The curator Mohammed Elfecky, he is an 'alter ego cipher', he is the protector of the mummy here on earth and himself a brother of the Fisher Kings.

Before you two arrived on this planet there were several other 'chosen' to be the face of the Magdalena on earth, and the face of the Baptist, Francis of Assisi, he carried the wounds of Christ as given to him by the Apostle John.

And Bernadette Sobiros, your so called Lady of Lourdes, she spent several days conversing with the holy lady who has rose petals upon her feet, both chosen for their ability to see beyond the normal spectrum of your earthly light.

Custodians generally emerge from these blessings as normal people, but modern DNA has somehow infected the process of 'Assignation' and your kind, well, they suddenly become super human. Their physical beings or their composition will simply just not erode. Let me tell you that there are, 'one hundred and four' mortal corpses that adorn the many bone yards and cemeteries on this planet. But today, Miss Gammay, you are almost at a perfect sister quality of DNA replication. You are as close as any human could ever resemble the Apostles Apostle."

There was an acute tension between the three, as Kemp stared back at Darlene with a huge smile on his smug face. As Wishart walked across to Darlene and touched her cheek with his pinky finger on his left hand, then stroked her cute little nose with his thumb. Then carried on explaining his role in God's playpen.

"My basic duty is to place all unearthly things back into a certain order, for continuity of process. But in the interim period, Darlene, you had inadvertently or deliberately touched the 'Sanctos Epistula' and triggered yet another transition phase that created a blip in spiritual continuity, you were gifted with etheric vision, a talent where you can see between two different dimensions, in your case time and space, and now somehow the afterlife.

So, I had to place you and Kemp somewhere, where I could get access to you both, very quickly, and without too much fuss, and here you both are. And before you ask. I do have the original Sank Real portrait from that infernal gallery. Miss Gammay, you should have a similar portrait I assume? And you can trust me when I say it is absolutely identical to the original, not even Rossetti himself could tell the difference."

Darlene gazed upwards. "I do have it, it is tucked up safely in my apartment under my bed."

Kemp interjected. "You hid a twenty million pound painting under your bed? What were you thinking girl?"

Darlene turned and shot Hastings the most serious of expressions that Kemp knew just when to shut up. He pursed his lips and grabbed her hand, then gave it a gentle squeeze.

"Sorry, if this is so important, then we need to get custody of it soonest."

The Monk placed a hand on Darlene's shoulder then spoke. Hastings automatically stood back, the presence of this monk just made him very uneasy. "Don't worry about the artwork. We have the oil painting securely back in the afterworld. But sadly you and Mr Hastings, well, we had to arrange an event that would exit you both from society. And fortunately for you both it was sad that you were hypothetically caught up in the most dreadful and horrendous of fires, and sadly the intensity of which, engulfed your complete house and your poor charred bodies, everything was burned to tiny cinders as the structure of your home, Darlene, was burned to the ground—fuelled by the fires of hell."

Darlene's mouth momentarily dropped open. Then started to shake her head in disbelief. "But what about my belongings, all my personal things, my study papers my antiques collection." She turned and gazed at Kemp who could only reach out to console her.

Wishart took a deep breath then spoke again. "Darlene, Kemp, if we did not act in this way then the Black Order—The Grand Lodge of Cairo—would simply hunt you down like a pair of rabid dogs and kill you both. You have much more serious entities to deal with. But we have retrieved a lot of things we thought were important for your future life. The GloC are hell bent on stopping you, Miss Gammay, from basically informing the world at large that there is a middle gateway twixt the river Styx and Mother Earth.

This is corroborated with a series of Egyptian myths and legends which cannot be dismissed, as they are fuelled with truth, these events have indeed actually occurred, and our faith is as real today as it was five thousand years ago. People want to keep secrets; secrets and one more human death is insignificant in their eyes.

This way they will simply stop searching for you two as they will think that you are both dead.

One cannot just open a time gateway a couple of times then just stop opening it up, the ancient world of Earth would be over populated by people like me. We are time keepers, and we must strike a sensitive balance of things whilst keeping the time gates alive and aligned.

But we cannot achieve this with your human kind around in existence, your genetic groups. They keep affecting change, you, they keep tampering with time and space, a fault in your drive for knowledge and enlightenment, there is simply too much information around and it is becoming very dangerous."

Kemp spoke up. "So what do you want from us now, then?" he asked.

Clasping his hands the monk Wishart took a step backwards toward the altar then spoke. "I need several things to happen to bring events up to contemporary control, but firstly, trust me when I say Death is already stalking your world with the demise of the human race at the top of his agenda. The Grim Reaper is on a blood driven rampage. He is searching for your direct progenitors Miss Gammay, he is after your DNA lineage, your line if existence, it is because you are the second line of descendant from Christ, Mary and Joseph of Arimathea.

The Soul collector wants that lineage terminated. Death is trying to reconcile history, he wants you out of the way, and we have strategically intervened and placed the Hellfire Cross Sword in existence, a move to dispel him from showing any interest in the custodians of such a weapon. As I have said, Death will not hang around where this sword is located! Death does not like it; he fears its very existence! He will not remain within fifty feet of its location. You may catch him on the periphery of your vision, but for him that's close enough. So logic says make one of you a custodian of the Hellfire.

Another thing we must consider is your new identities. Doctor Gammay, I think blonde is a good colour for you. Mister Hastings, not sure what we are going to do with you; you will have to decide how you want to look in the future. Anyway, come, let me show you what I mean, and whilst we are at it, let me tell you about or leverage.

This sword is this steel blade that once belonged to the Emperor Constantine. Then it was acquired by the Great Charlemagne himself who had it molded into the actual sword and had embedded a nail from the crucifixion within its actual configuration. Let's face it, any article that has touched the Holy body of Christ will undoubtedly hail great properties.

Even the Templars during the early crusades used this amazing instrument at Antioch, whilst fighting the infidel, they were granted a vision of where the Holy sword in its earlier configuration lay. Actually, it was me who showed the monk where to find the Holy sword and told them to venture forth and reign over your enemies. The enemy being controlled by Satan himself."

Wishart retrieved the sword and made his way to the huge set of oak doors that led out into the Abbey courtyard. Holding the sword aloft, he opened the door. It was then, as the door swung open, a huge, black misty face was caught unawares, it appeared to have been startled and pulled back very quickly.

What stood before them in the graveyard was something that even Wishart himself had not anticipated. Death had resurrected every unearthly soul in the boneyard, two hundred black mist spectres hovered over their respective graves and gazed blankly at the Abbey's entrance way.

Wishart lowered the sword just as Death began to come forward out from the dense clouds that had appeared. He then hovered motionless, then hummed another set of deep haunting tones.

"My children just want you to know or understand what you are up to Wishart. And they are waiting to hear your answer."

Wishart tapped the sword once into the concrete step without any warning, sending a single acoustic pulse across the churchyard, the visible ring of power could be seen rippling through each stone epitaph and up into each entity as it hovered with no intent on doing much, apart from looking dangerous and intimidating.

After a few seconds, the pulse had sent all the souls into a sudden, frightened panic stricken frenzy, and they began flying all over the boneyard, eventually ending up with each soul returning to its respective grave, and returning the sleepy clutch of ghosts to almost serenity. That was apart from Mister Death himself—he was not amused.

The Reaper was still hanging around, and was intending to hang around for a quite a while or so it seemed. It was then that Wishart grabbed the sword handle and spun the pommel piece or end stud of the sword at the hilt and waited.

Death's big, yellow and red eyes instantly widened as he realised that the 'apple' was the end cap of the holiest of articles, and he was gone in a hail of wind and whistle. Wishart screwed the apple back into the hilt

"And that folks is how we deal with Death. Now, Mister Hastings, you must be very careful when you raise the sword higher than your head, she is very sharp, and very heavy although it is quite fragile, but once you have had some practice with it you will be fine."

Wishart offered the steel to Hastings as he stood awestruck at what had just occurred.

Kemp Hastings reached out then took the 'Tartarus Inferni' sword in his left hand and raised it aloft just as Kyle Wishart disappeared out of view in a cloud of dust.

Hastings stopped gazing upwards then lowered the sword and walked toward the altar. He stopped and faced Darlene. He appeared to have had no choice in his new role and quickly took on the mantle of custodian of this unique God killing sword.

But his instant thoughts were drawn straight back to 5th century Briton, when life was cheap and unruly Kings were raping the nation of their wealth, and the Celtic folklore and mystery of the most famous sword on the planet 'Excalibur' was brought into existence to stem their unholy greed for wealth and power.

He wondered whether or not this was the same killing instrument that had been passed up through the ages, and how many Kings and Queens and unwanted tyrants had it despatched to the river Styx in the heavens, and now it appears to have evolved into the 21st century.

Darlene Gammay watched on as Kemp slowly lowered the sword and placed it by his side then casually walked back into the chapel and laid the sword flat back on the altar top.

"So, Doctor, I believe the sword is recharging itself? What do you make of that?" he asked, then sat down on the cold stone floor.

Darlene stepped up to the altar and was about to lift the sword when it slid across the altar top to a point just beyond the reach of her womanly grasp. She stepped back and gazed towards Hastings; he had not moved an inch or appeared to be remotely concerned.

"Hell's inferno Kemp, did you see that, the sword, it moved, that sword actually just slid across the altar top—look! That is really bizarre, strange even, mind you, then again what we have been through the past few weeks has certainly been far more than just bizarre, whatever next?"

Darlene moved slowly toward the investigator as he sat with his head coupled in his hands. Then she spoke very softly. "Look at us? We are a fine couple of misfits are we not. Me with this damned tattoo and you with your big new knife . . . what have we done to deserve these curses being bestowed upon us? Tell me what did the Apostles say?" she asked expectant of an answer.

Hastings slowly turned around and beckoned her to sit down beside him. After a few seconds they were both sitting, staring at the huge set of oak doors in front of them.

Hastings took a deep breath then spoke. "Well, young lady it appears to me that we both have been singled out for some higher purpose in life, we certainly cannot argue about that, but, you know what I really think, I believe that this whole charade was just a cosmic scheme to bring us together. What do you think?"

Darlene clasped both of his hands and placed her head on his shoulder. That was the point when the couple became aware that the cloister's area of the church had begun filling up with a light blue, gaseous haze that had somehow engulfed the altar and the choir area. The smell of rosewood suddenly filled the Nave as a warm wind spread through the chapel in a swirling fashion.

There was an echo of angels singing somewhere in the back of the House of God, just as the candles suddenly began to light in sequence one at a time, each candle pulsing into life, the sequence running from the main lectern and onto the four main gold candle standards that sat adjacent to the effigy of Christ. Then onto the two, large white candles that sat either end of the altar.

Hastings and Gammay stood by and watched in amazement as the church evolved into something more of a cathedral than a chapel. Darlene spoke softly and watched as the illumination of candles ensued.

"Oh my goodness, Kemp, I have certainly seen this before, remember, I told you my that in my bath. Well, here she comes again . . ." She cut herself short as a flurry of sparks erupted from the altar top and cascaded into the brightly lit church.

After a few minutes, one hundred and forty candles lit up the inner choir area of the wee chapel of St Columba. Darlene and Hastings moved closer to one another then watched as a succession of 'entities' appeared one by one and stood in a line by a range of pews which ran along the back edge of the choir area.

Eleven figures—eleven angels—stood in silence and gazed upon the couple who moved slowly backwards towards the sacristy doorway. Both humans were embroiled in a state of conscious thought. Hastings accepted that each figure appeared to be a solid person, not an apparition or a ghostly form, as before, but a physical presence made of flesh and bone.

A few moments had passed when one figure stood up; Darlene recognised this figure as the Apostle Paul. Then he was followed by the other Apostles, each in succession and were holding a single, golden chalice with their names heavily embossed in red lettering upon its jewelled surface.

The tallest of the assembly, John, smiled, then muttered the names of his biblical colleagues. "May I introduce my colleagues in life and my brothers in death: Mathew, Mark, Luke, Acts, Thomas, Thaddeus, Andrew, Mathias, Bartholomew and James."

Behind the assembled 'knot' of phantom Apostles, a single apparition of a woman had appeared and was waving her arms from left to right across her body. She was still holding a basket of white roses, and she was indeed a very beautiful, angelic figure of a woman—her skin was whiter than white, her eyes bluer than blue, and her fragrance an overwhelming aromatic fragrance of rose water.

Her mass of flowing red hair, which matched Darlene's own, appeared softer and livelier and was cascading down over her shoulders and onto her bosom. The medieval white-robed figure cast her right hand over the assembled eleven, white-clad individuals then she spoke very softly. "These are the storytellers, their words are my words, these prophets are my prophets. And they are now yours, your words will be their words and the Lord will know all."

The lady stared on as Darlene reached out somehow to try and touch her, but she was not there and yet she was.

"Who are you, my lady? Why have you come here to us?" Darlene asked, then waited patiently for an answer.

The white lady smiled a smile beyond all smiles and blinked her big, blue eyes. "You have been chosen to carry the gospel of the 'one', for I am the Silent Apostle, a consort of Jesus and Apostle to Andrew, for I am the twelfth Apostle and perhaps deemed the Apostles' Apostle, for I am Miriam, the lady of Magda, Princess of the afterlife," she said, then turned to face her collective Saints and Apostles in Arms.

Hastings had dropped his head and was now heavily in prayer. He felt a sudden urge not to stare directly at the beautiful maiden. He was not worthy to gaze upon the righteous, and he was not worthy as a male to gaze upon the face of the Magdalene. Then the angelic singing had started to get louder and louder and had subtly changed from female voices to a boys' choir of voices, then each pitched heavenly, as it began hailing a series of higher pitches that could literally burst the human inner ear.

Then, the entity of the Magdalene floated toward a single statue and took a position at the feet of the Magdalene figurine. The stone statue stood over ten feet in height and sat on a huge octagonal plinth. The stonework adorned the altar wall of the chapel.

The Holy entity began swaying from left to right as if becoming totally immersed in something alien to the scene that was literally unfolding before the assembled group of people and phantoms.

Hastings found himself being drawn toward the stained glass window at the east end of the chapel and watched as the face that once dominated Darlene's back and shoulder began to slowly appear on the window as an etched silhouette on the glass. To his total amazement the visiting spectre shared the same face as the glass image. Hastings was suddenly very numb. Darlene appeared to be as calm as ever and was staring directly at the beautiful face of the holiest of holy.

The Magdalene turned and smiled, then addressed her attentions toward Darlene directly. Although she appeared to be conversing with her, Kemp Hastings could hear no dialogue—in fact he could hear nothing at all for he was totally deaf.

Darlene stared and watched as the Magdalene's lips conveyed her holy words. "My Apostles have laid my path to the new world. The afterlife is a quieter place for now, you have served me well. You will be rewarded with eternal peace and be granted with child, this is my token of love and thanks to you, this child will have a significant royal standing one day."

Another warm breeze slowly swept across the cloisters and Hastings could hear again, but this time it was Darlene who had become deaf as she stood and watched as the twelve Apostles formed a circle of bodies around Kemp Hastings. Each man appearing to engage the religious investigator in-conversation. After a few moments, the Apostles had simply merged into one figure and vanished into the altar top in a haze of blue mist and sparks.

The Magdalene meanwhile, was spreading thousands upon thousands of rose petal leaves across the abbey flooring; a blanket of roses creating, a carpet of flora was spreading out in front of her as she walked down the aisle. She passed by both Kemp and Darlene, turned slightly and smiled at the couple, then disappeared as quickly as she had materialised.

Another great thrust of wind swept through the house of God and the candles were extinguished. The chapel was quiet and the air was slightly colder. Hastings walked backwards to the altar and picked up the sword then stood next to Darlene Gammay.

Darlene was taking deep breaths and wiping her brow. She had become overwhelmed with emotions, and had streams of tears running down her face. She started to talk through her soft weeping. "I really have no idea Kemp, but I feel so relieved, and I have no idea what has just occurred, but I do know that I have been through hell's half acre and back again, and I am too tired, too weak. I am glad that the return of the Sanctus Epistula is back with its rightful owner—which is good news and the beloved face of Magdalena is back, also returned with its rightful owner in Cairo, but they are one of the same. But this sword thing, well, from what we have just witnessed, well . . . I am certainly confused, the Magdalene, she says . . ." She decided to cut off her speech at that point.

She watched as Hastings rubbed the handle of the Hellfire Cross Sword and spoke, "Do not tell me, Darlene, I do not need to know your enlightenment spoken by the Magdalene in her astral tongue—it will not make any sense to me anyway, as will my revelation from the Apostles will to you. It will all sound like total gobbledygook. Their heavenly tones have been encrypted only to your understanding. Tuned to our ears only.

It is known as the language of the Apostles or the 'Sanctus Illuminati Verbati'—a hidden esoteric set of rhythms that are tuned to your specific DNA. All very complex stuff I am afraid, and you a scholar too. But, I think we have to go out into the big, wild world and face our fears, my fair maiden.

We must confront the demons that stalk our wonderful world and send them back to Hades, and we have the powerful 'Lancea Longini,' or this 'spear of destiny to assist us. And, hey, we have some very intense biblical back-up at our disposal. This Hellfire Cross Sword to assist us for good purpose, and yet I think we do not even have to have the weapon nearby us, well, that is according to St Paul and the boys, and in honesty, who the hell am I to argue with the Apostles?"

They both then slowly made their way out of the sacred church, and as they reached the huge Oak doors they automatically swung open and the world was a much quieter place.

There were no demons, no spirits, loitering around with menacing intentions, no sign of death himself to confront them, it was just a quiet, lazy cemetery laid out before them—just the way bone yards are generally designed to be.

Hastings was first to speak. "I think this Spear of Charlemagne has done its job. I don't feel threatened anymore, do you?" he said, just as Darlene stopped in her tracks and gazed up at the sky and smiled a lovely smile toward the heavens above. The sun had risen and the heat was warm and comforting on her soft skin; she felt her face tingle in the sunlight. She felt good inside in a very odd sort of spiritual way.

They had both endured so much anger, pain, emotional turmoil and now, they had to find a certain reality in their new world of investigative pursuits. Hastings closed the gate to the Kirk behind him and momentarily stopped.

"Wait a minute though. I have something to do first," he said, then walked back into the street of the dead, and found a single grave that sat adjacent to the 'Green Man' epitaph. The stone had no name and no writing etched upon it. It was just a headstone with a single rose clearly etched into its front surface

It was then that he recalled the 'original' Latin text that had been written in the ancient Deunos inscription. It read:

Absconditus, ac adepto admonition angelus. Concealed at the statue in the Abbey within a coffin is the important church letter of Magdalene.

The Angel to obtain divine doctrine, I say deceitful warning, sign at the grave is squared. Fear the Church, stand in the highest part, then commit oneself, in silence, this is of great importance. The table of my lineage and testimony of Magdalene.

To carry in front of the Tartarus Inferni—Hellfire Sword and deposit in my holy grave.

Now he was able to decipher the information that had been troubling him since the advent of this strange, yet wonderful experience. Darlene would certainly not have agreed but she was now more subdued and a very much more a wiser woman; albeit she had endured what can only be described as a biblical phenomenon event.

Hastings was reciting the Latin text out loud and was making simple but rational points as he filtered each line in successive order. "In the abbey interred in a grave, of course, that was the resting place of the Magdalene, which was now not a million miles away. The manuscript of the saints, well, that was clearly now etched into a stained glass window in the Chapel on Iona, and was ironically painted by Rossetti, who also dabbled in magic. The parchment is now secured in no particular grave per se. The angel had delivered this unique doctrine, not an angel of Christendom but an angel from the afterlife, in the form of an ancient, mummified entity.

The sign and warning of the 'square' most certainly pointed to the Grand Lodge of Cairo, and being on the square as any freemasonry ritual of the modern day will clearly depict, and the base dimensions of the pyramid, well, that was easy for Hastings to work out. It was easily a square based on an octagonal foundation.

The next line read: And to fear the Church is to prostate oneself in prayer and ask for guidance and forgiveness.

The Holy lineage of the Ancient nomads and the people of 'Magdal' have indicated that Mary Magdalene was most certainly a Princess for some and a Queen for others in her own right and of course she crossed into the world of Christendom, and was anointed by Christ but appointed by her peers as the Apostle's Apostle.

Hastings thought for a few more moments longer and toggled with the Latin portion of the final transcript. He was now the custodian of the Hellfire Cross Sword, and for this brief moment in time he was probably the most powerful human being on the planet of Earth. Esoterically, he had become a 21st century 'Thor figure'.

The words: 'Deposit in my Holy grave' echoed in the back of his mind as the final stages of illumination and raising the Hellfire sword above his head, he drove the steel blade deep into the bowels of the soft sands of the gravesite, and waited.

After a few brief moments, he could feel the sword physically being pulled downwards and absorbed into the soft mud and was literally being torn out of his grasp.

He knew that the sword was designed to 'protect' the holiest of relics and where else better to be, but with the holy steel's rightful owner?

As he watched and waited, he would swear that the headstone was suddenly embossed with an identical carving of the sword, just where the etched picture was sitting next to the Agnus Dei—Lamb of God icon.

Then a face appeared on the grave stone, it belonged to Mary Magdalene. "I thought that was where you belonged," he whispered, then made his way back to find Darlene who had walked a little bit further down the beaten track to death's doorway and was busy sniffing the sweet scent of the red and white roses that adorned the long colourful embankment.

Then she paused and spoke. "Kemp, I can see the angels and cherubs dancing within the mists over here, and over there I see a multitude of fairy queens and nymphs. You know what though, I always thought they existed—now I know for sure."

The End.